Cool Water, Hot Desire

"Uh, Jesse," she said shakily, "before you come in, would you mind just handing me my clothes and turning your back?"

He took one step further into the pool, letting the water level reach his abdomen . . . "Don't think that's a wise idea, M'randa," he said softly.

"Why . . ." She cleared her throat. "Why not?"

"Well, for one thing, I ain't got my pants on."

"Oh, Lord," she whispered, and blew a stream of bubbles into the water.

"So, if I go get you your clothes, why . . . you'd see me naked! The shame'd prob'ly kill me . . . Is that what you want?"

She shook her head. "No, Jesse."

"What *do* you want, Miranda?"

He took one step further into the pool. The muscles in his jaw twitched slightly before he asked again, "What do you want, Miranda?"

Miranda swallowed heavily. She knew what he wanted her to say. A deep, shuddering breath racked her body and she struggled to keep her voice steady.

"You, Jesse. I want you."

Diamond
Wildflower
Romance

A breathtaking line of
searing romance novels
. . . where destiny meets desire
in the untamed fury of the
American West.

NEVADA HEAT

ANN CARBERRY

DIAMOND BOOKS, NEW YORK

This book is a Diamond original edition,
and has never been previously published.

NEVADA HEAT

A Diamond Book / published by arrangement with
the author

PRINTING HISTORY
Diamond edition / July 1993

ISBN: 1-55773-915-3

Diamond Books are published by The Berkley Publishing Group,
200 Madison Avenue, New York, NY 10016.
The name "DIAMOND" and its logo
are trademarks belonging to Charter Communications, Inc.

PRINTED IN THE UNITED STATES OF AMERICA

10 9 8 7 6 5 4 3 2 1

To my brother, Ed Carberry, Jr.,
his wife/my sister, Dianna,
and my niece, Maegan.
With love,
Muska

NEVADA HEAT

CHAPTER 1

"I'm tellin' you, Jim, women just cause trouble."

Miranda Perry turned as the deep voice filtered through the restaurant door. When it swung open, she stared at the man who stepped inside. Tall and broad-shouldered, he filled the open doorway. His white shirt and black, unbuttoned vest were crumpled as if only recently unrolled from a tight pack. The black pants covering his long legs were covered with trail dust and his battered, wide-brimmed brown hat sat low across his forehead, keeping his eyes in shadow.

Miranda's gaze moved over him quickly. His shaggy dark brown hair curled over the back of his collar, and his square jaw as he faced her was tight, as though he was clenching his teeth.

Slowly he reached up and ran one hand across his face. The languid movement shook Miranda from her musings.

Who is he? she asked herself uneasily. And how did he come to be in Bandit's Canyon? Was there something wrong with the lookouts at the mouth of the canyon? Could he be the law?

She gave a quick look around her at the empty restaurant. The one lamp she'd lit earlier flickered unsteadily in the sudden breeze from the open door. For the first time in her life she regretted having given in to her midnight hunger. Miranda took a half step back then stopped as a familiar face with a shock of flyaway blond hair came out from behind the big man.

"Jesus, Jesse! It's damn cold out there, you know?"

Miranda's pent-up breath rushed from her lungs. Jim Sully. She might have known. Somehow the Sully brothers always managed to show up at the most awkward times. Her shoulders slumped in relief and she felt the beginnings of a smile when Jim continued ranting.

"Move aside, man! Let the rest of us out of the danged wind. Don't that wind *never* stop blowin' down this damn canyon?" His voice broke off suddenly, then he grinned and called, "Well, hey, Miranda! You still gettin' the late-night hungries, are ya?"

The stranger called Jesse shifted his gaze from hers and Miranda reluctantly turned to Jim. "Yes, and you should be grateful! I've got a pot of fresh coffee boiling."

"That surely sounds good." He sniffed the air and smiled. "Smells good, too. Wouldn't happen to have somethin' in the kitchen for us to gnaw on, would ya?"

Despite her best intentions, Miranda's gaze kept flicking back to the silent man still standing in the doorway. He looked lean and strong. Competent. She couldn't help wondering how a man like him came to be riding with the Sullys.

"Miranda?" Jim was watching her curiously.

She forced herself to look away from the stranger. "Good to see you, Jim. It's been quite a while."

"Sure has." Jim snatched his hat off. "The boys and me figured it was time to put our boots up for a spell. If that's all right?"

She nodded. "I'll tell Birdwell. You go on and put your horses away. Plenty of feed in the supply house." She turned for the kitchen. "Meantime I'll fry up some steaks."

"You got you a deal, Miranda. Oh!" Jim's voice crept up a notch. "Hold on a second. 'Fore you go, I want you to meet this fella."

Slowly she turned back and looked at the tall man.

Jim's easy grin creased his freckled face. "Miranda Perry, this here's Jesse Hogan. Picked him up a while back around Tucson. He's ridin' with us now."

She watched as the man called Jesse pulled his hat off. Free of the shadows, his green eyes glittered brightly against his sun-darkened skin and she was sure she saw them soften just a little when he nodded an answer to her smile.

"He's pure hell with that gun of his and not a bad camp cook neither!" Jim punched the bigger man in the shoulder.

"He just doesn't care much for women?" Miranda asked quietly, remembering Jesse's first statement.

"Uh . . . well," Jim stammered.

Jesse smiled lazily, reached up, and ran one tanned, long-fingered hand through his tousled hair. "Didn't say I didn't care for 'em, ma'am. *Said* they were trouble."

"It's not the same thing?"

"No."

Jim's head turned this way and that as he followed the strange conversation. Finally, when the two people paused, he cut in. "Now, Miranda, Jesse didn't mean nothin' by that. 'Sides, it ain't right holdin' a man to somethin' he says when he thinks nobody can hear."

Jesse held Miranda's gaze. In the clear green depths of his eyes, she read a challenge. Her lips curved slightly as she said, "Nonsense, Jim. It's when a man thinks he's alone that you can find out what he's really like." She cocked her head. "Don't you agree, Jesse?"

He leaned negligently against the door frame, his arms crossed over his broad chest. "Couldn't say, ma'am. But I *do* know that when a woman thinks she's alone, she's a lot less careful about how she looks!" His gaze moved down, sweeping over her.

A flush of heat spread up Miranda's throat and across her cheeks. He was right. She hadn't given a thought to her appearance. Without looking, she knew that her pink satin dressing gown hung open, revealing the sheer white nightgown that Black-eyed Joe had brought her from El Paso. Now that she was aware, Miranda felt the night breeze sigh through the doorway, pushing the soft fabric against her body, outlining every curve.

She met Jesse's amused, hot gaze and deliberately moved slowly as she reached for the silken cord, pulled the edges of her robe together, and tied it closed. Quietly she said, "You're welcome here, Jesse." She paused. "If Jim and the boys vouch for you and Birdwell agrees, of course."

Jesse's green eyes narrowed at her sudden change.

"Hell, yes"—Jim spoke up—"where *is* Birdwell, anyway? Like to get this settled so's we can bed down. Had us a long ride today."

Miranda tore her gaze away from Jesse's and turned. "You know Birdwell. He doesn't sleep much. I expect you'll find him at Big Pete's saloon." She started walking toward the kitchen. "First you get the horses put away then come eat. Birdwell'll be along. He likes his late-night coffee, too."

Booted feet stepped heavily on the porch outside. Jim's brother, Bill, stuck his head in the restaurant. He glanced quickly around the room. "Howdy, Miranda."

"Bill." She nodded, then started cooking.

"You two about ready?" Bill asked. "The boys and me are about froze solid waitin' on you."

"Yeah," Jim said, "we're ready." He started for the door, then stopped and slapped Jesse with his hat. "C'mon, Jes. Let's get agoin'."

Jesse shoved his hat back on and only reluctantly turned away from the woman he could hear rattling pans. Outside, the men held the reins of their horses and led them quietly to the stable. Bill Sully and the two others who rode with them walked a few feet ahead of Jim and Jesse.

"Who is she?" Jesse stared straight ahead and waited for Jim's answer.

"Huh?" Jim tugged slightly at his horse's reins to hurry the animal. "Oh. Miranda. Miranda Perry. Like I told you."

Jesse shook his head. "Not her name. Who is she? What is she doin' here?"

"*Doin'* here?" Jim's breath puffed out into the cold desert air as he looked at his new friend in surprise. "Hell, she *runs* the place!" He chuckled softly and hurried his stride as they neared the stable.

A woman? Jesse turned and stared at the lamplit windows of the restaurant. A *woman* runs Bandit's Canyon? A small stab of disappointment coursed through him unexpectedly. For just a moment, when he'd first seen her, feelings that he'd thought long dead had sprung to life again. Her smooth skin, freckled nose, and the soft, sweet scent of her had sparked a hungry desire that had made him wish he were a different man.

It must have been the lack of makeup, he told himself. It was a long time since he'd seen a woman without her war paint on. He smiled wryly. Of course, the kind of women he'd been spending time with in the last couple of years were not the sort to let *any* man see what they *really* looked like. Jesse remembered the flush of embarrassment on her cheeks when she'd realized that he could practically see through her nightgown. Quickly he told himself to forget it. It meant nothing. His lips twisted in a frown. An experienced whore could summon up tears and blushes at will. And what else could she be? She not only lived with the outlaws, she was in charge.

Suddenly Jesse snorted out a laugh and pulled at his horse again, hurrying his steps. Who the hell was *he* to judge? Wasn't he riding the bandit trail now himself? Wasn't he looking to hole up in the canyon for as long as he could?

As they entered the stable Jesse glanced around at his new riding partners and hid a half smile. The Sully gang. Why, Jim and Bill Sully and the two knotheads who rode with them were about the worst excuse for badmen that Jesse had ever seen! He'd never forget his first encounter with them nearly four months ago. He still smiled at the memory.

They had tried to hold up a stage on which Jesse was traveling. After being told there was no cash box onboard, they'd decided to take whatever they could get from the passengers. Fortunately they'd started with an old woman. Jesse fought down a chuckle as he remembered Jim Sully asking politely for the woman's purse. When the old lady started in moaning and crying about how she hardly had a nickel in the world and how she didn't know how she would get by if the bandits took her last little bit, Jim Sully had thrown in his cards.

The young bandit helped the old lady back into the coach, then turned around and took up a collection from his brother and the others. The half-starved outlaws finally managed to scrounge up about ten dollars, which Jim presented to the old lady with his apologies for upsetting her.

As the would-be bandits rode off and the stage started rolling again, the old woman looked up at Jesse in confusion. Carefully then, she tucked the crumpled bills and a handful of coins into her reticule. Right alongside a wad of bills thick enough to choke two horses.

And when they reached their destination, Jesse had discovered that not only was there a cash box . . . but it was loaded with gold. Payroll for some miners. Smiling to himself, he acknowledged silently that the Sullys were more likely to starve to death than hang.

It hadn't taken him long to buy a horse and track down the Sully gang. With a small show of his talent with a six-shooter and a few elaborate lies, Jesse had won their confidence and joined their "gang." And though he was forced to pose as an outlaw to accomplish his goals, he was just as pleased to be with a group that made the likelihood of actually committing a crime very slim.

"Hurry up now, you bunch!" Jim ordered, and Jesse snapped his attention back to the present. "We got hot coffee and good food awaitin' on us!"

Deliberately Jesse Hogan pushed all thoughts of

Miranda Perry aside and went about his own business.

The coffee was strong enough to stand by itself. Just the way Jesse liked it. Hot as hell and black as sin. He took a small sip and glanced covertly at the other men gathered around the stove in the corner of the restaurant. Besides Jim and Bill Sully and the two men who rode with them, there were three men gossiping in low tones. Carefully Jesse looked them over.

The first was an older man with gray-streaked hair and tired eyes. Another had long, dark brown hair pulled back with a piece of rawhide and tied at the base of his neck. The last, a blond man with a mustache, was much too thin to be the man Jesse was looking for.

He lowered his gaze again and cursed himself for a wishful fool. Had he really thought it would be that easy? After two years of searching, had he really expected to stroll into the bandits' stronghold and find his man right off?

Patience, he told himself. Patience. No matter how long it took, he would be patient.

He sighed and took a long gulp of coffee. Restlessly he let his gaze wander over the small restaurant. Though the paint was peeling and one of the window-panes had a rag stuffed through a broken corner, the place was clean. Floor neatly swept, tables scrubbed until the soft pine was near white, lamp chimneys sparkling—hell, even the drinking glasses had been washed. And in the kind of company Jesse'd been keeping for the last couple of years, that was quite a treat.

Again his mind returned to Miranda. Somehow he knew it was *her* doing . . . the neatness of the place.

The warmth, the homeyness. It was something he hadn't expected to find in an outlaw hideaway. He glanced at the empty kitchen and found himself wishing she hadn't left right after setting the food out on the tables. At the same time, though, he knew it was better that way. For both of them.

"You seen Birdwell?" Jim threw the question at the knot of men huddled around the stove.

"Nah," gray hair answered. "'Spect he's with Miranda."

Jesse gritted his teeth and his thumb tapped against the side of the china cup. So that was the way of things, he thought. She wasn't free with the whole place. Just this Birdwell fella.

"The way he looks out for her," Jim said, "I'm surprised he gets anything else done atall."

"Well," the gray hair said again, "you know what it's like around here. Folks comin' and goin'. New ones comin' in all the time . . ." He nodded at Jesse. "Like him."

Jesse's eyebrows rose slightly.

"Birdwell likes to teach 'em right off that Miranda ain't to be bothered."

Jesse shook his head slowly and stared at the older man. "He don't have to worry about me. I ain't about to fight any man over a woman. Least of all a town whore."

Gray hair leaped to his feet, his face a mask of fury. "Listen here, you, you got no call to talk about Miranda that way. Why, I got half a mind to let Birdwell know just what you said and let *him* deal with ya!"

Jesse's eyes widened. For chrissakes! What kind of bandit town *was* this? Was he supposed to use Sunday-school language?

"Now, Ezra . . ." Jim Sully jumped up and grabbed the older man's shoulders. "No need to carry on so, like you said. Jesse's new. He don't know about Miranda. He didn't mean nothin'."

Jesse hadn't moved. He rocked his chair slightly on its back legs and kept his steady gaze on the old man. Ezra's face had lost some of its purple coloring, but his lips were still thin and rigid.

"Then you best tell him, Jim. Quick before Birdwell comes along, hears somethin' like that, and snaps this fella like a twig." Ezra glared at Jesse and plopped back down.

Jesse calmly stared back, even though his mind was working furiously. Hell, he couldn't afford to get thrown out of the damn town! Not after spending two years of his life on the trail of a man who *had* to be known to some of the folks around here.

"I shoulda told you 'fore we rode in, but . . . well. Don't matter." Jim shook his head and plopped back down on the seat opposite Jesse. He glanced at the closed door uneasily, as if expecting someone to come in, then started speaking in a rush. "It don't pay to say things like that, Jesse. Specially not here. See, Miranda's got a lot of friends . . . me included."

Jesse's eyebrows shot up again.

"Not *that* kind of friend," Jim said, plainly disgusted. "Look, we ain't got much time. Birdwell's bound to show up soon. I'll just say this quick. Miranda ain't no whore. Hell, it'd be impossible, what with the way Birdwell rides herd on her! But that ain't the only reason. She's"—he paused and stared off into nothingness—"special. Her pa built this place when he got out of the outlaw business. Birdwell helped her old man, and when he died, Birdwell kinda took over bein' her pa."

Jesse waited, sure there was more.

"Anyhow," Jim continued, "the fellas that come through here, hell. We all know what we're like. Got nobody. Nowhere. No home. No families." He shrugged and grinned sheepishly. "Miranda is kinda family to all of us. Sister, mother—"

"Wife?" Jesse interrupted.

"No." Jim shook his head. "You ain't listenin', Jesse. She ain't like that, and if you ever say different, Birdwell's liable to thump you so hard you'd have to wear your hat on your boot tops!"

If all this was true—and he had no reason to doubt it—Jesse was even more curious than before about Miranda Perry. Why would a woman like her stay in Bandit's Canyon? From what Jim said, she sure as hell didn't belong there!

In spite of himself, he felt a surge of curiosity. That first attraction he'd felt for the woman flickered back into life and he squashed it back down. It had been two years since he'd allowed himself even to *notice* a "good" woman. And now, he told himself fiercely, was *not* the time to start. Not when he was finally so close. Besides, he wasn't going anywhere. If he should change his mind . . . He stifled a chuckle.

"What's so funny?" Jim asked, smiling.

"I was just thinkin'," Jesse countered. "Not that I'm interested or anything, but if I *was*, how much trouble could a fella with a name like *Birdwell* give me?"

Jim's lips pursed. He glanced at his brother, then at Ezra, before turning back to Jesse. "Let's just say you was wrong about Miranda . . . don't you make the same mistake about Birdwell."

Miranda pushed the image of Jesse Hogan from her mind. Instead she picked up her latest copy of *Godey's*

Lady's Book and flipped idly through the pages. Heaven knew, she'd already read it enough to have the blasted thing memorized, but somehow, reading about fancy dinners or how to take stains out of satin took her mind off the problems at hand.

She chuckled softly and told herself that she could probably tell the people at Godey's lots of things they didn't know. Like how to fit ten flapjacks on a griddle made for eight . . . how to keep desert sand out of your baked goods . . . how to allow for wind when taking a shot at a deer, or even, thanks to some of the men in town, how to rob a bank.

Miranda sighed, slapped the book closed, and let her head fall against the high back of her favorite rocking chair. She stared up at the ceiling and played the game that had entertained her since childhood.

Against the whitewashed wood, her mind created the image of Bandit's Canyon. Not as it was now, but as it could be. Clearly she saw women walking down freshly swept boardwalks, chatting happily to busy storekeepers. She saw children laughing and running in the street. Curtains hung at every window, flowers planted in boxes along the hitching rails, and even a church. Yes, she told herself. A church painted a fresh, clean white, with a tall steeple and a bell. The bell would ring out every Sunday for services, and during the week they could use it to call the kids in for school. She even knew where the church would be built. Right where Big Pete's saloon now stood.

She closed her eyes and still saw her dream town. A place where no one was hiding. Where there were no gunfights.

Then suddenly, down the main street of her dream, she saw herself, strolling arm in arm with a tall, dark-haired man who smiled down at her as if she were the only woman in the country. And though she couldn't see his face, she knew it was Jesse Hogan.

Miranda's eyes flew open and she straightened abruptly. For heaven's sake, she told herself. You only just met the man. Unwillingly, though, her mind conjured up her meeting with the strange man. She saw him again, travel weary, dusty, his green eyes moving over her familiarly as though he'd done it many times before. She remembered the spiraling curl of excitement that started in her stomach and grew rapidly at the sound of his deep voice.

Stop it. She stood up and carried her teacup back into the tiny kitchen of her small cabin. A cold wind whispered under the partially opened window and the starched red calico curtains fluttered in response. Miranda shivered, reached across the plank counter, and slammed the window shut. She shook her head and rubbed her arms vigorously, trying to dispel the chill creeping over her flesh.

What was it about the man that kept his image so fresh in her mind? Lord knew, she'd been around men all her life.

And none of them had ever affected her like this!

Determinedly she drew the cord of her red flannel robe about her waist and pulled it tight. As she jammed her hands into the pockets she reluctantly admitted that he'd even had an influence on her *clothing*!

Somehow it had never occurred to her before that her satin robes and sheer nightgowns were *quite* so revealing. But then, no other man had ever looked at her the way Jesse Hogan had. Her breath quickened and her heart pounded. She remembered how his eyes had glittered and how his gaze had raked over her body as though he could see right through the flimsy coverings she wore.

And for the first time she began to wonder if maybe her mother had been wrong. Maybe giving your heart to an outlaw didn't necessarily mean trouble and heartache. And if it did, maybe it would be worth it.

The front door flew open and crashed into the inside wall. Miranda forgot everything else and ran toward the sound.

Buck Farley, one of the new men in town, stood in the open doorway.

"What is it?" Miranda said quickly. "What's wrong?"

He gulped in air and pointed back down the street. "It's Bobby. Bobby Sawyer. He's finally come back."

Miranda took another step toward the man. "And . . . ?"

"He's hurt bad, Miranda." The man swallowed and shook his head. "Real bad. Took a bullet a couple days ago and been ridin' ever since tryin' to get back here." Buck's lips twisted into a disgusted frown. "Damn fool kid."

Miranda was already turning for the stack of bandages she kept ready in a cupboard near the door. She filled her arms with as much as she could carry, then said, "Where is he?"

"Little bunkhouse."

She nodded and started moving. Then she turned and ordered, "Go to the restaurant. Boil some water. Bring me a bowl of it and ask Jim Sully if he'll give me a hand, will you?"

"Sure thing, Miranda." He pulled the door to. "But why Jim? I'll help."

"I know, Buck. And thanks." She smiled and patted his arm. "But Jim's done this kind of thing lots of times." Miranda turned and hurried down the lop-sided boardwalk toward the bunkhouse at the end of the street. "Now hurry up, Buck," she called over her shoulder.

She heard the man take off for the restaurant, and though she didn't slow her steps any, Miranda took the time to glance skyward and mumble a plea for help.

CHAPTER 2

Miranda stifled a gasp when she lifted the edge of Bobby's sodden shirt to look at his wound. She heard him hiss through his clenched teeth and knew she was hurting him.

"I'm sorry, Bobby," she whispered, and let go of the dirty fabric.

"'S all right, Miranda." A half smile curved the corners of his full lips. "Got to be done. I know that. You go ahead on. Don't worry 'bout me."

Miranda bit her lip and reached for the shirt again. The unnaturally quiet bunkhouse seemed to close in around her. Two lamps, one on either side of the narrow cot, dappled the two people with an uncertain light that flickered and fought against the darkness.

Miranda squelched a rising sense of dread. She'd never seen a wound as bad as Bobby's. She wasn't sure what to do.

Where was Jim Sully and the damned water? If she could soak the edges of the material, it would come free from the dried blood a lot less painfully. But did she dare wait any longer? "I've got to get this shirt off you, Bobby."

"I know. . . ." He shuddered and swallowed. "Go on."

The bunkhouse door opened and Miranda looked up, relieved. But it was Jesse Hogan, not Jim Sully, who stepped inside. He carried a bowl of hot water in one hand and a whiskey bottle in the other.

"Where's—"

Jesse cut her off. "Jim and the boys're already asleep. I'll help."

"Thanks, but you don't have to. . . ." Miranda's words faded off when she looked up into his eyes. Instead of the raw desire she'd seen there earlier, sympathy and sorrow now shone in the green depths. The man was watching Bobby Sawyer's struggles as if he shared them in some way.

"Randa?" Jesse Hogan forgotten, she whipped back around toward the young man lying on the narrow bed. "You still here?"

"I'm here, Bobby. I won't leave you."

From the corner of her eye, she saw Jesse kneel down across from her. She saw his features tighten as he studied Bobby's wound. And she saw the gentleness in his touch as he carefully pulled the fabric free of the wound and eased the boy's shirt off.

"I reckon I really done it this time, ain't I?" Bobby swallowed and another long, shuddering breath shook his body. He groaned and reached for Miranda's hand.

"You'll be all right, Bobby. Just like I told you."

She ignored Jesse when his gaze snapped up at her obvious lie.

"Surely is cold tonight," the boy said haltingly.

"I know, I know." Miranda smoothed his sweat-dampened sandy blond hair off his brow. "As soon as Jesse's finished, I'll cover you up with a warm blanket."

Bobby's head rolled to one side and he stared at Jesse for a moment. "Do I know you, mister?"

"Nope." Jesse smiled at the boy briefly, then went back to work on his wound. "Just got here tonight."

"Fine welcome!" Bobby snorted a laugh and groaned softly at the action. His wide blue eyes suddenly focused on Miranda. "Don't go nowhere, Randa. Please."

"I won't, Bobby. I'll stay." She laid one hand on his clammy forehead. "You calm down now."

"Reckon the boys'll figure I'm some kinda green baby—actin' all scared like. . . ."

Miranda met Jesse's regret-filled glance, then turned back to the young man. "No, Bobby," she whispered. "No, they won't."

"Hell." Bobby closed his eyes and sighed. "Wasn't s'posed to turn out like this."

She forced a smile into her voice. "You remember all this next time you try to hold up a bank all on your lonesome."

"Oh"—he licked his lips—"yes, ma'am." His soft chuckle became a moan. After a few long, agonizing seconds he added, "But who woulda thought that old man banker would pull a gun?"

"I know," Miranda whispered, and smoothed her fingertips along his jaw. "Don't try to talk, Bobby. Hush now."

Not for the first time Miranda wished she knew more. Wished that she knew enough to make his chest wound stop bleeding. To get that damned bullet out of him without tearing up his flesh any more than it already was. To make him live. Sudden tears welled up in her eyes and she blinked furiously. He didn't need to see her cry. She glanced again at Jesse, only to find him staring at her, waiting, it seemed, for her attention.

An unspoken question filled the silence between them, and though she'd been expecting it, when Jesse slowly shook his head, Miranda wanted to scream.

But she didn't. There was nothing either of them could do. And there was no doctor. Not in Bandit's Canyon. Probably not a *real* doctor for a hundred miles. Bobby Sawyer was going to die. And there wasn't a blessed thing she could do about it. It was a miracle that he'd made it back to the canyon at all with a wound as bad as his.

She bit her lip and tore her gaze away from Jesse's. Pain, regret, and frustration were etched into the tall man's features. His eyes seemed to hold all the sorrow in the world. And it didn't help her to know that he shared her pain. Miranda looked down at Bobby and shook her head. Such a waste.

"Randa?" His fingers tightened slightly on hers.

"Yes, Bobby?"

"I ain't ready to die yet. . . ." He opened his eyes and tried to focus on her. He couldn't see her clearly, but it didn't matter. Bobby held an image of her firm in his mind. Soft brown hair that sparkled in the sun, freckles across her small, always sunburned nose, and blue-green eyes that flashed when her temper was lit, but were usually calm and shining with the kindness she showed to everybody. He didn't need to see her with his eyes. Just hearing her voice again was enough. No matter what happened to him now, it would be all right.

Bobby twisted wildly for a moment before slumping into stillness. His insides were on fire. And he didn't have the strength anymore to fight it off. Instead his tired body drooped with each flaring burst of agony and he held his breath until it subsided.

Bobby'd ridden through waves of pain for almost two days just to reach Bandit's Canyon—and Miranda. As soon as the damned banker'd shot him as he was riding out of that town, Bobby'd known that he'd caught a death bullet. Nothing to be done about it. But at the same time, he'd forced himself to stay in the saddle. To stay conscious. To get to Miranda. To get home. Bobby didn't so much mind the dyin', it was missin' out on the livin' that bothered him. But hell, he'd known all along that it would prob'ly end like this. At least he wasn't alone. Miranda was there.

The pain eased up some and he took another shaky breath. Had to ask her something.

He smiled inside. Funny how it took dyin' to give him the guts to say what he'd always wanted to say.

Summoning up what strength he had left, Bobby muttered, "Don't feel bad, Miranda." His lips twitched slightly. "I know I'm goin'. It ain't bad, y'know. Long as you're here."

She bit the inside of her cheek. "I'm glad, Bobby."

"You're 'bout the only decent woman who's spoke to me in the last couple of years. . . ." Shouldn't never have left home, he told himself fruitlessly.

Miranda's smile was strained, but he didn't notice as she wiped his cheeks with a cool cloth.

Something twisted inside him and Bobby groaned at the red-hot pain slicing through his body. Miranda's fingers tightened around his hand and he tried to concentrate on her presence. He had to hurry. He *had* to know before he died.

"Randa?"

"Yes?"

"You recall that dance"—he coughed and Miranda winced in sympathy—"at Big Pete's place? Couple months back?"

She'd leaned down closer to him. He couldn't see her in the growing darkness, but he smelled her perfume. That soft, flowery stuff she always wore.

"I got to know somethin', Randa. 'Fore I go . . ." Bobby paused. Why didn't somebody light a damned lamp?

"What?" Miranda's breath fanned his cheek.

"If I'da asked you to partner up with me . . ." He licked his dry lips and struggled for another gasp of air. "Would you have gone along?"

"Yes, I would, Bobby." He heard her take a trembling breath. "I was waitin' on you to ask me."

Bobby smiled. "Well I'll be goddamned." He sighed.

He felt her perfume surround him. Thousands of flowers blossomed and spread everywhere. Why, he could *see* 'em. Clear as anything. Acres and acres of 'em. And *him* right dab in the middle. The flowers went on forever—far as he could see and more. And the sunshine was so bright. A soft breeze caressed him and he took a deep gulp of the sweet air, surprised to find that his chest didn't hurt anymore. Bobby started walking through the colorful fields of flowers swaying in the gentle wind, toward the sunlight that seemed to call him.

"Bobby?" Miranda laid her head on his chest and listened. Nothing. Slowly she rose and looked down at him. As she pulled the blanket up over his face, Miranda hoped the Lord would forgive her the lie that had brought the smile still curving Bobby's lips.

Jesse sat unmoving in the silence. Without the boy's labored breathing, the quiet was almost too much to bear. He watched Miranda pull the brown blanket up over Bobby Sawyer's face. His chest tightened painfully as he saw tears fill her eyes and roll down her cheeks.

Breathing raggedly, Jesse sat back on his heels, his hands lying uselessly in his lap. He'd known from the moment he'd first examined the wound that the boy would die. And Lord knew, it had taken every ounce of his will to remain there to watch it. He continued to stare at the woman opposite him, vaguely surprised that his first instinct was to comfort her. She still knelt by the bed, her shoulders bowed, head down, and he knew that she was hiding her tears.

From him.

Jesse let his head fall back on his neck. His wide, staring eyes fixed unblinkingly at the ceiling, where the feeble light from the two lamps dipped and swayed. The boy had been as good as dead when he was shot. And somehow he'd managed to make it back here to this nest of outlaws.

Why? Why was it so important for the kid to die here? With her?

He looked at her again and tried to understand. But all he saw was that she needed someone. That she needed the comfort she'd given to the dying boy just minutes ago.

Jesse straightened up and pushed himself to his feet. Slowly he walked around the bed and stopped when he reached her side. She hadn't moved. It was as if she were alone. Jesse knew what she was feeling. The helpless rage. The overwhelming grief at an unnecessary death. Suddenly it wasn't just *her* need that touched him. Jesse wanted to help. It had been so long since he'd felt anything at all, he was overwhelmed by his sudden urge to comfort her. To somehow ease her pain, if only for a moment. He knew from his own past that her sadness would fade away. Her life would go on.

It wasn't grief that lasted forever, he reminded himself grimly. It was guilt.

He stooped, cupped her elbows with his hands, and drew her to her feet. When she turned to look at him, Jesse's heart stumbled. Her watery eyes and trembling lip shook him to his core. How could she feel so deeply and manage not to shatter?

Slowly he pulled her against him and his arms closed around her. She laid her head on his chest and wrapped her arms around his waist. As she cried softly Jesse rested his chin on the top of her head and found himself patting her back reassuringly as he would a child.

He forced his breathing to slow even as he mentally ordered his body to ignore the warmth of her. The delicate scent of flowers clung to her and he couldn't help noticing how soft and clean her shining brown hair was. Or how well she fitted up against him. Or how good she felt in his arms.

It had been far too long since he'd held a woman for the right reasons. For comfort. For love. He'd been too much in the company of women who were only interested in his money. Jesse took a deep breath, filling his lungs with her scent, and smoothed her hair back from her face. Her tears had increased and she held him with a fierce grip that surprised him with its strength.

For one precious moment he allowed himself to pretend that he was the Jesse Hogan he used to be. That Miranda Perry was his woman. That she held him not for comfort but for passion.

Where had it all gone? he wondered. Where was the

life he'd planned so carefully? He closed his eyes and clamped his lips together. He'd wanted a wife. Children. And now all he had was a moment of make-believe while holding a woman who cried for another man.

Miranda's tears slowed. He felt the tension leave her and regretfully noticed that she'd released her hold on him. Accordingly his own arms loosened and he looked down at her as she pulled slightly back.

"I'm sorry. . . ." she started to say.

Jesse's arms dropped to his sides. "Don't be."

She nodded and glanced over her shoulder at the still form on the bed. "It's only that . . . he was so young."

His gaze followed hers. The blanket-covered body stirred too many memories for him, though, and he looked quickly away. "Yeah. Young and stupid."

Miranda's eyes snapped back to him. "He was my friend."

Jesse's lips quirked. He felt the customary coldness pour back into him and welcomed it. Her face was much too vulnerable. Her warmth too tempting. Her heart too big. Deliberately he said the one thing he knew would spark an angry response from her.

"Must've been a mighty *close* friend for him to ride two days with a wound like that"—he leaned closer—"just to die in your arms."

His ploy worked. Jesse watched, disgusted with himself, as her features froze into a mask of distaste. She took a step back from him as though he were covered with muck. Solemnly she pulled the cloth belt of her ugly red robe tighter around her narrow waist and tossed her loose, flowing hair over her shoulder. He found himself wondering what had happened to the pretty nightclothes she'd been wearing earlier.

Making a supreme effort, Miranda stiffened her spine and lifted her chin. "Thank you for trying to help, Mr. Hogan."

If he could have figured out a way to do it, Jesse would have kicked himself in the gut. Hard. What the hell was the matter with him anyway? Did he have to make everybody as miserable as he was? Did he have to destroy everything soft so that he could remain strong?

The look in her eyes chilled him. It shouldn't have mattered to him *what* she thought of him. But it did. For some strange, goddamned reason, it did. And now he'd fixed it so that all she'd want to see of him was his backside, leavin' town. So? his mind answered. That's how it should be, isn't it? You weren't exactly planning on staying at Bandit's Canyon, now, were you?

No. He wasn't. But had it really been necessary to make her hate his guts? His eyes quickly raked over her tall, shapely form. Yes. It had been necessary. If she hated him, then he would be safe. Safe from his own cravings for a normal life. If he didn't keep a careful guard on them, they would escape the dark pit in his soul that he'd shoved them into and demand release.

And then he would never find the one man whose capture could bring him peace.

He straightened his shoulders and pulled his hat down low over his eyes. "Sorry it didn't do any good."

Her eyes filled again and he felt himself weakening. He wanted to reach out and pull her into his arms again. To hold her until her tears dried. But he couldn't.

"So am I," she whispered.

His right hand moved as if to touch her but stopped

halfway. Heavy, rhythmic pounding sounded outside. It was coming closer. Jesse glanced at the oil lamp closest to him and saw it flicker. At every stomp, the shaky wood floors and walls seemed to vibrate. Each hurried crash was louder than the one before as the intruder came ever nearer.

Jesse looked quickly around the bunkhouse. Even in the half-light he could see that there was no other way out. Unless he shoved Miranda through one of the far windows then followed her. He shot a look at her and saw that she'd hardly noticed the sounds. Or if she had, she was too grief-stricken to care. And in that case, he would have to look out for both of them.

Jesse whirled around to face the door and pulled Miranda behind him. His long legs spread wide apart, he lifted the gun from the worn holster on his hip. When the bunkhouse door flew open, Jesse held his pistol steady, waiting for his target to step inside.

"Holy shit!"

"Jesse, don't!"

Miranda's voice drowned out his curse and her arm snaked out from behind him to knock his pistol down. Jesse hardly noticed. His attention was centered on the man in the doorway.

Standing at least five inches over six feet, the barrel-chested man filled the doorway with his massive shoulders and powerful arms. The red and black checks on the shirt he wore seemed to shrink and grow with the man's forceful breathing. A wild-looking salt-and-pepper beard covered the lower half of his face and the dim lamplight gleamed off the surface of his shiny bald head. The man's hands were curled around a Colt revolving shotgun and Jesse didn't have the slightest doubt that he would use it.

Above the full beard, the giant's eyes, as hard and black as two chunks of wet coal, glared at Jesse.

"What the hell's goin' on here?" the big man's voice thundered.

Jesse stared openmouthed at the intruder and finally noticed that he himself was no longer holding a gun. The thought of going up against a shotgun— unarmed—in such close quarters wasn't a comforting one. Miranda scurried out from behind him, giving him a look that said plainly she thought he was crazy.

Jesse made a grab for her and the giant lifted the shotgun.

"Stop it. Both of you." Miranda looked from one to the other of them, shaking her head in wonder. "For heaven's sake. Hasn't there been enough dying for one night?" She looked pointedly at Bobby's body.

Jesse saw the big man glance at the bed and wondered briefly if he could reach his pistol before his opponent could aim his shotgun. As if he could read minds, the man in the doorway turned back and pointed his weapon directly at Jesse.

"Put that thing down." Miranda shook her finger at the man. Then she spun around, picked up Jesse's pistol, and handed it to him. "And you, put this away."

Reluctantly both men did as they were told. But still, they kept a watchful gaze on each other.

Miranda spoke first to the big man. "This is Jesse Hogan. He rode in tonight with the Sullys." The man cocked his head and narrowed his eyes. "Jesse says the others are asleep . . . so you'll have to wait till morning to talk to them." She ignored his distrustful stare and turned around once more. "Jesse . . ."

Somehow he knew what she was going to say even before it came out of her mouth.

"This is my uncle. Birdwell Cates."

Dawn was just streaking the eastern sky with slashes of pink, orange, and scarlet when Miranda and Shelly Port sat down with their usual morning coffee. Neither of them spoke until they'd had a few sips of the strong black liquid.

"Well, it sounds like you had a helluva night." Shelly smiled when her friend got up slowly. She followed Miranda's progress around the cabin with her eyes. She didn't miss the little signs of agitation. How Miranda's hands shook slightly. How she couldn't seem to sit still for longer than a minute. In the two years they'd been getting together for a chat in the early-morning hush, Shelly'd never seen the other woman like this.

Intrigued, Shelly determined to find out what . . . or *who* was behind the strange behavior.

Miranda carried the coffeepot to the table and poured her friend another cupful. "It was certainly a long night. Between poor Bobby dying and then Birdwell and Jesse Hogan squaring off at each other . . ."

"It *is* a shame about Bobby, all right," Shelly said quietly. "He was always so . . . polite. A nice kid."

"Kid?" Miranda chuckled. "He was a year older than you."

"No foolin'?" Shelly shook her head. "Sure didn't seem no twenty-five to me." She sighed and took a sip of coffee. "But I guess I put a lot more livin' into my years than he did, huh?"

Miranda smiled, reached across the table, and patted the woman's hand. Most of Shelly's past was still a secret from everyone in town. The only thing Miranda was sure of was that the young woman had come to Bandit's Canyon three years ago with a cardsharp named Slick Stephens. When Slick left a couple of months later, Shelly stayed. Slick had never been back, and there'd even been a rumor about a year ago that he'd pushed his luck on a riverboat and gotten shot for his trouble.

Miranda looked at her friend and smiled. Shelly's long dark hair was brushed into an upsweep and held in place by a silver comb adorned with pretty blue stones. Her green gingham dress was much plainer than those she wore when serving drinks at Big Pete's saloon, but it seemed to suit her far more.

Whatever it was that had brought the woman to the canyon, Miranda was grateful. Shelly was the only friend she'd ever had and she couldn't imagine a better one.

"So," Shelly said softly, "you gonna tell me about this Jesse fella?"

Miranda's cheeks flushed. "I don't know much. Just that he rode in late last night with the Sullys." She took a deep breath. "And he helped me with Bobby."

"That all?"

"What do you mean?"

One corner of Shelly's mouth tilted in a wry grin. "Only that I don't recall ever seein' you blush over anyone else around here."

"I'm not blushing . . . well, if I am, it's not because—"

"Yes . . ." Shelly leaned her elbows on the table and propped her chin in her hands.

"Stop it, Shelly." Miranda slumped back in her chair. "He's no different than any of the others who drift through here."

"Oh." Shelly nodded abruptly. "So he's fat and old and smells like he hasn't had a bath in a year?"

"No." Miranda smiled and shook her head. "No, he's handsome. And tall. And thin. And has the saddest green eyes I've ever seen."

"Uh-oh."

"What do you mean, uh-oh?"

"I mean it was bound to happen someday, honey." Shelly chewed at her lip.

"What?"

"Oh, some smooth-talkin', sad-eyed cowboy comin' here and makin' you go all soft inside." Shelly leaned toward Miranda. "Then he'll start tellin' you how he's not really an outlaw . . . never meant no harm . . . it was just 'evil companions' got him in trouble. All he needs is the love of a good woman and he'll be fine."

"Shelly, I—"

"No, I've heard the stories. I've seen the sad eyes. And let me tell you. Nothing changes. They are who they are. Nobody holds a gun to their heads and *makes* them turn outlaw. They do it 'cause they want to do it. And no 'good' woman is gonna stop 'em. All that happens is the good woman goes bad right along with 'em."

"Shelly." Miranda swallowed uneasily. She'd never seen her friend like this. Her usually smiling brown eyes were solemn and bitter. "I don't know what it is that happened to you."

The other woman looked away, her lips twisted mutinously.

"But I *do* know," Miranda continued, "what will *not* happen to me. And I'm not about to fall in love with a man on the run from the law." She stood up and carried her coffee cup to the kitchen of the town restaurant. "First off, that's the one thing I promised my mother. And secondly . . ." She spun around. "I've lived here my whole life, Shelly. I've known probably every bad man who ever traveled through the west. I've listened to their stories, patched them up when they come in shot, and buried 'em when I couldn't save 'em. I may be two years younger than you. And maybe I haven't seen or done everything you have."

Shelly snorted.

"But I've seen enough to know that *this* is not what I want. I want a home. A man of my own who's home at night. I want to be able to light a lamp after dark without worrying about making myself a target. I want children." Shelly didn't look convinced, but after the night before, Miranda was more sure than ever how she wanted her life to go.

Oh, she was willing to admit that Jesse Hogan was an attractive man. All right, she conceded silently, *more* than attractive. But he was also an outlaw. Miranda took a long, deep breath. And that one fact made thinking about him impossible. She would treat him no differently than the others. She couldn't. If she ever started to weaken, she would simply force herself to remember Bobby's face as he lay dying. It had been hard enough watching a friend die like that. She vowed that she'd never have to watch a man she loved go through the same thing.

Miranda shook her head firmly and smiled at her friend. "No, Shelly. I want nothing to do with an outlaw." She spread her arms wide. "Someday I want Bandit's Canyon to be a *real* town. With nice people. And box picnics. And church socials." She stood up, walked to Shelly's side, and met the other woman's gaze steadily. "So don't you worry about me, Shelly. What I want, no sad-eyed cowboy can give me."

Shelly rose slowly and hugged Miranda. She blinked back the tears in her eyes and made a silent vow. She would personally see to it that no handsome drifter did anything to make Miranda's dreams die.

CHAPTER 3

Jesse glanced at the dozen or so men sprinkled around the dining room. As his gaze quickly moved over each of them, he mentally checked them off his private list. Too fat, too tall, too thin, too dark . . . it went on and on. This quest of his had forever changed the way he looked at people. No longer did he bother to find out if they were liars or good folks. Drunks or teetotalers. Lazy or hardworking. It didn't matter. All that mattered now was the one man he sought.

He leaned back in his chair and took a long drink of coffee. So far he hadn't seen anyone in town that came close to the brief description he had of his quarry. One more time he silently repeated that information. The man he was looking for was of average height, with dirty blond hair and wide shoulders. He had a knife scar on his left forearm, a tattoo of an Indian war lance on his back, and he rode a big gray horse.

And the most important piece of information. Only a few months ago he'd learned that the man he was hunting had been known to hide out in Bandit's

Canyon. Though Jesse was fairly sure the man wasn't there now, with winter coming on, there was a good chance that he would be soon.

Disgusted, Jesse sat forward and slammed his coffee cup down on the table. Not much to show for two years of searching. He ran one hand over his face in a futile attempt to wipe away the frustration that had become his constant companion.

Jim Sully laughed at something his brother said and Jesse grimaced. He remembered clearly the outrageous stories his own brother, Carter, had loved to tell. And with each telling, the stories grew until not even Carter recalled the actual facts. Jesse stared down into the dregs of his coffee. In his mind's eye, though, he was seeing his sister-in-law, Della, swatting her husband with a dish towel, then allowing herself to be captured and tickled into submission.

One corner of his mouth lifted in a halfhearted smile as Jesse heard again the soft whispers coming from Carter and Della's room late at night. He remembered teasing Della about her girth as the baby within her grew, and he remembered Carter's quiet pride in his wife and coming child.

"It's good to see you smile, Jesse!"

His thoughts scattered, Jesse looked up at Jim Sully. "Huh?"

"I said"—Jim grinned and propped one foot on the nearest chair—"it's good to see you smile. Usually you got such an almighty fierce look about you."

Jesse shook his head and stood up. He would have to be more careful. Be more friendly to the outlaws if he wanted these people to trust him enough to talk. Lord knew, if he didn't find what he needed here in Bandit's Canyon, he didn't know where else to look. Deliberately he forced a light tone into his voice.

"That's my 'bad man' look, Jim. Figure if I can scare folks, they'll hand over their cash quicker."

"Hell." Jim laughed. "If I had any money, *I'd* give it to ya!"

"See? Workin' already." Jesse shoved one hand in his pocket, fumbling for a coin. "Who do we pay for breakfast around here? That's the best meal I've had in quite a spell."

Jim shook his head. "Don't pay nobody."

"What?"

"This"—Jim waved his arms about—"ain't a reg'lar restaurant, Jesse. It's like . . . a town kitchen." At Jesse's blank look, Jim continued. "Miranda, Shelly, and sometimes a couple of Big Pete's girls do most of the cookin', although a few of the boys lend a hand now and again." He leaned forward and grinned. "I try not to be here then. Anyhow, you don't pay for your meals. When you come into town, you put however much you can spare into the jar yonder."

He pointed and Jesse turned to look. A big, red clay jar sat on a table just to the side of the front door.

"When somebody goes out for supplies to stock the kitchen and such, they take what they need from there." He shrugged. "That way nobody goes hungry and the food here belongs to any of us that needs it."

Jesse shook his head slowly. He could hardly believe it. A town full of sneak thieves, rustlers, and bank robbers run on the honor code. "Whose crazy idea was that?"

Jim's brows shot up. "Crazy? Why the hell is it crazy? It works."

"And all you bunch . . . *trust* each other?"

"Well . . ." Jim paused a moment then smiled. "I wouldn't say 'trust' is the right word. 'Put up with' is

most likely. 'Sides, if we steal here . . . where else we
gonna go?''

That was true enough. And looking around, Jesse
could see plainly what this place meant to most of the
men. It was a haven. A safe place where they could let
down their guard somewhat. Where they didn't have
to be constantly on the prod, waiting for trouble to
start or a lawman to sneak up behind them. Even he
had felt it, Jesse acknowledged silently. He knew that
he was perhaps closer to his prey than ever before,
and an uneasy calm had settled over him almost as
soon as they'd entered the canyon. At least until he
met Miranda.

Shrugging, he followed Jim out of the restaurant.
But when the blond walked toward the corral and
stable, Jesse stayed behind. Leaning against the half-
finished porch railing, he reached into his pocket for
his tobacco pouch.

After he'd rolled his cigarette, he scraped a match
across the nearest post and touched it to the tobacco.
He took a deep pull, dragging the hot, acrid smoke
into his lungs and expelling it in a cloudy blue stream.
This early in the morning, there weren't too many
folks wandering about the town. So far the only
people he'd seen were those in the dining room,
hovering over coffee, hoping to wake up.

Jesse's gaze moved over the empty, one-street town,
and despite himself, he felt a grudging admiration for
whoever had put Bandit's Canyon together. The tiny
village lay nestled deep in the rock canyons of the
desert, surrounded on all sides by high cliff walls.
Clumps of mesquite and sage clung tenaciously to the
rocks, sprinkling the red rock with patches of gray and
green. A cursory look at the cliffs and a man would
think there was no way out of there. But Jesse knew

that wasn't so. There were so many caves and tunnels twisting through the rock canyons, a man could get lost in there for years.

He lowered his gaze and looked at the neat buildings lining the street. One story, with two-story false fronts, most of them looked as though they could use some care, though the place looked a sight better than he'd expected it to. Wind, sand, and the desert sun had done plenty of damage. The paint on most of the plank buildings had been swallowed by the wood grain, leaving only a hint of their original color. But scattered here and there was evidence that someone was trying to change all that.

Jesse's gaze lit momentarily on the bright green door of the general store. The paint job was fresh, the color shiny in the early sunlight. His eyes moved on, absently noting a flower box, a half-finished boardwalk, a decidedly crooked hitching rail, and even, he observed with surprise, gingham curtains at the bunkhouse windows. Idly he wondered why he hadn't noticed them the night before.

Because, he told himself firmly, he was too busy noticing Miranda. He gave himself a good shake to clear his mind and went back to studying the outlaw hideaway. His gaze stopped on a particular sign. He snorted. Jesse never would have thought that a bandit town would have a store marked LADIES' APPAREL! Just under that sign, a door opened.

Jesse watched as a nicely rounded behind backed into view. Despite his best intentions, his gaze fixed on the woman dragging a huge box out of the store. Miranda was wearing a pair of men's pants that had obviously been altered to fit. And fit her they did. The fawn-colored trousers hugged her behind and clung to her long, shapely legs. At her calf they disappeared under a pair of knee-high moccasins that even from a distance he could see were decorated with beads and fancy stitching. She stood up, put her hands at the small of her back, and stretched.

Jesse's gaze moved unwillingly over the white, open-throated shirt straining across her high, full breasts. His breath ragged, he tore his gaze away and focused instead on her shining brown hair that hung in one long braid down the center of her back, ending just at her narrow waist.

He rubbed the back of his hand across his mouth and clenched his teeth. If Birdwell Cates was so damned concerned about men leaving Miranda alone, why the hell did he let her dress like that? In all his life, he'd never see a woman so . . . *bewitching*. That was the only word for it, he knew. Nothing else could explain his interest in the woman. After all, for the last two years he'd had no trouble at all avoiding the very same feelings that were swamping him now.

When she raised her arms high above her head and twisted first one way then the other, obviously working out the kinks in her muscles, Jesse groaned softly and turned away.

In the cool desert morning, he was dripping with sweat. He felt it roll down between his shoulder blades, sticking his gray shirt to his already too hot flesh. Deliberately Jesse kept his back to her, walked to the edge of the wide porch, and sat down.

Whatever was happening to him, he'd best find a way to stop it. He pulled his hat off and fanned himself slowly as he shifted around on the uneven porch looking for a comfortable position. Then Jesse smirked at his own thoughts. He knew damn well what was making him uncomfortable and it *wasn't* the good-for-nothing porch! Well, he told himself wryly, at least *now* he understood why Birdwell was so dang touchy about Miranda! Hell, lookin' like she did, it was amazing that the men around her left her alone. And yet maybe it wasn't so amazing. Jesse leaned his head back against the railing and remembered his little "chat" with Birdwell.

Miranda hadn't been gone from the room more than an instant when the big man started in.

"I saw the way you was holdin' her," he said, "and I'm here to tell ya . . . that there'll be the *last* time!"

Jesse's eyes hadn't left the shotgun, still aimed in his direction. "You didn't see a damned thing, mister."

Birdwell took one ponderous step closer. "Don't tell me what I seen with my own two eyes—"

"I was holdin' her while she cried for that damn fool kid over there." Jesse forced himself to meet the other man's cold black glare.

Slowly Birdwell nodded. "Maybe. M'randa *does* go on about such things." The shotgun lowered a hair. "But that don't mean you wasn't thinkin' somethin' different."

"Shit," Jesse countered as he realized he wasn't as near to being shot as he'd thought, "you gonna shoot a man for what he's thinkin' . . . then you'd best stock up on an almighty lot of ammunition."

Birdwell studied him for a long, breathless moment, then slowly lowered the shotgun. "Awright. Reckon I cain't shoot you for what you think . . . but, mister, you ever try to do somethin' about it and this here gun will smash you into so many pieces, nobody'll be able to walk without steppin' on ya."

Jesse nodded.

"You say you come in with the Sullys?"

"That's right."

"How long you plannin' on stayin'?"

Jesse shrugged indifferently. "Till Jim's ready to pull out, I s'pose."

"I'll be talkin' to him about you." Birdwell's voice lowered and rumbled in the quiet room. "And I best like what I hear."

Jesse straightened his hat and headed for the door. To get there, he had to walk directly past Birdwell. When he was next to the big man, he stopped and looked up. "Don't worry about me, mister. I don't want her." Birdwell started to speak, but Jesse cut him off. "I got things to do and a woman's got no place in my plans." He took another step, then stopped and looked over his shoulder. "But just so's you know." Birdwell looked up. "If I *did* want her . . . not you *nor* your damned shotgun could stop me."

Before the big man could answer, Jesse turned his back and walked away.

A curse rang out in the still air and Jesse snapped out of his recollections. Hesitantly he looked around at Miranda and saw that it was as he'd expected. It *was* her cussing. As he watched she kicked the box in front of her then, hands on her hips, glared at it expectantly.

He sighed. If he knew what was good for him, he'd head off and do *something*. Rub down the horses, clean his guns—hell, even wash his clothes. He knew he ought to stay as far away from that woman as he could. Even as he pushed himself to his feet and started toward her, he called himself every kind of fool and wondered if Birdwell would take pity on a crazy man.

Birdwell fingered the shotgun's trigger thoughtfully. He cradled the gun in the hollow of his arm and watched Jesse Hogan cross the street to Miranda. Birdwell's gaze flicked quickly to the young woman he thought of as a daughter and he noted, not for the first time, how she'd filled out in the last few years.

His coal-black eyes narrowed when Jesse closed in on her. Birdwell didn't much care for the way the younger man looked at Miranda. Like a hungry kid at a peppermint stick. Lord knew, he'd seen other men stare at her with wishful eyes and itchy hands . . . but there was something different about this one. Something more. In Jesse Hogan's eyes there was a craving.

He watched as the outlaw lifted the wooden crate easily and began to follow Miranda down the half-finished boardwalk toward the general store. He heard Miranda's laughter, soft and gentle in the early-morning air, and could hardly credit that "his" little girl was a full-grown woman. Birdwell left the shadowy alley and walked down the street in the opposite direction of the store. Miranda would be safe enough for now. Not even Jesse Hogan would try something foolish in broad daylight in the middle of town.

When he reached the oversized, slat-backed chair in front of the main bunkhouse, Birdwell plopped down. Tilting the chair onto its back legs, he lifted one booted foot and propped it on the porch railing. He reached over and leaned his shotgun against the side of the bunkhouse, then ran one beefy hand over the smooth surface of his scalp. Where had all the time gone? How had the years slipped by without him hardly noticing? And when had Miranda become the woman she was? In his mind's eye, Birdwell saw her as she used to be. All long legs, knobby knees, and spirit. Like a Thoroughbred filly. And as she grew she'd fulfilled every promise he'd seen in her and more. Maybe too much more.

He glanced around the quiet street and felt again the

odd sense of foreboding that filled him more and more often lately. Times were changing. Or maybe he was just getting old. He'd been out of the outlaw life for so long, he hardly knew any of the young sprouts comin' through the canyon anymore. Shit, he told himself, most of the ones *he'd* started out with were either in jail or dead.

And in just the last year or so, he'd begun to see a change in the kind of men lookin' for shelter in Bandit's Canyon. Oh, sure, there was still some of the regular crowd—like the Sullys for instance . . . and Ezra Banks and a few others. But along with them was a bunch that Birdwell wouldn't give two bits for. And he couldn't think of a rightful way of keepin' 'em out of the canyon.

He shook his head and smoothed his full beard down over his red flannel shirt. Ol' Judd Perry would be some disgusted if he was to come back from wherever he'd gone after dyin'. One of the first rules Judd had lain down for his bandit town was "no killers allowed." Birdwell snorted. Oh, Judd understood how some folks kinda stumbled into the outlaw life. How rustlin' a few head of cattle because you were hungry could stick the name of outlaw on a man. And gamblers and cardsharps—well, Judd always figured if a man was stupid enough to get himself fleeced by the likes of them, it was his own fault. Even bank, stage, and train robbers had their place, Judd figured. Kept those rich fellas on their toes. But he never could abide a killer. Wasn't no reason for it, he'd always said.

And Bandit's Canyon had worked just fine. Over the years it'd been home to most of the wanted men west of the Mississippi at one time or another. And not a killer in the bunch. Until now. Birdwell's eyes moved restlessly over the street. He felt in his bones that some of the men hiding out in town *were* killers. But there was no way to prove it. And as long as they caused no trouble in town, he had no reason to throw them out.

Birdwell heaved a sigh and directed his dark stare toward the general store where Miranda and Jesse had gone. With a snort of admiration, he recalled Jesse's bravado the night before. Standing up to a man holding a shotgun on you was either real stupid or damn nervy. Either way, though, Hogan's actions had made Birdwell face the fact that there might come a day when he wouldn't be able to protect Miranda. That one day somebody might just shoot him down to get to her. Without Birdwell, she'd be all alone. In a town full of men you couldn't trust further than you could spit.

He had to try again to get Miranda to leave the canyon. It was the only way he could be sure of her safety.

"What the hell have you got in that damned thing anyway?" Jesse straightened up and glared at the huge wooden box sitting on the plank floor in the middle of the general store.

Miranda chuckled again but quickly bit the inside of her cheek to stop herself. Her laughter only seemed to annoy him and Jesse Hogan was cranky enough already. "All sorts of things," she answered, dropping to her knees.

"Hmmph! Looks like junk to me."

She frowned up at him then went back to the box. "It only looks like junk if you've no imagination!"

"What the hell's imagination got to do with any-thing?" He stepped closer to her and peered into the jumble of things he'd just carted what seemed like miles. "Dented pots, old lamps, mangy-lookin' curtains, and half a butter churn! If that ain't junk . . . I don't know what *is*!"

"Nonsense." Miranda lifted one of the dented copper pots. With one finger she rubbed at the caked-on grease and soot. "With a little hard work"—her finger smoothed over the deep furrow in the metal—"and perhaps a hammer here and there, this old pot will be like new!"

"Well, why the hell don't you just *buy* new?" Jesse moved over to the rough-planed counter, turned his back on it, and leaned his elbows behind him. "Why you want to waste your time on that old stuff?"

Miranda set the pot down and reached for a scarred brass lamp. "It's not easy to get out and buy new things, Jesse. Why I can't even remember the last time I left the canyon." She threw a quick glance at him over her shoulder. "Besides, I'll appreciate everything more if I work hard for it."

He shook his head and she could see that he still didn't understand. And she wanted him to. For some reason, it seemed important. Miranda felt his gaze on her and tried to concentrate on unloading the crate in front of her. But it was difficult. Ever since he'd walked up to her and offered her his help, she'd had a hard time concentrating on anything but him.

There was something about the man that called out to her. His brilliant green eyes and the loneliness behind them touched her as nothing else ever had. Miranda glanced at her hands and noticed that despite the clenching grip she had on the side of the box, she was trembling. Good heavens. Where were all the fine intentions she'd told Shelly about only that morning? What had happened to her firm resolve to be nothing more than casually friendly to Jesse Hogan? To treat him no differently than she did any of the other men hiding out in the canyon?

Was Bobby's death fading from memory so quickly then? Had she forgotten the promise she'd made to her mother? And what about the vow she'd made to herself? Could she allow all these things to fade away because of an unreasonable attraction to an intriguing outlaw?

No. She swallowed heavily, forced her heartbeat to slow down, and took a deep breath. Deliberately she reached into the box and drew out the crumpled, dirty blue fabric that had once been curtains. Keeping her voice level, she commented, "These will wash up nicely, I know it. And they'll look so nice hanging in the shop."

She kept her head averted, but she heard him shift his feet and desperately hoped he stayed where he was. It was hard enough to gather her wits with him at a distance.

"What shop?" he asked, and Miranda sighed her relief. He hadn't moved.

"The one we just left."

"Oh." A long, silent pause and then: "Ain't never heard of a ladies'-apparel store in a bandit town. There other women around here?"

Miranda's lips twisted slightly, but she didn't turn. "A few. Big Pete's girls, down at the saloon—Shelly, me. Oh. And Serena Dexter. But she doesn't live here all the time. She came in a couple of months ago with her husband, Pike."

"*Pike* Dexter? *Arizona Pike?*"

He sounded so astonished, Miranda looked over her shoulder at him. His jaw hung open. He'd pushed away from the counter and was staring at her as if she'd grown another head.

"Well, yes, Arizona Pike." She cocked her head. "Is there another Pike Dexter?"

Jesse pushed his hat back and shook his head slowly. "No. Leastways I hope not. One of him is surely enough."

"Oh, I agree."

"You 'agree'?"

"Certainly." Miranda leaned forward into the box, pushing items around and occasionally lifting one for a closer inspection. "Heaven knows, Pike isn't the most gentlemanly man I've ever met. And he has the most awful temper. Really. Why, I could tell you some stories about Pike that would really surprise you!"

"I doubt it."

She looked up and saw he'd leaned back against the counter.

"Pike's wanted in more places than rain." Jesse stared at her. "Shoot, even his own men *hate* him!"

"Oh, I know." Miranda nodded and sat back on her heels. "It's such a shame."

"A shame?"

"Oh, yes." She looked up at him again. "See, he wasn't always like this. Oh . . . he always had a nasty temper. But he didn't used to be so . . . hard."

Jesse snorted.

"It's true." Miranda turned her gaze on the far wall and stared blankly, remembering the past. "He used to have a lovely smile. And when Pike laughed, well. You just couldn't help laughing along with him." Her features fell. "But not anymore. Not since his brother was hanged." She glanced at Jesse and saw she had his complete attention. "A vigilante mob dragged Mort out of a saloon somewhere in Arizona and hanged him on the spot." She shook her head slowly. "Ever since then, the only person Pike treats decently is his wife, Serena. And it's a good thing, too."

Jesse's voice was strained. "You sound like you mean that. What would you do to him if he didn't treat her decent?"

"Oh." She grinned sheepishly. "I don't know. But I'd think of something. A woman in her condition should be treated with care." Miranda folded her dirty hands in her lap. "Thankfully, though, Pike seems to realize that. It's why he left Serena here with us while he went out on business."

"Her condition?" Jesse's voice seemed even more strained.

"Yes. It's so exciting! Her baby is due in just a week or so now!" She looked up at Jesse Hogan, and if she hadn't known better, she would have sworn that the man paled.

Son of a bitch! Unbidden, visions of Della raced through Jesse's mind. His sister-in-law had been so proud of her rounded belly. She used to pat her unborn child and talk to it off and on throughout the day.

What was it Miranda'd said? That a woman in that condition should be treated with care? His insides twisted. No woman should be treated as Della had been. Especially not a pregnant woman.

Oh, Jesus, he groaned silently. He didn't know if he could stand being around a pregnant woman. Memories of his lost family already hovered over him like a thick winter fog. Seeing a woman enjoying what Della'd been denied . . . no.

Jesse straightened up. He'd have to find out all he

could in the next week or so, then get out of the damned canyon. Maybe once he found the man responsible for shattering his life, he'd be able to build a new one.

But not before.

CHAPTER 4

Buck Farley snorted, reached across the table, and slapped his partner's shoulder. "You been starin' at that woman for close on an hour now. Don't you never give up?"

"Nope." Dave Black flicked a glance at his friend then turned back to watching the dark-haired woman by the window.

"Shit, Dave." Buck shook his head and gulped at his coffee. "We been here a couple months now and that female ain't so much as smiled at ya!"

"Don't matter."

"I seen some hard heads in my time, partner, but you do beat all of 'em put together."

Dave shrugged. "Hard head or not . . . I ain't about to quit on her."

"Sometimes you don't make no sense at all." Buck leaned forward, his long, brown hair falling across his shoulders. "Don't you think you'd best remember why we come here in the first place?"

Dave glared at his friend. "I ain't forgot. And you best keep your voice down, Buck."

After a glance around at the nearly empty dining room, Buck continued. "Nobody's listenin' to me. *Includin'* you. You got no call to be worryin' over that woman when there's business to take care of."

"What business?" Dave faced his friend. "Like you said, we been here a couple months already and don't know a damn sight more than we did when we got here." His voice dropped to a whisper. "So instead of hangin' around here tellin' me what to do, why don't you go get busy?"

Buck frowned, reached up, and yanked his hair free of his collar.

Dave shook his head. "And while you're at it, why don't you cut that damn hair of yours before some Indian beats you to it. I've known some would look at that mess like quite a prize!" He pushed himself to his feet and snatched his hat from the table. Looking down at the other man, Dave frowned and added, "Didn't your mama teach you to take off your hat when you're inside?"

The other man's eyes rolled up and he looked at the brim of his dirty black hat as if surprised to find it still on his head.

"I swear, Buck, you been out ramblin' too long." Dave turned and walked slowly to the table where Shelly Port sat, still staring out the window.

They'd been in the store for a long time. Shelly's fingers twisted together, but her gaze didn't shift. She would watch that general store for as long as she had to. A curl of worry spiraled through her body. Shelly knew she wouldn't be able to relax her guard until

Jesse Hogan had left not only the general store, but Bandit's Canyon.

Her full lips twisted and she clenched her joined hands tighter. She was afraid for Miranda. Oh, Shelly knew that the woman had been raised right there in the canyon. That she'd been surrounded by all types of men all her life. But despite everything, Miranda remained an innocent. Shelly smiled wryly, thinking of her own lost hopes and dreams. Maybe it was because her own innocence had long since gone that Shelly was so determined to protect Miranda's.

Miranda's trusting nature had survived even living in a town where liars, cheats, and thieves were the only citizens. Shelly shook her head. Three years she'd been in the canyon. And this was the first time Shelly had seen Miranda's interest in a man go beyond kindness.

Shelly chewed at her lip. Miranda didn't understand. She didn't know what a smooth-talkin' man could do to a woman. How he could slip up behind her before she knew what was happening and rearrange her whole world. She squeezed her eyes shut. Then, when he tired of her, he'd leave her. Alone and unfit for anything besides the life he'd introduced her to.

She took a deep, shuddering breath and glared at the general store opposite her. None of that would happen to Miranda. Shelly would see to that. The woman was the best friend Shelly'd ever had.

"'Scuse me, ma'am."

She jumped and looked at the blond man as he sat down across from her. Somehow she wasn't surprised to see him. Ever since he and his saddle partner had hit town, the lean, blond man turned up everywhere.

"Don't mean to bother you, but . . ."

Deliberately ignoring him, Shelly looked back out the window.

"You just looked so pretty, sittin' there in the mornin' sun and all . . ."

Shelly shifted uncomfortably. She'd heard pretty words too many times before. From too many men. Still, there was something about this one . . . she smoothed her pale blue skirt self-consciously.

"I . . . uh . . ."

"What is it?" She glanced at him and saw that for an outlaw, he was mighty nervous looking.

Dave ran his fingers over the brim of his hat. Dammit, he'd had everything he wanted to say right there on the tip of his tongue and now that she was lookin' at him . . . Hell. He couldn't remember his own name! Those big brown eyes of hers cut right into a man's soul. And he fancied that he saw the same shadows haunting her eyes that he suspected were in his own. Painful reminders of a past that wouldn't stay in the past. Her thick black hair was caught up in a severe knot at the base of her neck, but she didn't fool Dave. He'd seen that hair free and wild once. It was during a storm, shortly after he and Buck had come to the bandit holdout. Shelly, thinking herself alone at the edge of town, had taken the pins from her hair, turned into the fierce canyon wind, and let the steamy, desert gusts pummel her from all sides.

Dave was on guard duty that night, high on the cliffs. From his perch he'd watched her, facing into the wind and rain. Thunder crashed down around them and lightning streaked across the sky. In the strange half-light of the lightning bolts, Shelly had allowed nature the caresses she denied to every man in the canyon. As long as he lived, Dave would remember her as she was that night. Soaking wet, her face turned up to the sky, and the hot blasts of wind molding her dress to her body like a lover's hands.

A chair leg scraped across the wooden floor and Dave shook himself. She was leaving.

"Wait." He half stood, his hand stretched out toward her. "Don't go. Please."

Shelly watched him through narrowed eyes. "Why not?"

"I thought we could . . . uh . . . well," Dave stammered, trying to come up with a reason, *any* reason to convince her to stay.

She threw a quick look out the window then turned back to Dave. Slowly, reluctantly, Shelly sat down again. "What is it you want from me, mister?"

Dave eased down onto his chair and took a deep breath. Well. There it was. What was it that he wanted? Hell, if he told her that, he had no doubt that she'd hightail it for the nearest hole and crawl right in. This was not the time to tell the woman that what he wanted was *her*.

"I figured maybe you and me could be . . . friends?"

"No."

He blinked. "No? Just *no*?"

"That's right."

"Why the hell not?" He leaned back in his chair, a slow grin lifting one corner of his mouth. He certainly hadn't expected *that*! "You got so many friends you can't stand one more?"

"No." Her gaze dropped to the tabletop.

"That all you're gonna say?"

Nothing.

Dave frowned slightly. This wasn't going the way he'd planned at all. Now she wouldn't even look at him. But like he told Buck. He wasn't about to give up.

"Well, then, if you ain't gonna talk . . . *I* will." He leaned forward, his elbows on the table. She was so stiff, it was like she had a poker stuck up her corset. He took a deep breath and plunged ahead. "I ain't askin' for nothin' special here, Miss Shelly." At least not yet, he assured himself. He lowered his voice. "I just thought that we could talk sometimes, *you* know. Hell, I know I ain't much to look at." Dave shrugged. She still stared at the table. "But that don't matter none to friends, does it?"

Suddenly she looked up, glanced at him quickly, then let her gaze slide away to the window.

"Tell you what." He rubbed one hand over his freshly shaved jaw. "How 'bout if I do the talkin' and you just listen sometimes? How'd that be?"

She started and Dave turned to follow her gaze. For an instant he saw Jesse Hogan outlined in the doorway of the general store. Then the man turned and disappeared inside again. Dave wondered if she was interested in the new man. But he discounted that notion quickly. That wasn't interest shining in her eyes. It was worry. She was clearly frettin' over something.

Dave's brain worked at a fever pitch. Mentally he went through the names and faces of the most notorious of the wanted men in the area. He was fairly sure Jesse Hogan wasn't one of 'em. Then what was it about the man that upset Shelly so? Her features were stiff. Her hands clasped tightly together. *Something* had her real skittish.

Suddenly the answer dawned on him. Miranda was in that store with Jesse. Shelly was mother-henning the woman.

Dave chuckled softly. "You know, that boy's been

warned some already about leavin' Miranda alone. Reckon he's one that's got to learn the hard way."

Shelly turned and looked at him. Her features blank, she slowly stood up. Looking down at him, she said softly, "Seems like most men got to learn the hard way." She didn't give him time to answer her, just spun around and walked across the room and out the front door.

Dave stared after her for a long moment. A leisurely grin curved the edges of his mouth. Seems he owed Jesse Hogan a thank you. At least she had finally *talked* to him. It was a start.

Miranda's eyes followed Jesse as he walked from the counter to the doorway then back again. His color was no better and his mouth was now a grim, hard line. Silently she went back over what she'd said, looking for a clue to his sudden change of manner. He'd been all right until she'd mentioned Serena.

Miranda looked up at him. Did he know her? Or Pike? Would there be trouble when Pike returned? There were so many things about him that she didn't know.

"Are you all right?" she asked quietly.

"I'm fine!" Jesse snapped at her. He managed to look everywhere but directly at her. Finally he settled his gaze on a shaft of sunlight just above her head. Pale light filtered through a dirty windowpane over the door and sliced through the gloom of the store. Tiny flecks of dust floated and danced in the light and Jesse tried desperately to concentrate on them. This was all *her* fault. Dammit anyway, she had no right to make him feel things that were better off dead! It didn't do any good at all to let himself grieve for Della. For Carter. For the baby. Nothin' did any good. Except putting them out of his mind. And he would have done just fine at that if not for this woman and this damn town! Who the hell would expect to run into a pregnant woman in an outlaw hideaway?

He glared at Miranda. She reacted to his stare and looked up. Jesse's fists clenched as his teeth ground together. Why did she have to look at him like that? Her turquoise eyes all big and wide, concern written all over her face . . . who asked her to care?

"Like I said," Jesse grumbled, "I'm just dandy. It's *you* that ain't right!"

"Me?" Her head cocked to one side and her long, brown braid fell over her shoulder. "What do you mean?"

"This!" Jesse pushed away from the counter and marched in a wide circle around her. He raised his arms to encompass the store and the surrounding town. "All of this! What the hell are you doin' in a place like this?"

Miranda smiled and shook her head. "You mean what's a nice girl like me doing here?"

"Well, yeah!"

"Oh, Jesse, I'd thought better of you than that." She pushed herself to her feet. "I can't tell you how many times I've heard that question."

"That right?" He took a step back, trying to keep a safe distance between them. "You got an answer?"

"Of course." Miranda looked at him. Nervous, fidgety, he'd managed to turn the conversation away from himself. She knew he'd done it purposely, too.

He pushed his hat back further on his head. "And that there's another thing! How come if you been livin' in this hole all your life . . . how come you talk like a durn schoolmarm?"

"I do?" Her brow wrinkled slightly and she tapped one finger against her chin thoughtfully.

"You sure as damn well do." Although she sure as shootin' didn't *look* like one. At least none he'd ever seen. He tried to keep from admiring her figure, but those damn trousers and open-necked shirt made it almighty hard.

"I never realized." Miranda shook her head. "Isn't that funny?" She looked up at him and smiled. "No one's ever told me that before. I wonder why not."

"Most likely they was afraid they'd say it wrong."

"Oh, no," she said quickly. "That couldn't be why, could it?" Her eyes widened even more. "I'd feel terrible if I thought for a moment that I'd made anyone uncomfortable."

Jesse let his head drop back on his neck. He stared at the ceiling helplessly. What was it about her? Even when he's bein' mean to her, all she can think is that mayhap she's upset some other folks. He chanced a quick look at her. She still looked worried.

Something deep within him stirred and he found himself saying quietly, "You didn't bother nobody. Folks prob'ly never even noticed."

Miranda's features softened and Jesse felt an unreasonable warmth flood him. This didn't make sense. None of it did. And what was worse, he found he *really* wanted to know why a woman like her was living in the middle of the desert playin' nursemaid to men who'd most likely get shot on sight at any decent town.

"So," he asked in a tone more harsh than he'd planned, "you gonna tell me or not?"

"Hmmm?"

He sighed. "You gonna tell me why the hell you're livin' out here in this godforsaken hole?"

Miranda laughed gently and Jesse felt the sound smooth over him like bubbling warm water in a hot spring.

"If you'll carry this box over behind the counter, I will."

For just an instant a smile hovered on Jesse's lips before disappearing entirely. Figured she'd find a way to make him heft the durn thing again. Silently he lifted the crate once more and set it down where she told him. Then he turned and looked down at her, trying not to inhale the flowery fragrance of her. She smiled at him. A wide, friendly smile whose like he hadn't seen in longer than he cared to remember. Then she turned and walked to the open doorway.

She stared out at the street and began to speak. "This 'hole,' as you call it, is my home. I was born here."

"*Here?*"

Miranda glanced back at him and nodded. "Right here. My father built this place, you know. But I suppose you've heard that already."

He shrugged. "Some. Why don't you tell me?"

"My father, Judd Perry"—she turned back to the sunwashed street—"was a thief. He didn't start out that way of course."

"Of course," Jesse agreed, and let his gaze move over her leisurely.

"But when his farm failed and he couldn't get a loan, well, I suppose he got angry. Bitter. He started robbing stagecoaches and worked his way up to banks." Miranda shrugged and slid her hand up the side of the door she leaned against. "He made a lot of friends on the Owl Hoot trail, and after a few years, he was tired. He had enough money 'stashed away' and he wanted to find a spot he could call home." She looked back at Jesse and grinned. "But he was wanted just about everywhere, so he had nowhere to go. Then he remembered this place. He had hidden up here in the canyon once before when a posse was hunting him." She leaned her head back against the door panel and closed her eyes. "So he decided to come here and build his own town. Only it would be a town where outlaws would be welcome. He'd seen the lonely men riding trails by night, never able to rest, never able to close their eyes for fear of being caught unawares. He talked a few of his friends, like Birdwell and Big Pete, into coming with him and they built this town."

"I thought you said Birdwell was your uncle," Jesse interrupted her.

She shook her head. "He's not really. But in my heart, he is."

Jesse nodded and waited for her to continue.

"Anyway, they came here together and let word get around of what they were planning to do. Soon outlaws from all over the country were coming by with supplies. Every board, every nail was brought in from the outside by men who knew they would finally have a place to call home."

She opened her eyes and pushed away from the door. Walking slowly around the room, Miranda ran her hand over the shelves and chairs lovingly. "There's a natural spring here, you know, so there was plenty of water." She stopped, looked at Jesse, and smiled. "Of course, the Apaches didn't care for Judd and the others settling down right on top of the water. . . ."

"I'll bet." Jesse returned her smile but privately thought that Judd Perry and his friends must have had a helluva time convincing those Apaches.

"Even now," Miranda added, "we have an occasional raid."

He shook his head. She said that so simply. As if an Apache raid was no more important than a burned chicken dinner.

"And with outlaws coming in from all over the country, there was always a fresh supply of food for the men and grain for the animals. Although now we even have a good-sized garden in springtime. We put up the extra so there's plenty of vegetables for winter." She smiled proudly. "*That* was my idea. And it's not easy getting the men to take their turn at hoeing, either. But one of the town rules is, if you don't help out, you don't stay."

"Rules?" Jesse said softly, not wanting to break the spell of her voice.

"A few." She shrugged her shoulders again. "But they're very simple. The one I just told you about helping out . . . and another is, no killers are allowed sanctuary in the canyon." Miranda stopped and watched him seriously. He looked so surprised at her last statement, she felt she should explain. "My father understood how a man might be forced into stealing to survive and he thought any man fool enough to play cards with a professional gambler *deserved* to be cheated. But he wouldn't tolerate a killer." She smiled again. "Judd didn't trust them. Another rule is that there be no stealing or fighting in town. Judd always said that everyone had a right to feel safe here."

"Any more I should know about?" he asked softly.

"Just one." She stopped a few feet from him. "Leave me alone."

Jesse's brows shot straight up.

"Judd added that one to the original list when I was born."

"Don't blame him." He couldn't seem to keep his eyes off her. "But none of this tells me how come you sound like a schoolteacher."

She took a deep breath and stepped up closer to the counter and Jesse. Idly she ran her fingertip along the scratch marks on the plank counter. "My mother was a schoolteacher." Miranda flattened her palms on the rough wood. "Her family was fairly wealthy, living in Independence, Missouri, when Mother decided to become a teacher." Miranda smiled. "Naturally her family was against it. They wanted her to marry and settle down nearby. But Mother wanted adventure. So she went west and finally found a position in a tiny town outside Placerville. In California."

Jesse nodded.

"While she was teaching, a young man would drop by from time to time and they would talk. Mother used to say they talked about *everything*. And he was so handsome. And so polite. So kind and gentle." Miranda inhaled sharply and went on in a rush. "One day the young man asked her to marry him. But he said, before she answered, he wanted her to know the truth about him. And so he told her. But Teresa McGraw didn't care that Judd Perry was an outlaw." Miranda's chin went up. "She loved him. And knew he loved her."

Miranda turned to face Jesse, a soft smile on her face. "After they were married, Judd came here, built this place, then brought my mother here. I was born two years later."

"Where are they now?" Jesse asked, though he was fairly sure he knew the answer.

"They're both gone now." Miranda took a step closer. Only inches separated them. "Mother died when I was fifteen and Father was killed only two years ago."

"Killed?" Jesse whispered. Her perfume drifted up to him and he took a long, deep breath of it, letting it fill him.

"Hunting accident. Just outside the canyon." She licked her lips nervously and watched Jesse's mouth.

"Shame."

"Yes." She breathed. "I miss them both."

"'Course." Jesse held perfectly still for a long moment. His gaze moved over her face like a gentle touch. Her eyes held him and he felt himself falling into the clear blue-green depths. Slowly, tenderly he raised one hand and touched the sprinkle of freckles across the bridge of her nose. Her skin was so soft. Her warm breath teased the inside of his wrist and his heart began to pound furiously.

She tilted her head back and seemed to invite his fingers to smooth down the length of her cheek and jaw. The silence in the room screamed at him. All he heard was the rushing of his own blood and the quickening of her breath.

He bent lower and dipped his head close to her. The fresh, clean scent of her flooded him, and when she cocked her head to one side, he moved and claimed her lips with his own.

His mouth moved over hers almost reverently. His hand moved to the back of her head, his fingers pushing through her hair. The length of her braid felt heavy against his palm. He wrapped his left arm around her waist and held her with a gentle strength. She sighed into his mouth and Jesse's throat closed with the rush of long-denied emotion. When she lifted her arms to encircle his neck, something deep inside Jesse's chest snapped.

He tore his mouth away and buried his face in her hair to muffle his quiet groan. Like a drowning man, he held on to her as though his life depended on it. He couldn't understand what was happening. He only knew that something was different. Something about him had changed.

And it was because of her.

CHAPTER 5

He released her so suddenly, she almost fell over. Jesse stared at her, his chest heaving with his effort to calm his breathing. What had happened?

Miranda reached out a hand for him, but he stepped back. Her hair was coming loose from her once neat braid. Long, soft tendrils curled down around her face. Her cheeks were flushed, her lips parted as her breath came in short, harsh gasps. Her turquoise eyes were shining as she watched him, and Jesse felt a vague sense of dread creep through him.

Oh, Lord, what was goin' on? He reached up and rubbed one hand over his face. He ignored the trembling in his fingers and tried to remember why he'd come to the canyon.

He had to get out of that damned store. He was after vengeance. Justice. He couldn't let *anything* distract him.

Not even Miranda.

He had to think.

His gaze flicked to her and he knew he'd never be

able to think clearly around her again. The memory of that kiss and what it had done to him would always be with him. Deliberately he turned away from her. It was hard enough trying to figure out what she'd done to him. With those eyes of hers looking at him, it was impossible.

"Jesse?"

He flinched but didn't turn. "What?"

She took one step closer and it was all he could do not to run.

"Jesse, what's wrong?"

Jesus! Her voice sounded so small and hurt. He dragged a deep gulp of air into his lungs and desperately fought to keep from looking at her.

"Nothin's wrong." His throat closed. Jesse swallowed heavily and added, "I got to go, Miranda."

"But . . ."

She took another step and Jesse couldn't bear it any longer. Without a word, he stalked to the door and hurried outside.

Miranda listened to the sound of his bootsteps as they faded off down the boardwalk. Suddenly alone, she tried to make sense of everything.

But there wasn't any sense in what had happened. None at all.

She touched her own lips with her fingertips in memory of his mouth against hers. If she tried, she could recapture the warmth of him. The smooth feel of his lips. His breath on her cheek.

Stop it! she silently ordered herself. Instead of recalling every detail, she should be trying to wipe it from her mind. No matter what the kiss had done to her . . . *and* him. In a few moments with Jesse, Miranda'd betrayed every vow she'd ever made—both to her mother and to herself.

She looked at the empty doorway and shivered slightly. Jesse Hogan had done with one kiss what a lifetime of living with outlaws hadn't accomplished. Miranda was afraid. Afraid of what he made her feel when he was near. She would have to be on her guard. Slowly, deliberately Miranda crossed the room and closed the door.

Miranda handed the cup and saucer to Serena and smiled. "How are you feeling today?"

The tiny blonde looked down at her swollen stomach and grimaced. "As big as a cow."

Miranda laughed and handed over another cup of tea to Shelly.

"I swear," Serena added as she ran her palm over her belly, "if this child doesn't show up soon . . ."

"What will you do?" Shelly asked. "Change your mind?"

"Guess it's too late for that, huh?" Serena took a sip of tea then gasped, her hand shooting to the side of her belly.

"What is it?" Miranda set her cup down and knelt beside her friend. "Serena? Are you all right? Is it time?"

After a moment Serena shook her head gently and sighed. "You're gonna have to settle down some, M'randa. You can't get to jumpin' every time the little fella gives me a mule kick!"

Shelly chuckled and Miranda looked from one woman to the other before smiling reluctantly. "All right. I know I'm a little flustered over the baby. . . ."

"A *little*?" Shelly's brows went straight up. Glancing at Serena, she said, "Do you know that she's

plannin' on havin' a pot of water boilin' all the time
from now until whenever that child arrives?"

"What're you plannin' on doin' with all that water,
Miranda?" Serena's eyes shone with gentle laughter.

Miranda paused, thought for a moment, and finally
admitted, "I don't know." She glared playfully at
Shelly. "It's *your* fault!"

"*My* fault?"

"Yes." Miranda shook a finger at her friend. "I
heard you a couple of weeks ago down at Big Pete's
place." She turned to Serena. "Shelly was telling Fat
Alice about the time she helped deliver a baby and she
said it was a lucky thing they had plenty of hot
water."

Shelly grinned. Strange how remembering the hard
times she'd lived through didn't hurt nearly as much
as it used to. Had to be because of the friends she'd
found in this place. "You should have listened to the
whole story, Miranda." She turned to Serena and
winked. "Why that hellhole the baby came into was so
filthy dirty, I used up oceans of hot water just scrub-
bin' the place down."

"*That's* what the water was for?" Miranda's brow
wrinkled. "Well, I'm glad to know that!" She looked
slowly and deliberately around the little cabin they'd
fixed up for the Dexters. Only two rooms, the tiny
place was sparkling clean and Miranda had rooted
through all of her treasures to find little things to make
their home more cozy.

Yellow curtains hung at the windows, a bright rag
rug covered the middle of the plank floor, and on it sat
two chairs with a small table between them. A wash
table with a pitcher and bowl stood in the corner and
she'd even found an old painting of a mountain sunset
to hang over the fireplace. In the other room was a

narrow feather bed with a good warm quilt atop it and two lamps hung on either side.

She smiled, pleased with her efforts. Serena had a nice home and people who cared about her. She would be fine.

All she lacked was her husband. And there was nothing any of them could do about that.

"I won't worry about boiling water again," Miranda said firmly. "This house fairly gleams."

"It does that," Serena agreed, and let her eyes roam around the little room. "Miranda," she said softly, "I don't know if I ever thanked you for all you done for me, but I . . ."

"No need for that, Serena." Miranda patted the other woman's hand and smiled at Shelly. "We were glad to, weren't we?"

"Yes." The woman nodded.

"Besides," Miranda said brightly, "I can hardly wait for the baby to get here! It's all so exciting!"

"Oooh . . ." Serena gasped again.

"Another kick?"

The pregnant woman smiled and nodded. Reaching out, she took Miranda's hand and held it firmly against her belly.

Miranda held her breath. Her fingers spread out over Serena's taut skin, she waited, hoping she'd know it when she felt it. Then something hard poked her hand fiercely and Miranda's jaw dropped. She stared at Serena's unborn child and waited again, hoping for more. This was the first time she'd ever been around a woman about to give birth. The baby obliged and Miranda laughed delightedly.

"That's *wonderful*!" She glanced at Shelly. "Don't you want to feel it?"

Shelly shook her head. "No . . . I've uh, felt it before."

Miranda shrugged, turned back to Serena, and reluctantly pulled her hand back. "What does it feel like from inside?"

"Oh, that's hard to say." She smiled and pushed herself to her feet. "Guess it would be kinda like swallowin' a jackrabbit that's all the time hoppin' around . . . it's somethin' you've got to feel for yourself. But I'll say this. I've seen the inside of an outhouse more in the last few months than ever before in my life!"

She walked slowly to the backdoor, her hand at the base of her spine. "I'll be back directly."

When she was gone, Miranda sat back on her heels and looked at Shelly. "I hope someday I'll get to know what it's like to have a child inside me." But when she did, it wouldn't be in a bandit town with an outlaw husband, she reminded herself firmly. No. She wanted a husband that would be there with her when she needed him. Then she dismissed that thought and added, "It must be a joyful thing."

"Not always."

"Hmmm? Why not?"

"Well, take Serena." Shelly glanced at the still-closed door. "I reckon it's mighty hard to be 'joyful' with your husband out doin' Lord knows what and maybe gettin' killed by some posse or other."

"Yes," Miranda agreed. After all, hadn't she just thought the same thing herself? "But Serena *seems* happy."

"What else can she do? She sure as hell can't change Pike. And there's no stoppin' that child from comin'."

"But I *know* she's happy about her baby," Miranda

protested. She'd watched Serena's face as the baby
kicked. She'd seen her pleased, proud expression.

Shelly exhaled in a rush. "Oh, I expect you're right,
Miranda. Don't pay me no mind."

"Is anything wrong, Shelly?" Miranda looked at her
friend closely. She seemed a little pale.

"No." Shelly took a deep breath. "Everything's just
fine."

As the other woman reached for the kettle hanging
on a hook over the fire, Miranda watched her thoughtfully. Despite what she said, there *was* something
bothering Shelly. And why not? There was certainly
something bothering *her*, and his name was Jesse
Hogan.

Miranda frowned. There were altogether too many
damned secrets all of a sudden in Bandit's Canyon.
Shelly's behavior. Jesse's kiss and dismissal only that
morning. Even Birdwell hadn't been himself lately.
What in heaven was happening to everyone? Herself
included.

She hadn't told Shelly about Jesse's kiss. And for the
first time in her life, she hadn't gone running to
Birdwell with her problems. This was something she
was going to have to figure out for herself.

And now, watching Serena preparing all by herself
for the birth of her child, Miranda told herself that
maybe Jesse walking away from her was the best thing
that could have happened.

"Hang on, man!" Jim Sully shouted, and waved his
hat high over his head in excitement. "C'mon, Jes!
You're doin' fine!"

Whether Jesse heard him or not was hard to tell. Jim
shook his head and grinned. His forearms on the top
rail of the corral fence, he leaned forward, his eyes

never leaving the man on horseback. Some of the men had brought in a pack of wild horses they'd come across and now the outlaws had to face up to the chore of breaking them. It would be a lot of work, but when they were finished, they'd have a supply of fresh horses right handy in the canyon.

"He's havin' him quite a ride, ain't he?"

Jim looked up as his brother Bill stepped up on the rails, swung his leg over the top, and straddled the fence.

"I'd say so!" His gaze turning back to Jesse atop the wild, bucking horse, Jim chuckled. "For some dang reason, Jesse appears set on breakin' every damn horse himself!"

Bill pushed his hat back and watched.

The chestnut mustang arched his back, jumped in the air, and spun in one vicious move. Jesse's left arm high in the air, his right hand curled around the lead rope, he gripped the horse's sides with his knees and stayed with it. The horse leaped forward suddenly and just as quickly stopped dead, its forelegs stiff and head down. Jesse sailed over the animal's head and landed with a crash against the fence on the far side of the corral. Free of its unwanted rider, the chestnut trotted docilely around the open area.

Bill jumped into the corral and, with the help of two others, grabbed the horse and held it steady.

"You 'bout had enough, Jes?"

Jesse staggered to his feet, shaking his head as if to clear it. He bent over, snatched his hat off the ground, and slapped it against his thighs. He glanced up at Jim. "Not yet." Miranda's kiss and his own reaction were still too vivid a memory. If he stayed with the horses long enough, maybe their wildness would calm him.

"Shit, boy. That horse from hell ain't about to let you get back on! Give one of the others a chance, why don't you?"

Jesse frowned and walked across the corral toward the wild-eyed animal already prancing nervously. "Stay out of this, Jim. I'm gonna ride the damn hardhead if it kills me."

Jim propped one boot on the bottom rail and shook his head gloomily. "It just might at that, y'know."

Bill and two others held the horse steady as Jesse climbed back up. As soon as he was set, the three men jumped clear and just managed to avoid flying hooves.

"'Lo, Jim."

Jim Sully looked over his shoulder and smiled. "Hey, Birdwell. Fine day, ain't it?"

"S'pose." Birdwell laid his shotgun on the top rail, both hands on the weapon to steady it.

Jim's eyebrows went straight up. "Huntin' bear, are ya?"

Birdwell didn't answer. Instead he asked quietly, "What do you know about this Jesse fella, anyway?"

Jim shrugged. "Not a helluva lot, I reckon. Why?"

Birdwell swung his head to look at the other man. His cold black eyes stared hard at the blond man. "Any reason why you ain't answerin'?"

"No." Jim cleared his throat. "Hell, Birdwell. You know as well as me that most men on the run don't talk about theirselves."

Birdwell gazed at him steadily . . . waiting.

"Well." Jim coughed again and turned back to the corral. Looking at Birdwell's surly face was enough to make a man jumpy. "Let's see now . . . we picked him up around Tucson a while back."

"How?"

"Huh?"

"I *said* how'd you come to hook up with him?"

"Oh." Jim's forehead wrinkled as he tried to remember the exact set of circumstances. The whole
thing was almighty fuzzy. As a matter of fact, he
couldn't rightly recall just how Jesse happened to find
them. "He just rode up to the fire one night, clear as I
can remember. Helped hisself to coffee, talked some to
me and the boys . . ."

"Yeah?"

"Well, shit, Birdwell!" Jim straightened up and
forced himself to look into the big man's eyes. "I
didn't know you was gonna give me no test on it or
nothin'. How the hell am I s'posed to recall every
blasted thing?"

Birdwell sighed and shook his head. "What *do* you
know?"

"Let's see . . . " Jim shoved his hands in his pockets, pursed his lips, and narrowed his eyes in thought.
"He don't hardly never complain." He nodded
abruptly. "And that there is a good thing. Lord knows
between Bill and them other two, I hear enough
gripin' already."

"What else?"

"He's right even-tempered. I 'preciate that in a
ridin' partner. Get a hothead in your bunch, and he's
liable to shoot off his gun or his mouth at the wrong
time and get ya into a peck of trouble." Jim glanced
into the corral and saw that Jesse had about whipped
that durn horse into shape. And he'd missed the last of
the fight because of Birdwell's danged questions. He
turned, frowning, back to the man on his right. "And
I'll say this for him. Jesse always does his share.
Whether it be takin' a turn as camp cook, sittin' night
guard, or draggin' Bill outta some saloon when he's

dead drunk. He's a hand, Birdwell. I got no complaints."

Birdwell nodded thoughtfully and picked up his gun. Cradling it in the hollow of his arm, he turned and walked away just as Jesse stepped up to the fence.

His hat in his hand, Jesse used his sleeve to mop sweat off his forehead. Squinting after Birdwell, he asked Jim, "What'd he want?"

Jim shrugged and grinned. "Askin' questions about you, son!"

"Me?" Jesse's gaze snapped back to the baby-faced outlaw. "What kind of questions?"

"Durn it! You, too?" Jim took a deep breath and exhaled sharply. "What the hell's goin' on here anyhow? How come all of a sudden I got to remember ever'thing that a body says?"

"What kind of questions, Jim?"

"Shit. Just the usual. Who are ya? What do I know about ya? That kinda thing." Jim reached across the fence and punched Jesse's shoulder. "Don't pay him no mind, Jes. It's just his way. Sometimes Birdwell's like a old woman."

"Yeah. A old woman with a revolvin' shotgun."

"Yeah, well . . ." Jim turned the subject to something more interesting. "You gonna have another go at one of them mustangs now that you settled that one's hash?"

Jesse put his hat on and tore his gaze away from the big man's broad back. "Yeah. Yeah, I am." He turned and walked back to the far side of the corral, where the next wild horse waited.

Somehow Jesse managed to keep from turning and taking another look at Birdwell's retreating figure. He didn't like this one bit. Hell, he'd guessed that the big man was wary of him, but it sounded now like his suspicions were growing.

What if he found out somehow that Jesse wasn't an outlaw at all? That he'd been pretending so's he'd have a way of gettin' into the canyon?

That's not all you should be worryin' over, his brain reminded him. What do you think'll happen if Birdwell finds out about you kissin' Miranda this mornin'? Jesse kicked at the dirt, disgusted. He knew good and well what would happen. He'd get thrown out of town. Or worse.

Dammit. Jesse rubbed his jaw viciously. What the hell had he been thinkin'? He had no business kissin' that woman! And why in the Sam Hill had she kissed him back?

Suddenly every awakened, unwanted feeling he'd experienced in that kiss came rushing back. His heart pounded, his breath quickened, and his palms itched to hold her again. He came up alongside the next horse he was set to ride and motioned one of the men to get out of his way. Grabbing hold of the saddle horn, he pulled himself up and settled in. His fingers wrapped around the rope. He gritted his teeth. Jesse was determined to rid himself of the feelings Miranda sparked if he had to ride and break every damned wild horse on the place.

Even if it meant breaking a few of his own bones.

The men let go and the horse charged. Jesse's body snapped back and forth. Jarring, pounding pain coursed through his body, and when the horse made a sharp left turn, Jesse flew off into the dirt. Landing on his back, Jesse took a long moment to get to his feet. When he finally managed it, he heard Jim call out, "Hey, Jes. Forgot to tell ya. M'randa wants us all out to the graveyard this afternoon. We got to bury Bobby."

Jesse brushed his hands against his thighs disgustedly. Damn near broke his back that time and it didn't do no good at all. Miranda was still in his mind. Not only that, he would have to see her again much too soon. At a burial.

He sighed and walked to the horse. Just what he needed. Another funeral.

The sandy-haired man rolled over onto his side. Reaching out, he grabbed the naked woman lying next to him and pulled her closer. She muttered sleepily as his hand moved over the curve of her hip.

His head propped up on one hand, the man idly explored the woman's body with the other. As he did, his gaze moved over the room he'd been in for the last two days. Bloodred drapes hung over the two windows, effectively shutting out daylight. The walls were covered with a garishly colored flowered paper and a painting of an ugly, nude woman reclining on a chaise hung on the far wall. A blue haze of cigarette smoke drifted through the air and blended badly with the stale smell of whiskey and sweat. The sheets beneath him were wrinkled and hot, the feather pillows long since flattened into uselessness. On the left side of the bed, a full-length, standing mirror faced him. Deliberately he tossed the covers off the woman beside him and stared at her backside reflected in the mirror. His tanned, work-roughened hand cupped her snow-white buttocks and he smiled at the image it made.

She stirred slightly and he gave her a little pinch. She moaned and moved closer. He grinned at his own reflection. Lottie'd been good fun. Not too bad a way

to pass the time, he told himself. Lord knew she was
eager enough. And still . . . he frowned and the man
in the mirror glowered back at him. His gaze moved
over the reflected image of her back. From shoulder to
calf, she was a well-built woman. But her hair was red.
Her eyes a murky brown. And she had too much meat
on her willing bones.

Deliberately his brain created another woman's
image. In the shining glass, the man now saw a
smaller, curvy woman with soft brown hair and
blue-green eyes filled with desire. For him. In his
mind's eye, the woman reached for him hungrily and
he watched her hands move over his thick body.

His breath coming fast, the sandy-haired man felt
the steady pulsing in his loins and groaned deep in his
throat. Lottie stretched out along the length of him
and in the mirror he stared as her pale, grasping hands
moved over his hairy thighs. Her teeth nipped at his
nipples and the blond man moved his hand up to the
back of her head. His fingers threaded through her
dyed copper-red hair and pulled her head back.

She looked up at him, running her tongue over her
lips, her brown eyes still half-shut with sleep. The man
allowed himself to pretend that those eyes were the
deep, blue-green ones he wanted them to be. Lottie
turned her head suddenly in his grip and moved her
lips over the long scar on his forearm. Her tongue
smoothed over his skin and he sucked in a deep
breath. She never seemed to forget how sensitive that
old knife wound was and how it affected him when
she teased it with her mouth.

Slowly he lay down on his back and gave Lottie free
rein to his flesh. Carefully, with practiced hands, the
woman stroked his heated skin with her palms, occasionally scratching gently with her long, sharp finger-

nails. The man stared up at the ceiling and imagined the entrance to Bandit's Canyon.

Lottie's mouth touched the inside of his thigh and his body jerked slightly in response. He smiled lazily. She moved on, running her lips and fingertips over his calves. Deliberately he closed his mind to her actions and concentrated instead on his plans.

It was coming on to winter, he told himself. About time to find a spot and settle in. Mayhap now was the time to head for the canyon. It'd been a while since he'd been back. Miranda ought to be quite a sight now. All filled out good and proper.

Lottie's teeth worked at his abdomen and he stroked the back of her head idly. He glanced at her, watched her large breasts dance with her movements, and felt himself swell eagerly.

Yes, it was time. Time for him to go back to the canyon and claim what was his. Time for Miranda to realize what he'd known all along. She was meant for him. He was the only man worthy of her. And by God, this time he would have her. He grinned up at the ceiling and remembered the last time he was there.

Ol' Judd Perry had actually had the nerve to refuse him. And after he'd done the right thing by talkin' to the old man first and all. Well, Judd wasn't around no more. And Birdwell was gettin' too damn old to worry about.

This time nothing would stop him.

Lottie's mouth closed around him and he allowed himself a brief moment to savor the damp warmth of her mouth before he pulled her off.

"What'sa matter, honey?" She grinned at him lazily. "Don't ya want it like that this time?"

"Yeah." He smiled back at her. "Yeah, I do. But I want to watch. I want to see you."

She straightened up, lifted her chin, and shook her wild tangle of hair back from her face. Sitting on her heels, her hands on her milky thighs, she sighed, "Why didn't ya say so, hon?" Slowly, with the concentrated glide of a snake, the woman eased her body down off the bed. Once she was kneeling on the floor, she crooked her index finger at him.

The blond sat up and swung his legs over the edge of the mattress.

"Before we start, darlin'," she whispered, her fingernails dragging over his nipples, "let me see it again. You know what that does to me."

He grinned and half turned. He felt her finger move over his shoulder, following the design traced there.

"Ooh." She sighed heavily and moved her mouth over his shoulder and around to his chest. Her tongue darting quick, wet strokes on his flesh, she mumbled, "I just *love* that thing. I ain't never seen no Indian-lance tattoo before."

He pushed all thoughts of the canyon away. No reason why he shouldn't pay attention and enjoy what Lottie did so well. The man lifted her slightly and took her nipples into his mouth, one after the other. When he released her, she slid down the length of him, brushing his chest with her breasts.

He stared into the mirror opposite him. Her hair tumbled freely over her shoulders and back. She sat on her heels, her rounded buttocks smooth and somewhat flattened. Her waist was narrow and the soles of her feet as pink as the rest of her. His gaze fixed on her, he threaded his thick fingers through her hair and drew her mouth to his member.

When her lips closed around him and her tongue moved over his swollen flesh, the man sucked in a gulp of air between clenched teeth. His fingers tightened and he held her fast. He concentrated on the image before him. Of the naked woman on the floor before him. Servicing him. Enjoying it. Wanting it as much as he did.

But in the vision he saw, the woman had soft brown hair.

CHAPTER 6

"He wasn't a bad youngster, Lord." Ezra Banks stood at the head of the freshly dug grave, staring up at the heavens. Storm clouds scuttled threateningly over the wide, desert sky, and the distant rumble of thunder grew closer with every passing moment.

A sharp, cold wind snapped around the small group of mourners, snatching at hats and moaning deep in the red rock canyons. The afternoon sun had dipped beneath the edge of the cliff face, leaving the small, quiet group in deep shadows.

"He didn't lie to his friends . . . didn't never cheat at cards . . . and was always plumb helpful when it come time for work." Ezra's voice grew louder as he competed with the thunder.

Miranda glanced up in time to see Jesse shift his gaze from her hastily. His face pale, his features strained, he looked as though he'd rather be anywhere but here. She looked away from him and let her eyes move from one disgruntled, sulking face to the next. Miranda knew that none of the men relished a burial.

It was always too clear a reminder of what could happen to any of them.

One last time she glanced at Jesse Hogan. One day it would be him lying at the bottom of a hole carved out of the earth. Shot or hanged, Jesse would end his days like all other men who lived outside the law. She had to remember that. She had to keep telling herself that he was no different from the others.

Deliberately she turned her gaze back to Ezra as he finished his prayer.

"I can't tell ya what to do o' course, Lord, but I'm thinkin' ya ought to let the boy warm hisself at your fire. Ya won't be sorry." The older man lowered his gaze to the blanket-wrapped figure lying at the bottom of the grave. "Amen."

"Amen." A chorus of half-whispered, uneasy responses answered him. The dozen or so bandits in attendance shifted from foot to foot, clearly anxious to be away from the graveyard. Their eyes moved constantly, almost as if the men were afraid to focus for too long on the weather-beaten crosses and the rock-lined graves.

Ezra, however, was the first to turn from the dark hole in the rocky ground. His pale blue eyes, red-rimmed and watery, skittered over his companions as he led the way to Big Pete's saloon.

Shelly tugged on Miranda's arm, anxious to leave the graveyard behind them. But Miranda looked at her friend, forced a half smile, and shook her head. "No. I'll stay until it's finished. You go on ahead. I'll see you at Big Pete's in a little while."

Reluctantly Shelly moved off, holding her skirt down when the rampaging wind teased at the hem. Miranda watched and noticed that Dave Black was only a step or two behind the woman. She also noted that Shelly was deliberately ignoring the outlaw.

Miranda turned back to the two men standing on either side of the open grave, shovels in hand. Birdwell and Jesse stared at each other grimly. Miranda shook her head, disgusted. Of all the men in town, why had these *two* been the ones to choose the short straws? Why not Dave and Ezra? Or even the Sullys? She looked down at the body of Bobby Sawyer. Poor Bobby. He won't even have any peace when they lay him to rest.

"You don't have to stay, y'know." Even though Jesse'd shouted at her, she barely heard him. The wind carried his voice away as quickly as he spoke.

"Yes, I do," she called back. No matter how hard it was to remain in the little cemetery, staying was the least she could do for Bobby.

"Leave her be," Birdwell shouted.

Jesse didn't answer the other man, but Miranda saw his fingers tighten around the shovel's handle. "Birdwell, please!" Miranda yelled to the older man, and grabbed at her black scarf. She was too late. The wind plucked it from her head, sailed it across the graveyard, and wrapped it around one of the crosses. Miranda walked toward it, the wind at her back, pushing her . . . prodding her.

She stumbled and fell, landing on one of the white rocks she'd used to outline the edges of the graves. A sharp pain shot through her knee and tears filled her eyes. She plopped down, yanked her scarf free, and used it to brush away the dirt and pebbles embedded in her palms. Her stinging flesh gave her the excuse she'd needed to let her tears fall. Surrounded by the dead, Miranda felt the first stirrings of her need to get away. Away from the place of so much death.

Always before, it had been enough to dream of changing Bandit's Canyon. Making it a real town. Now she wasn't so sure any longer. Even if that dream came true . . . wouldn't the spirits . . . the souls of the outlawed men still remain? Wouldn't there always be a sadness here? A desperation? A loneliness?

Her gaze moved to the crosses marking her father and mother's graves. Judd had done his best. Miranda knew that. But still, he'd lived his life hiding. Just as his wife had. And now they would lie together forever, hidden away from everything and everyone.

She sniffed and pulled a long strand of windblown hair out of her eyes. Wasn't this the very thing her mother'd been trying to tell her so long ago? That this kind of life was not what she wanted for her? Maybe she should do what Birdwell wanted and leave the canyon. She glanced over her shoulder and saw that Birdwell and Jesse had almost finished shoveling the loose sand into Bobby Sawyer's grave.

It was so hard to believe that she'd never see the boy's reckless grin again. She'd seen too many endings in Bandit's Canyon.

Pushing herself to her feet, Miranda leaned into the wind and walked to the fresh grave. Her long black skirt clung to her legs, pushing her back for every step she took. Desert sand flew up and pelted her face and hands with tiny pinpricks of pain. She welcomed the needle-sharp jabs and tried to concentrate on them.

While Jesse tamped the dirt down with the flat of his shovel, the first of the raindrops fell. Slowly at first, huge, cold drops danced on the dry earth, their heavy *plops* the only sound. A long, jagged slash of lightning lit the sky and thunder crashed overhead. In the next instant the heavens opened and rain fell as though God had upended a bucket.

Jesse stared at her. Through the gloom of the afternoon, the pouring rain, and the intermittent bursts of lightning, he felt her gaze lock with his. Only a few feet separated them, but it might as well have been miles.

All through the short, sad funeral, he'd fought to keep his eyes from her. And lost. Despite his best intentions, it was as if he was drawn to her. Walking away from her hadn't helped. Damn near killing himself on the wild horses hadn't helped. Not even a *burial* was enough to crush his growing need to be with her. To touch her. To hold her.

His grip tightened on the shovel. Why the hell did he have to meet her *now*? Why couldn't it have been two years ago? When he was still alive.

Jesse turned away and walked clumsily across the muddy ground, back to town. To the outlaws. Where he belonged.

Without a word Birdwell stepped up beside Miranda and draped one beefy arm over her shoulders. Together they went back home.

As if to defy death, the men were noisier than usual. They drank more, laughed louder, and fought harder.

Jesse sat in a corner of the ramshackle saloon. A bottle of whiskey and a full shot glass on the table in front of him, he looked around the busy room. The steady, pounding rain thudded against the leaky roof and, inside, fell into three widely spaced tin wash pans with plinks and splashes. A blue haze of smoke drifted lazily in the air, and in the far corner, one of the men pounded enthusiastically on a battered piano. Scarred tables and chairs, tobacco juice on the floor, and bullet holes in the walls were displayed almost proudly in the light thrown by dozens of candles and lanterns.

Big Pete, with his bushy red hair and full, gray-streaked red beard, stood behind the bar, futilely trying to keep up with the demand for drinks. No sooner did he fill one glass then another empty slammed down on the plank counter.

In one corner, Bill Sully, weaving drunkenly, fought one of the others for Fat Alice's attentions. Buck Farley stood, elbow propped on the bar, talking to Birdwell. Ezra Banks was dealing a poker hand, even though his pale blue eyes flicked frequently to Jesse. Dave Black sat at another table, talking and laughing with a clearly uninterested Shelly. Jesse shook his head. He gave the man credit. Dave didn't know the meaning of the word "quit." Jesse's gaze moved on and he saw Jim Sully slip from the saloon, his arm around Wilma's thick waist. With all the women who worked for him busy, it appeared that Big Pete would be doing his own serving that night.

The front door swung open, letting in a blast of cold wind and rain that threatened to extinguish the candles and lamps. Jesse turned to frown at the fool responsible and Miranda walked in. She'd changed her clothes. As she pulled her wet rain slicker off, Jesse sighed. She was back to wearing those damned trousers again. Deliberately he looked away and picked up his glass. Tilting his head back, he tossed the raw whiskey down his throat and quickly poured another. After he'd swallowed that one, he lowered his gaze to the tabletop and studied the glass as he spun it in his fingers.

He shouldn't have come to the saloon, he knew. She was bound to show up there. Hell, he told himself as he tipped a splash of amber liquid into his glass, if she was right, he probably never should have come to the canyon at all.

It had been botherin' him most of the day. That one little niggling piece of information that he hadn't thought about at the time. When Miranda was telling him the "rules," she'd mentioned one that had surprised him but hadn't struck him hard until much later.

No killers were allowed in the canyon.

Jesse gulped down the shot of whiskey and clenched his teeth against the raw bite of it. The only reason he'd come to the canyon at all was that the man he was seachin' for supposedly hid out here for a time a couple years back. Jesse'd figured that if he'd done it once, he'd do it again. But if no killers were allowed in . . . dammit. He rubbed at his eyes and tried to think.

The loud chatter around him faded away. And instead he heard only Miranda's voice. Big Pete said something and she laughed gently.

Jesse forced himself to keep his lowered eyes fixed on the tabletop. Idly his fingers traced the deep carvings in the wood, made by some bored former customer. Miranda laughed again and Jesse's fingers curled into a fist. His chest tightened. If he'd come to this place for nothing . . .

No. Jesse pushed the sound of her voice away and ordered his brain to work. If a killer wasn't welcome here, that meant one of two things. Either his information was wrong and the man he wanted had never been here . . . or the man had lied and no one in town knew him for the killer he really was.

That seemed the most likely. After all, not every bad man in the territory was known on sight. *Jesse* was proof of that. Hell, he wasn't an outlaw, and they'd accepted him as one. But if he was right, it would make his search even harder. Now he would have nothing at all to go on. No one in town would know anything about the man.

Jesse let his gaze move over the men in the room. It was possible that his man was already here. But he didn't think so. A man who killed as easily and viciously as the one Jesse was looking for wouldn't be able to hide his true nature that easily. There would be *some* sign. Temper, edginess, an eagerness to fight . . . something.

This was getting him nowhere. Jesse stood up, poured himself one last drink, and tossed it down his throat. His eyes shifted to Miranda. She was leaning against the bar talking to Big Pete. One moccasined foot propped on the rail, elbows on the plank counter, her chin in her hands, she was completely unaware of him. And maybe that was best. Jesse shoved his hat on and turned to the door. He stepped outside quickly and never saw Miranda swing her head around to watch him leave.

He hadn't gone more than a few steps when a woman's voice stopped him. Jesse turned around reluctantly, but it wasn't Miranda hurrying to him. It was Shelly.

The woman dipped her head down to avoid the slashing rain. Her arms wrapped tightly about her, she came up to within a step of him before she stopped. Her dark blue dress already near soaked, her black hair hanging in strings about her face, she looked up at him and Jesse just managed to keep from stepping back a pace. Anger fairly blazed out of her dark eyes. And he had no idea what he'd done to deserve it.

"Yes, ma'am?" he said.

"You can save your pretty manners." Shelly pushed

her hair out of her eyes and glared at him. "I know your kind. And manners don't mean spit to ya!"

"Ma'am?" Jesse looked over her head toward the saloon he'd just left, hoping someone would come out and get her. She sounded feverish.

"I want you to leave Miranda alone, you hear?"

Miranda. Jesse snorted. Of course. He stared at the angry woman, hardly noticing the small slice of light behind her that came and went in an instant.

She poked a finger in his chest. "I know all about your kind." He backed up and she followed, her voice getting louder to carry over the rain. "You with your soft talk and sad eyes."

What the hell . . . ?

"Tellin' a woman everything she wants to hear just so's you can have somethin' warm besides your horse to cuddle up to for a couple of days . . . or weeks."

"Now, ma'am—"

"Don't 'ma'am' *me*!" Her index finger jabbed at him. "I heard it all. And I *believed* it!" Her mouth worked furiously and the anger in her eyes was softened by a sheen of tears that she refused to let fall. "But no more. And *not* Miranda!"

Jesus! What the hell kinda town *was* this? No killers allowed . . . pregnant women . . . a woman boss with a bald mountain for a bodyguard . . . played-out gamblers and worn-out whores and now a she-devil about ready to tear his heart out for something that happened to *her* long before he got there!

"Lady . . ."

"I ain't no *lady* neither. Just a woman." She leaned toward him, her chest heaving, eyes narrowed. "But, mister, I make you a promise here and now. You do anything to hurt Miranda"—she paused and looked him square in the eye—"and I swear I will shoot you stone dead."

Jesse's jaw dropped. As she pushed past him he stepped aside quickly. She crossed the narrow street and was swallowed up almost instantly by the rain. Still dumbfounded by what had happened, Jesse jumped when someone else spoke up from behind him.

"Ain't she somethin'?"

Dave stared off after her, an admiring smile on his face.

"She is that." Jesse just wasn't sure *what*.

"That woman's got more fire than anything I ever seen before. 'Magine her sayin' she'd shoot ya!"

The man looked *proud*. Jesse shook his head. "Mister, I *believe* her."

Dave grinned at him. "Shoot, son, so do I. That's why I mean to have her. Who the hell wants some mealymouthed woman that's all the time afraid to say what she thinks?"

"It'd be some safer than livin' with a woman who'd just as soon shoot ya!"

"Yeah." Dave's eyebrows quirked. "But not near as excitin'." He moved toward the edge of the boardwalk. "I'll see ya, Jes. Got to make sure she gets home all right."

"Hell, who'd bother a woman like that?" Jesse smiled.

"Only me, I reckon." Dave chuckled and jumped into the rain. "And that's just how I like it."

Jesse watched the other man set off after Shelly and felt a wave of jealousy rush through him. He glanced over his shoulder toward the saloon and found himself wishing that he could go after the woman he wanted as easily.

Then he told himself he was being foolish. Between Birdwell and now Shelly, he probably wouldn't survive the courtin' even if he tried.

For a solid week Jesse'd watched her. He'd never seen a busier, more determined female in his life. She worked on the town daily as if expecting it to become the way she wanted it to be. And it seemed that no job was too big or too small to pass up.

He shook his head slowly. Standing in the shadows, he could watch her without being seen himself. For the third time in a week Miranda was washing windows. It didn't seem to bother her that as soon as she finished, the ever-present desert sand and dirt flew up and coated the panes all over again.

He glanced just to Miranda's left and admired once more the nice job she'd done completing the half-finished boardwalk in front of the empty general store. She hadn't asked for help. She hadn't whined or complained about bein' tired, he told himself. Hell, she prob'ly didn't even notice that nothing she did made much of a difference!

And reluctantly Jesse found himself admiring her stubborn determination to build the town of her dreams.

Miranda bent over then to rinse out her rag in a bucket of clean water. Jesse let his gaze move over her for a long moment before cursing softly and turning away.

The heavy scent of wet sage filled the still, afternoon air and Miranda breathed deeply, leaned on her broom, and looked out over the muddy street. She wasn't quite sure why she bothered to sweep up the boardwalks. Especially after a rain. As soon as everyone was up and about, they'd only track the mud all over everything again. Glancing back over her shoulder at the already dusty windows she'd washed only that morning, she sighed and went back to work.

There was something comforting about the steady brush of the bristles against the wood. Or maybe it was simply the peace of a familiar chore.

The air was cool and quiet. Sunshine poked sullen fingers through the gaps in the clouds, bathing Bandit's Canyon with indistinct sunlight. Alone, Miranda let her mind wander. It was almost winter again. Soon men from all over the territory would start heading for the canyon. And for the first time in her life, Miranda wasn't looking forward to it. It seemed to her that in the last few years, things hadn't been going as smoothly as they used to. There were more fights now. More trouble. It was as if the men couldn't bring themselves to leave their violence behind anymore. Now they brought it with them to the canyon.

She admitted silently that last winter there were several men staying in the canyon she'd never seen before. Some of whom scared her. Although, she told herself, it could have been worse. At least Tom Forbes hadn't spent the winter with them again. Miranda shuddered slightly and pushed the broom even harder. Chances were very good that Tom would be riding into town any day. He rarely stayed away longer than a year at a time. And that meant she would have to spend the winter finding ways to avoid him. Just the thought of his cold gray eyes filled her with dread. If there was only some way to prevent him from coming. If she could only prove her suspicions.

Miranda shook her head and attacked the boardwalk with short, sharp jabs of the broom. She *knew* that Tom Forbes was a killer. She felt it in her bones. It was in his eyes. It was in the way he moved, like a mountain lion . . . always stalking, watching. Miranda shivered again and the sun ducked behind a black, wispy cloud.

The solid smack of a hammer against wood smashed the afternoon quiet. She stood still, cocking her head, trying to identify the direction of the sound. When she had it, Miranda hurried down the boardwalk.

She moved soundlessly in her moccasins until she could see around the corner of her own cabin. Just beyond stood the corral. And at the far side of the fenced area, a man crouched in the shadows, pounding nails into the crooked posts.

Miranda stepped down into the street, mindful of the mud holes. Delicately she picked her way along fence posts, her eyes darting from the man to the road and back again. Even before she could see him clearly, she knew it was Jesse. Somehow she wasn't surprised. Especially to find him alone. In the last week or so, Miranda'd noticed just how often the man managed to be on his own.

Not that he was unfriendly or standoffish. Her brow furrowed thoughtfully. The other men seemed to like him well enough and yet Jesse remained solitary. As if he *wanted* to be a part of things and at the same time keep himself distant.

When he stood up and yanked at the fence post, testing its strength, she swallowed heavily and almost retreated.

He'd taken his shirt off. The muscles on his chest glistened with sweat as he swung the hammer back for another blow. His broad-brimmed hat was pulled down low, throwing his face into shadow. His pistol and holster rode his narrow hips and his long legs, spread wide for balance, looked every bit as muscular as the rest of him.

Somehow Miranda managed to keep moving. Though she knew she should turn around and go back to work, she couldn't take her eyes off him. The now familiar racing of her heart accompanied the short, gasping breaths she took. No matter how many times she saw him, her reaction was always the same. And if she was to survive the long winter ahead *and* honor the vows she'd made to her mother *and* herself, she had to find a way to stop it.

She took a deep breath and told herself that now was as good a time as any. They were alone. No one to disturb them. Maybe they could talk. Talk about what it was between them and how they could stop it before it got out of hand.

He looked up suddenly as if sensing her presence. There was no welcome on his face or in his eyes. But Miranda kept walking. It was too important that they talk.

"Good afternoon," she said as she stepped up beside him.

"Afternoon." He glanced at her then went back to studying the post. He looked at her from the corner of his eye and kept working.

"Jesse . . ."

"What do you want, Miranda?" He dropped the hammer and turned to face her, hands on his hips.

He was so close she could have touched him. Instead she shoved her hands into the back pockets of her pants. Tilting her head back, she said softly, "I thought we could talk."

"About what?"

"Well . . ." She tried to read his eyes, but he kept

them half-shut in the shadow of his hat. "Perhaps we could talk about what happened in the store the other day." Just thinking about that kiss brought the blood rushing to her face and a curl of pleasure to the pit of her stomach.

He took a deep breath and a drop of sweat rolled down his flesh and disappeared into the dark curls that covered his chest. "What's there to talk about? It was just a kiss."

"*Just* a kiss?" She was beginning to feel a little foolish. Was it possible that she'd made more out of it than there was? No. She remembered his reaction. His heart pounding. How tightly he'd held her.

He was lying.

"Yeah. A kiss." He turned his back on her, bent, and picked up the hammer again. "Now I got to finish this."

"Not yet." She waited for him to look at her again. "I don't know why you're acting like this, Jesse. I only wanted to talk to you about this . . . feeling that's between us. Get it all straightened out in our minds."

"Feelin'?" He pushed his hat back. "What are you goin' on about now? Wasn't no *feelin's* involved." His sharp green eyes met hers then slid away quickly. His breath rushed out on a heavy sigh. "It was just a kiss, Miranda."

Funny, she should be glad to hear him say that. But she wasn't. It was one thing for them to talk and settle things between them. It was another for him to insist that nothing existed. Now she was determined to make him admit that there was more between them than either of them wanted.

"Prove it."

"What?"

"I said, prove it." She took a step closer. "Kiss me

again. Show me that there is nothing for us to talk about. Prove that it was just a kiss."

His eyes narrowed, his lips grim, he stared at her. Miranda waited, holding her breath. What had she done? For a long moment he didn't move. Finally he reached for her and drew her up against him. Just before his mouth came down on hers, she heard him mutter, "It's just a kiss."

CHAPTER 7

It was nothing like before.

The moment their mouths met, Jesse knew he was lost. So warm, so soft, her lips welcomed him and he swallowed back a groan of pleasure. His arms closed around her, his hands moved over her back of their own accord, responding to the need to touch her. The smooth, delicate material of her white shirt caressed his palms and Jesse splayed his fingers wide to feel as much of her as he could.

There was no gentleness in this kiss, there was only an urgent need. He smoothed her lips with his tongue until she opened her mouth for him and he slipped inside. Her breath mingled with his, and when she moved her own tongue against his in unpracticed passion, Jesse's heart stopped.

She leaned into him, pressing herself against his body, and he held her tightly. He felt her hands slide up his naked arms and over his shoulders. Her fingers plucked his hat off, then wove through his hair.

He couldn't get enough. He couldn't kiss her deeply enough. He couldn't get close enough.

His arms still wrapped around her, he turned her until her back was against the stable wall. With one arm cradling her head, he ran his hand up over the curve of her hip, past her narrow waist to the swell of her breast. She moaned softly when his fingers moved over her erect nipples and he tore his mouth away from hers, dragging air into his chest.

Jesse looked down at her as he slipped his hand into the open vee of her shirt. Her eyes slitted, her lips parted, her breath came fast and furious. Slowly his long fingers pushed the edge of her chemise aside and reached for the pink bud waiting for his touch. When his fingers moved lightly over her warm flesh, Miranda gasped.

He felt the same reaction shake through him. Jesse moved his gaze slowly down the length of her throat, and where his eyes moved, his lips followed. He trailed feather-light kisses down her neck and over the smooth ivory of her chest. Miranda's nails bit into his shoulders as he moved closer to her breast. Slowly, deliberately he held the dainty fabrics aside and dipped his head to taste her. As soon as his lips closed around her nipple, Miranda arched her body against his and he heard her breath coming in small, urgent gasps.

His chest too tight to breathe, Jesse settled instead for suckling at her breast. His tongue teased the tip of her and circled the pale pink ring of flesh. His body aching for her, Jesse groaned when her fingers threaded through his hair and held his head tightly against her breast in a demand for more.

His fingers reached for the tiny buttons of her shirt and quickly undid them. His mouth moved over her heated skin, kissing and stroking with his tongue every inch of flesh his hands uncovered. He felt her body trembling and knew that the same tremors were shaking him.

For a brief moment, when her shirt lay open and her breasts were bared to him, Jesse stepped back to look at her. His index finger moved delicately over her nudity and he felt himself swell with need. He'd never known such an overpowering desire before. And it was more than just wanting to lie with her. He wanted to bring her pleasure. He wanted to hear her cry out his name. He wanted to watch her face when the small explosions of delight shot through her.

And Jesse knew that all of these things were going to be denied him. He didn't have the right even to wish for them.

He reached out and cupped her breasts with his hands, kneading them gently with his fingers. He turned his gaze to her face and was undone. Her turquoise eyes, soft with passion, smiled at him. Her lips, parted and eager, waited for him. She lifted her arms to hold him and he stepped into the circle of them, burying his face against her neck.

Her bare breasts pressed against his chest and Jesse tightened his hold on her, reveling in the feel of her body next to his own. His lips moved to her throat, placing small damp kisses on her heated flesh. Miranda's hands moved over his back, pressing him to her, holding him, comforting him.

"Miranda . . . I . . ."

"Hush, Jesse," she whispered, her hands moving slowly over the muscled expanse of his back. "It's all right."

"No." He pulled away slightly so that he could see her face, but kept his arms around her. "No, it ain't all right at all." One hand moved up, stroked her jawline, and slid down her throat to her chest. Then he carefully and gently tugged the edges of her shirt together. Jesse pulled a deep, shuddering breath into his body and prayed for strength. He tried to avoid looking at her eyes. The passion there had been replaced with questions. Questions he didn't know if he could answer.

He cast a quick look at the still-quiet street, then took a couple of steps away from her. "You'd best, uh . . . you know."

He heard her move but kept his back to her. "Miranda," Jesse whispered finally. "I shouldn'ta done that. I'm sorry."

"It, uh . . ." She stepped up beside him. "It was just as much my fault, I'm afraid."

"Nah."

"Yes, it was." Miranda moved to stand in front of him and looked him square in the eye. "I knew, I think, what would happen when I told you to prove that there was nothing between us."

His brow wrinkled and he raised his gaze to a point over her head.

"I suppose I . . . wanted this to happen."

She sounded as confused as he felt. Jesse felt a sudden urge to hop on the nearest horse and get the hell out of town. None of this should have happened. None of it.

"And now that it has," she continued, "maybe you'll admit that we *do* have something to talk about."

He snorted. "*Talk?* Jesus! I'm scared to death to get too close to ya!" His whole body was on fire. He'd never felt anything *close* to this before. And she wanted to *talk?*

"Well, then," Miranda said with a forced smile, "we'll just have to keep a safe distance between us."

"And what do you reckon that is?" His lips curled. "About ten miles?"

"Hmmm."

"Yeah." He groaned and shifted uncomfortably.

"But, Jesse," she said hurriedly, "don't you see? We *have* to get this settled between us. Or neither one of us will have any peace this winter."

"Thunderation." He shook his head and slumped back against the stable wall. "I don't know if I can take this all winter long, M'randa."

She moved up to the rough planed wall and leaned against it herself. Keeping a foot of space between them. "Yes, it *will* be difficult."

"*Difficult?*" He laughed and groaned, dropping his head back with a thud against the building. "Lady, you don't know the half of it."

"What do you mean?"

He closed his eyes. No point in tryin' to explain the pain he was living through. She'd only want to "help." "Never mind."

"Jesse, we're simply going to have to find a way to ignore this . . . whatever it is between us."

"Ignore it?" He shook his head, eyes still closed. "From where I'm standin', M'randa, that's gonna be mighty hard to do."

"Hard, yes. But not impossible." She turned to look at him and didn't speak again until he'd cocked his head in her direction and opened his wide green eyes. "We could do it, Jesse. If we work together."

"How do you mean?"

"Well, first off, we agree on one thing already."

"What's that?"

"That this kind of thing can't keep happening."

"Amen, sister."

"Right. You don't want a woman hanging around, and I certainly have no intention of falling in love with an outlaw."

One eyebrow quirked. "What's the matter with outlaws? Your own pa was one!"

"Now don't be insulted! We're supposed to work together on this."

"I ain't insulted. Just curious."

"Well, I promised my mother that I would never marry a man running from the law." When he would have spoken, Miranda added, "Besides, I want a husband who's home with me, not running around the countryside getting shot at by outraged citizens and angry posses." Her face fell. "I've seen too many friends shot, hanged, or sent to jail to want that for myself."

"Sounds smart to me," Jesse whispered.

She looked at him and smiled. "Good."

"Don't see how that's gonna make much difference." He moved his hips slightly and winced. "Neither one of us wanted anything a few minutes ago, neither. And look what happened anyway."

She flushed and cleared her throat. "Yes, well. But we *let* that happen. We won't do that again."

"Oh."

"All we have to do, Jesse, is treat each other like friends."

"Friends?" He grinned helplessly. If she didn't beat anything he'd ever heard of. Jesse'd never had a "friend" who could turn his body into a pool of melted butter before. Wouldn't you just know that she'd come up with something like that?

"Yes." She took a step closer, her excitement overriding her caution. "If you're no more than polite, and

I treat you like I treat all the others in town, then I *know* we can avoid situations like this!"

"Polite."

"Polite." She nodded emphatically. "If we avoid being alone together . . . well, for heaven's sake, Jesse. We're both adults."

"I ain't sure, but I *think* that's what's causin' all this trouble, M'randa." His lips quirked. "Us bein' adults and all."

"Yes." She met his gaze for a long moment and leaned toward him before catching herself with a start. "I see what you mean. But I know we could do it. If we just try."

Jesse looked down on her smiling face and realized that she really believed what she was saying. She actually thought that what was between them would just go away if they ignored it long enough. It would be like wishin' away hot weather in a desert summer.

Even now all he wanted to do was grab her and crush her to him. To inhale the flowery fragrance of her, to taste the inside of her mouth, run his tongue over hers, to slip his fingers inside the damp, warm center of her and feel her arch against his hand. And when she was ready for him, to join his body to hers and bury himself in her warmth, to feel her muscles tighten around him when she found her release.

Jesse groaned softly and closed his eyes.

This wasn't going to work.

"Jesse?" She laid one hand on his arm and rubbed his flesh absently with her thumb. "Are you all right?"

He stared at her and wondered where he would get the strength to keep clear of her when her slightest touch shook him to his toes. She looked so worried. Her teeth bit into her bottom lip and her eyes were shadowed. For both their sakes, Jesse knew he had to try to do it her way.

But God knew, he couldn't make any promises.

"No, M'randa," he finally said softly. Gently he lifted her hand from his arm and stepped back a pace. "I ain't all right. I don't believe I'm ever gonna be all right again."

For almost two weeks they tried. Jesse'd never worked harder at anything in his life. He was polite. He was friendly. He was losing his mind.

He shook his head wearily and leaned back against the side of the stable. It was the only place in town where he could be alone. And yet he wasn't *really* alone there. The memories were too vivid. He and Miranda alone together, there beside the stable just after dawn. Memories of Miranda's breasts under his fingers, the taste of her, the soft sighs fanning his cheek.

Jesse hunched forward then back quickly, giving the back of his head a good thump against the plank wall. Late-afternoon shadows covered the ground, making the few rocks of the canyon still touched by sunlight stand out in stark contrast. Idly he picked up one pebble after another and tossed them toward the cliff face.

This little bargain that he and Miranda had made wasn't working. At least not for him. As far as he could tell, Miranda wasn't having too much trouble treating him like any of the other outlaws hanging around town. His lips pressed together tightly and he reached for a slightly bigger stone. He flung it viciously at the rocks and felt no better after. Watchin' Miranda smilin' and talkin' and even on occasion dancin' with the other men was about to drive him completely loco.

No matter how hard he tried, he couldn't seem to keep his eyes off her. Every move she made seemed destined to tug at him. To probe at the rawness of his too-long-ignored emotions. Jesse found himself finding ways to help her around the town. Carrying wood, patching roofs, hanging pictures, hell. He'd even swept the damn boardwalk just the other day. And still, it was hard to keep up with her.

Miranda worked like a demon night and day and still managed to be kind and friendly to everybody.

Oh, by rights he couldn't fault her any. It was just her way. His eyes squeezed shut and her face swam before him. Hell, he couldn't even blame the other men for wantin' to be near her. Isn't that what he wanted himself?

Jesse opened his eyes again and squinted at the canyon walls. When had it happened? he wondered. When had Miranda become first in his thoughts instead of the revenge he'd been thirsting for for two years? Like a feast laid before a starving man, Miranda's warmth and kindness had drawn him to her. She was everything he'd been denied for too long. She was everything he'd wanted and hoped for before Carter and Della died.

His fingers rolled another stone around on his palm. It pained him to know that if Carter and Della had lived, he'd never have met Miranda. He would have had no reason to pose as an outlaw and would never have learned about Bandit's Canyon.

Is that the kind of thing his old grandmother meant when she would say, "Things always work out for the best"? He snorted and pushed himself to his feet. Now his tired brain really *was* off target. How could he ever claim happiness for himself because of Carter and Della's deaths?

Suddenly disgusted, Jesse brushed his palms together. Maybe it would be better if he just left the canyon now. He could think of another way to catch the man he was after. There *had* to be another way.

Someone laughed and he turned to look. Miranda was crossing the street, heading for the restaurant. Unerringly his gaze went to Miranda. She had a smile on her face, her turquoise eyes were shining, and that long, thick braid of hers lay over one shoulder, across her breast.

Jesse took a deep breath and blew it out in a rush. He had to admit it, if only to himself. He couldn't leave the canyon. He couldn't leave Miranda. He wanted her too badly.

It was more than that, he knew. Jesse didn't just want her kisses, her embraces. He wanted to know how it felt to be loved by her. To be fussed over and worried about. To be welcomed after a long absence with a smile meant just for him. He didn't want to have to share her with a whole town full of misfits and troublemakers.

And he didn't want to have to worry about gettin' killed by Birdwell. *Or* Shelly. Jesse grinned as he thought about all the times during the last couple of weeks that those two people had just "happened" to be around whenever he and Miranda were together. Hell, if they only knew what all he was goin' through to keep away from her, they'd be able to let down their guard some.

Although, if they could read his thoughts, he'd be a dead man already.

After picking her way across the dry wash, Shelly stopped and cocked her head to listen. There was only the silence of the desert. Shaking her head, she kept walking, moving carefully over the stones in her path. She would have sworn that she'd heard the sound of footsteps close behind her. But she must have been mistaken. No one could get past the lookouts, and if there were Apache or Paiute in the area, they'd have seen some sign before this. Besides, whenever the Apache raided, they made straight for the big water hole and whoever might be there. Shelly kept her eyes fixed on the ground and stayed clear of the bigger rocks and boulders, knowing they would be the favored haunts of rattlesnakes.

She glanced up at the afternoon sky, pleased to see that the rain clouds had moved on to the neighboring mountains. Taking a deep breath of the sage-scented air, Shelly smiled. It was good to be alone for a while. As much as she loved her friends in town, sometimes she simply *needed* to be off by herself.

She stopped, spun around, and looked carefully behind her. That same sound again. A spiral of uneasiness flowed through her. She was far enough away from the town that a call for help would go unheard. And to get back to town, she would have to pass the spot where the sounds were coming from.

It had to be an animal. It could be a mountain lion. Or a hungry coyote. Shelly's mouth dried up and her throat closed. Her breath came in shallow puffs as she studied the land around her.

Slowly, carefully her hand moved to the hem of her skirt. Inching the material up the length of her leg, Shelly didn't stop until her fingers had closed around the wooden handle of the knife she wore strapped to her thigh. For the first time she desperately wished she'd listened to Miranda two years ago when her friend advised her to carry a gun with her outside of town.

When she had the knife in hand, she straightened abruptly and called out, "Who is it? Who's out there?"

The wind pushed through clumps of sagebrush and mesquite. Prickly-pear cactus and ocotillo bushes stood silently by. Shelly caught a rustle of movement from the corner of her eye and turned to meet whatever waited for her. Her grip on the knife tightened, and for the briefest of moments she wished heartily that she'd stayed in town to keep an eye on Jesse Hogan.

But, she told herself as her gaze moved inexorably on, in the last weeks he and Miranda had hardly spoken more than a few words to each other. And so she'd thought it would be safe enough for her to leave town for a little while. Safe! she snorted. Now it wasn't Jesse Hogan's intentions she had to worry about, it was . . .

"You?" Her knife hand dropped to her side, though she kept a firm grip on her weapon.

Dave Black stumbled out from behind an ocotillo bush and cursed softly when inch-long thorns on the long, tentaclelike branches caught at his shirt and hat. When he was finally free of the tall, spindly cactus, Dave glared at it as if it were a living enemy deliberately trying to trap him.

"Afternoon, Shelly." He smiled and walked toward her.

Miranda carried the coffeepot into the dining room. Her gaze flicked to Jesse, sitting at a corner table with the Sullys. Helplessly her heartbeat quickened when he smiled and shook his head at something Jim had said.

Deliberately she turned away and set the big tin pot on the main table, where the men could help themselves. Then she went back into the safety of the kitchen. She stood in front of the stove and gave the stew pot a few good stirs. Clouds of steam rose up and she leaned into them gratefully. The heat would explain away any redness in her cheeks.

She'd never realized before how long two weeks could be. She felt as though every nerve in her body was stretched to the breaking point and beyond. It had sounded so simple when she'd explained her plan to Jesse. But there was nothing easy about treating him with the polite friendliness she gave the others.

Even remembering the vow she'd made to her mother was becoming more difficult. Miranda moved away from the stove and walked to the back window. She held the stiff, white curtains aside and stared out at the cliff face. So many memories had come back in the last few days.

Things she hadn't thought of in years. Her mother and father holding hands and taking walks by the light of a summer sunset. Their shared laughter and whispers. The way they would look at each other, and even in a crowded room, Miranda knew that in their hearts they were alone together. And as much as they loved and doted on her, Miranda realized that their love for each other was a rare, deep emotion that even she couldn't intrude on.

Oh, she remembered the fear as well. Judd had pretty much retired when he built the canyon town and brought Teresa there to live. But every once in a while something would come over him and he would ride off. Either alone or with a few of the men from town. And during the days that he was gone, Miranda remembered clearly how her mother would spend most of each day near the mouth of the canyon, waiting for sight of him.

She dropped the curtain back into place. Those were the times when Teresa would talk to her daughter about her future. When she told Miranda that this was not the kind of life she should lead. That living with fear was too high a price to be paid no matter how much she loved a man.

Miranda walked over to the oven, pulled open the door with a towel-draped hand, and took out the two, golden-brown loaves of bread. She inhaled deeply, turned, and set them down on the wood counter behind her. As she lifted them from their pans Miranda reminded herself that as soon as Judd had come back from one of his "trips," Teresa's words of warning were lost in the happiness of her parents' eager reunion.

She sighed and folded the towel neatly. How many times, she wondered, had she sat alone in the restaurant in the middle of the night, remembering the love between her parents? How many times had she dreamed of finding that kind of love for herself? But she'd never met anyone who'd even come close to kindling that kind of feeling in her. Until Jesse Hogan came to the canyon.

But he was an outlaw. Exactly the kind of man she'd been warned against.

Miranda let her head fall back on her neck. As she stared blankly at the ceiling her brain conjured up the image of his face. Even the fates seemed to be working against them. It seemed that as soon as they'd decided to ignore the disquieting feelings between them, they were thrown together more often than before. Whether it be at Big Pete's saloon, helping to repair the roof after the storm or sorting supplies brought in by a passing bandit. No matter how hard they tried to stay apart, *something* had brought them together.

And Miranda was finding it harder than ever to keep her vow to her mother in mind.

As if to taunt her, images of Jesse raced through her mind. Miranda closed her eyes tightly to savor them. His eyes. His smile. The way he looked at her out of the corner of his eye when he thought she couldn't see him. How he'd helped her with the never-ending chores that no one but she ever bothered with. How he crossed his arms over his chest defensively as if that move would keep him separate from the others. And how butterflies filled her stomach when his mouth came down on hers.

Whether he liked it or not, Miranda felt that she was beginning to know Jesse Hogan very well. And it frightened her just a little to realize that the better she knew him, the more she liked him.

CHAPTER
8

"M'randa!"

She looked up, startled at the shouting voice. Someone was running toward the kitchen door.

"M'randa!" The swinging door flew inward, slammed into the wall behind it, and swung back into Ezra Banks's hysterical face. "M'randa!" he called again, and pushed at the door once more.

She came around the table quickly to meet him. Behind the older man, everyone in the restaurant was moving toward him, anxious and worried.

"What is it, Ezra?" She reached out and laid one hand on the shabby sleeve of his black coat. "Calm down now. Tell me what's wrong?"

His narrow chest heaved spasmodically while he tried to catch his breath. The man's normally neat gray hair stood out in a wild bush around his head and his faded blue eyes blinked rapidly.

His agitation was contagious. Miranda glanced up at the men behind him and read her own fears on their faces. Her gaze stopped on Jesse for a long moment and his green eyes soothed her, calming her rising sense of alarm. She turned back to Ezra.

Trying to help, she asked quickly, "Is it the law?"

He shook his head violently and took another shuddering breath.

"Apaches?"

Again his head shook negative.

She heard the men move restively, a few of them muttering disjointed sentences, "Crazy ol' coot . . . What the hell? . . . 'Bout stopped my heart . . ."

"Ezra . . . *please*," she said quietly. "What is it?"

He bent over, hands on his knees. Miranda heard the long breath he drew in, and as he released it he muttered, "Serena. The baby. It's comin'."

"Well, shit!" one man's disgusted voice from the other room echoed out hollowly.

"Hellfire and damnation, Ezra!" Jim Sully called out. "Thought there was a man with a rope headin' our way."

The older man straightened up and shot the men a disgusted glare before turning back to Miranda. He leaned toward her and whispered, "I didn't know what else to do, M'randa. She's cryin' somethin' awful."

Miranda glanced over his head and saw Jesse's strained, pale face. Quickly she looked away.

"It's all right, Ezra. She'll be fine. Why don't you go get Shelly while I—"

"She ain't here."

"She's probably at her cabin," Miranda offered.

"Nope. She ain't. Already looked." He frowned and pushed his hair back from his face. "Went there first. When I couldn't find her, came right to you."

"*Damn!*" Miranda scowled. "I forgot. She left town earlier this afternoon. Went for a walk." She shook her head. "Well, we'll just have to start without her. Hopefully she'll be back soon." She moved through the doorway, talking to herself more than Ezra. "I'll go get Fat Alice and Wilma. They should be able to help."

Ezra snorted. "Fat Alice is dead drunk . . . I don't know about Wilma."

A stab of worry clutched at Miranda. If she had to do this alone, she *and* Serena were in big trouble. She'd never even *witnessed* a birth before, let alone *helped* at one. Maybe Jim . . . no. For just a moment she'd considered asking Jim Sully. He was the one who took care of most of the cuts and gunshot wounds, when he was in town. But somehow Miranda couldn't imagine Jim's brash, loud sense of humor being of much comfort to Serena just now.

Then she remembered Jesse. How gentle, how kind he'd been to Bobby Sawyer. He'd seemed so sure of himself and what to do. Maybe he could help her now. She looked up. Searching for his face in the crowd. He was gone.

She didn't have time to wonder about his absence, only made a mental note to send someone to find him later. If she was the only one able to help Serena, she told herself, then she'd better get at it. And hope for the best.

Miranda stepped out onto the boardwalk into the dusky twilight. At the same time Buck Farley careened around the corner of the farthest building. His horse in a full run, Buck lay low over the animal's neck, urging the big black to run even faster. From the corner of her eye, she saw Jesse trot over to join the other waiting men.

At the restaurant, Buck sat up in the saddle, pulled back on the reins, and leaped to the ground before the horse had completely stopped moving. His eyes wide, he pointed back the way he'd come.

"Bill Sully's still on watch. I come to get ya!"

Jim stepped down from the boardwalk, hand on his gun. "What happened?"

"Indian sign." Buck nodded toward the canyon. "From what we could guess, a good-sized raidin' party."

"Apache?" someone asked unnecessarily.

Buck spat. "Who the hell else?"

Birdwell walked up to the crowd as Buck finished speaking. "They ain't gonna do much before daylight. But we best be set and waitin' long before then. You get on back to Bill. The rest of us'll be along directly."

"Yes, sir."

"Wait!" Miranda stepped up to Buck and grabbed his arm. "Shelly's not in town. She went out beyond the wash for a walk earlier."

He tugged at his hat brim and smiled reassuringly. "Don't you worry then, ma'am. If she crossed that wash, she's safe enough."

"What do you mean?"

"Flash flood. All that rain in the mountains, I reckon. Anyhow, she won't be comin' back real soon . . . but them Apaches ain't gonna be tryin' to swim that mess, neither!" He grinned and waggled his eyebrows. "'Sides, she ain't alone. I saw Dave followin' after her."

"Quit your talkin' now and move out!" Birdwell bellowed.

"I'm already gone!" Buck leaped onto his horse's back, yanked at the reins to turn the big animal, then thundered back down the street, his long brown ponytail flying out behind him.

"All you men!" Birdwell shouted. "Get your rifles,

shotguns, and somebody get the extra ammunition from the store." He looked from one man to the next. "Meet back here in five minutes! Get everybody out here!" As they started to move he added, "And somebody drag Fat Alice down to the cliffs. She'll be sober before sunup. With Shelly and Dave out of it, we'll need every extra gun hand."

The men started running in all different directions. Jesse turned to join them, but Miranda grabbed his arm. "Birdwell, I need Jesse to stay here."

The big man's black eyes narrowed. "Why's that?"

"Serena's having her baby. Shelly's not here—Fat Alice is drunk and I'm not so sure about Wilma."

Birdwell cursed softly and spat into the dust. "Wilma's a helluva lot better shot than she is a midwife. I was already figurin' on leavin' you here to stay with Serena. And maybe leavin' Ezra here to protect the both of you."

"I don't need Jesse for protection, Birdwell. I can shoot as well as anyone here. I *need* him to deliver this baby!"

"No."

They both turned to stare at Jesse. Even in the fading light, they could see how pale he was.

"I ain't deliverin' no baby. I'm goin' to the canyon with ever'body else."

Birdwell straightened up to his full, imposing height. "You'll go where *I* tell ya! *I* say who goes to the canyon." He narrowed his gaze and glared at the younger man. "You know what to do with Serena?"

"No . . . I . . ."

"I think he knows, Birdwell," Miranda broke in, and stared at Jesse as he spoke. "At the very least he knows more than *I* do. You can leave Ezra, too, if you want. Though if the Apaches get past you all, one gun around here more or less won't make that big a difference."

Jesse ran one hand over his face. Avoiding Miranda's gaze, he looked directly at Birdwell. "Don't I get any say-so in this? I never delivered no human baby. Just cows and horses and such."

His features were strained and tight, and Miranda heard the tiniest note of panic in his voice. Birdwell obviously didn't, because he countered, "That'll do. Cain't be that much different." He looked at Miranda. "All right. You can keep him here. But Ezra stays, too."

Jesse took a deep breath and opened his mouth to speak.

Birdwell cut him off. "You do what you can for Serena." His black gaze flicked to Miranda and back to Jesse. "And *nothin'* else! Y'hear?"

Jesse snorted, snatched his hat off, turned on his heel, and marched off down the street, mumbling fiercely.

"You be all right?" Birdwell's whispered concern pulled Miranda back from her speculation about Jesse.

"Yes." She reached up, pulled the bald man's head down, and kissed his bearded cheek. "We'll be fine. You take care, Birdwell. You're all the family I've got." She patted his broad chest nervously.

Birdwell closed his fingers over her hand and squeezed it. One of his rare smiles lit up his eyes. His voice gruff with emotion, he said softly, "Hell, it'd take a sight more than a pack of surly Apaches to do me in. 'Sides, it's prob'ly just a few young bucks lookin' to cut loose their wolf for a while." He grinned suddenly. "Hell, you know as well as me, them boys feel like they *got* to hit us a couple times a year . . . just so's we won't get too comfortable."

Immediately he turned for the cliffs. Then he looked over his shoulder and added, "You watch out for that fella. I ain't so sure about him, Miranda. Matter of fact, I'm a lot more sure about them Indians than *him*. There's somethin' that ain't right there."

She nodded. "I'll be careful." Miranda watched her honorary uncle until he rounded the corner, then she turned and ran down the street toward Serena's cabin. Her long legs moved easily in the buckskin trousers and every time her moccasined feet hit the dirt, they seemed to pound out Birdwell's concern. *Ain't right . . . ain't right . . . ain't right . . .*

Shelly glared at the smiling blond man opposite her. His sparse mustache rode his full lips and curved up at the corners of his mouth. Disgusted, she turned away from him and looked out over the roaring water as it rushed past them. Only an hour or so ago it had been bone-dry. Now it looked as though every drop of water the Good Lord ever created was gathered together there . . . all to keep her from escaping Dave Black.

"Really somethin', ain't it?"

She jumped. He was altogether too close. Shelly took a step to one side and nodded.

He moved up again. Pointing to the water, he said softly, "Look there . . . a big ol' cottonwood branch."

Her eyes followed the dipping, swaying tree branch, its wet leaves glistening in the late sun. The water turned it, pushed and prodded it until it was dragged beneath the surface.

"Wonder how far it come?" he murmured softly, just behind her ear.

Shelly stood as stiff as an iron bar. She felt his breath

on the back of her neck and tried to sidestep him. It
didn't work.

He touched her arm, and when she jumped uneasily, he let go. The flood in the wash seemed to get
louder, its thundering power filling the air around
them. Dirt-colored water swirled around rocks,
plucked at the roots of quivering mesquite bushes,
and went on. She took a step toward the rushing water
and he grabbed her arm firmly. This time he held on.

"What the hell are you doin'?" he shouted.

She turned quickly, met his gaze for a split second,
then turned away again. "Going back to town."

A gust of wind and the roaring river snatched her
voice the moment it left her throat, but Dave read her
intentions on her face. "Are you loco? You can't get
back to town. Me neither. We're stuck here for a while,
Shelly. Can't you see that?"

"No!" She yanked her arm from his grasp and
looked up at him through the eyes of a trapped
animal.

"What the hell did I ever do to you, woman?"
Dave's fingers curled helplessly into fists at his
sides. "Why the hell do you jump like a high-backed
cat every time I get too close?"

She looked around her wildly. Her hair slipped
loose from its knot and the wind picked up the
waist-length mass and swirled it around her features
like a black cloud of smoke. Irritably Shelly snatched
at it while at the same time stepping back from the
angry man across from her.

He took a step closer and she took two back.
Instinctively she moved to keep him at a safe distance.
Daylight faded quickly as the sun disappeared behind
the cliffs. Between the growing darkness and her own
hair whipping across her face, Shelly moved blindly in
a last-ditch attempt to get away from Dave.

Her right foot stepped back and landed on the cold surface of the raging water, causing Shelly to lose her balance. Her arms waving frantically, she hoped for something to grab onto as her body tipped toward the crashing torrent below.

Before she had time to scream, Dave's arm shot out and snaked around her. Instinctively Shelly grabbed him, her fingers curling tightly around his strong forearms. With two quick, backward steps, he had them both safely away from the edge of the wash.

For a long moment neither of them spoke. Shelly finally raised her gaze to meet his and briefly he saw a shy, feminine awareness shining at him. Then he watched helplessly as the haunted, distrustful shadows crept back into her eyes. When she tried to pull away, he refused to allow it. His grip on her waist tightened. He smiled down at her and continued to hold her close.

"Let me go."

"Not yet."

She glared at him and made one last futile attempt to wrench herself from his grasp.

"Now settle down, Miss Shelly." Dave shook his head gently. "You got no reason to be all upset."

She stiffened and her breath came fast and furious.

Dave felt the tension in her body and sighed. What could he do to convince the woman that he meant her no harm? Hell, she'd damn near drowned herself just to get away from him! He glanced at the rising water and looked back at her set, determined features. If he wasn't careful, he knew that she was just fool enough to try it again, too.

Gritting his teeth against what he knew was coming, Dave quickly bent down, put one arm under her knees, and scooped her up. Shelly's jaw dropped, but she recovered in a hurry. Both of her legs started kicking while she shoved at his chest.

"Turn me loose, mister, or so help me God, you're gonna be the sorriest bastard that ever walked!"

"Miss Shelly! That any way for a lady to talk?" He kept walking, intent on getting plenty of space between them and the floodwaters.

The flat of her hand smacked across his cheek and Dave moved his jaw uncertainly. "There ain't no call for that neither."

"I'll decide what's called for, you no-good—"

"Here now!" He frowned at her. "I'll set you down again. Just as soon as we're clear of that durn water. You got no call to go smackin' me or callin' me names!"

"And *you*," Shelly countered, finally giving up the useless fight for freedom and lying still in his arms, "got no call to go pickin' me up and totin' me all over the canyon like I was a sack of potatoes! I didn't ask for your help."

"No, you surely didn't." He shook his head and kept walking toward an overhang of rock. "You wouldn't ask me or any other man for help if it meant your life . . . which it almost did!"

She crossed her arms and flattened her lips together into a grim line. When he finally set her on her feet, she turned away only to be turned right back by his strong hands.

"Now, Miss Shelly," he said softly, and waited for her to look up at him. "There's somethin' I think you should know right off."

She stared at him suspiciously.

"I wouldn't never hurt you."

She snorted.

"And I won't allow nobody else to hurt you, neither."

Startled by the blunt declaration, she looked away. But not before Dave saw the sudden sheen of tears in her big brown eyes. A wave of tenderness tugged at his heart. He reached out and touched her cheek gently. Taking a deep breath, Dave said the words he'd wanted to say for weeks. "I love you, Miss Shelly."

He saw her shoulders stiffen, but he was too determined to quit now. She might not want to hear it, but he *needed* to say it.

"I reckon it'll take you a time to get used to that. Lord knows, it kinda took me by surprise." Dave chuckled. "But it's the truth. I *do* love you . . . and someday, Miss Shelly, you're gonna love me back."

She turned to face him slowly. Her eyes wary, her teeth biting into her bottom lip, she shook her head. "Mister, you shouldn't ought to be out on your own. I think you're outta your head."

He threw his head back and laughed, the sound echoing off the rocks surrounding them. She only stared at him while the last traces of his laughter faded away. Finally Dave looked at her again, bent down, and brushed her lips briefly with his own. "Maybe so, darlin'. It surely ain't the first time I've heard that."

Shelly touched her lips with the tips of her fingers and didn't move away when he reached to cup her cheek.

"But I *still* love you. And that ain't never gonna change."

The look she shot him left no doubt as to her feelings, but Dave didn't care. She hadn't shied away from him.

It was something.

* * *

Miranda was sure that she'd have to search for Jesse, but he was standing right outside Serena's cabin, staring at the closed door as if a grizzly bear waited on the other side.

His jaw clenched, his body rigid, he didn't even react when Miranda came alongside and laid her hand on his arm.

"Jesse?" She waited what seemed an eternity for him to look at her. When he did, she saw fear and pain in his eyes.

His fingers closed over her hand. "Miranda, I can't do this. Don't ask me."

She wanted to tell him that it was all right. That she could do it alone. She wanted to, but something inside her told Miranda that it would be the wrong thing to do. He didn't need her sympathy. He needed her strength. And that's what he would get. There would be time enough later to find out why a pregnant woman affected him so.

"You have to do this, Jesse." She met his gaze and refused to let him look away. "I don't know anything about it. And Serena needs help." She took a deep breath. "Serena needs *you*." She paused a moment, then added, "And so do I."

Another eternity passed before Jesse exhaled heavily and nodded. He crossed the boardwalk, pulled at the latch, and opened the door. From an open doorway on his right, Jesse heard Serena crying. As Miranda stepped into the cabin Ezra Banks came out of Serena's bedroom.

The older man's hand was shaking as he wiped his face with a rumpled, red bandanna. His red-rimmed eyes shot straight to Miranda gratefully then moved over Jesse. For the first time Ezra seemed pleased to see him.

"Praise heaven you come," the man mumbled softly. He took a few steps toward the young people in the doorway. "Oh, it's terrible," he said, shaking his head. "Terrible. She's hurtin' somethin' fierce! Poor Serena." He looked up at Jesse. "Do you know how to help her?"

Jesse shifted position uneasily. As far as he knew, the only thing that helped the pains was gettin' the baby out. He groaned silently. How in the *hell* had he gotten himself into this? His gaze flicked over the older man in front of him. Poor Ezra was a mess. And the man's panic was catchy. Jesse could feel the tremors begin in Miranda. She pressed close to him and held his hand tightly.

With his free hand, Jesse rubbed his jaw and glanced at the open doorway opposite him. Inside, Serena Dexter lay waiting. But would he see Serena . . . or would he see Della's image? Would the guilt that never left him keep him from helping someone else?

"Jesse?"

He looked down at Miranda and forced a smile. Her eyes were shadowed with worry and she was counting on *him* to set things right. The fear that had swamped him earlier faded slightly. There was no hope for it. He was good and caught. He *had* to deliver this baby. Otherwise all Serena had for help was Miranda and Ezra. "It's all right, M'randa. We'll do fine."

Faith and confidence shone in her eyes and Jesse drew on it greedily. She almost made him believe that he *could* do this.

"Ezra," he said, turning to the other man before he could change his mind, "you gonna be helpin' out?"

"*Me?* Oh, no. No, no, no . . ." Ezra's bandanna moved frantically over his flushed face. His pale eyes widened and his head shook violently. "That, uh . . . wouldn't be . . . uh, seemly, you know. No. Not at all. I, uh . . ." He hurried around the couple, grabbed the door latch, and pulled it closed behind him. As he stepped onto the porch they heard him say, "I'll be right out here . . . standing guard. That's what I'll do. Yes. Stand guard. Oh, Lord . . . *help* with a *baby*? No, no . . ."

The door clicked shut quietly. Miranda smiled. "I know how he feels."

Jesse's lips quirked. So did he.

Three hours later Miranda wanted nothing more than to go outside on the boardwalk with Ezra. In fact, she'd much prefer sitting on the cliffs watching for the Indians to attack. Anything would be better than this waiting, she told herself.

She looked over at the bed. In the soft glow of candlelight, Serena Dexter lay pale and ghostly against her pillows. An almost constant frown of discomfort rode her lips, but she hadn't cried out loud since they'd first arrived.

Miranda's gaze moved to Jesse, sitting on the edge of the bed, holding Serena's hand and speaking in quiet, reassuring tones. His long fingers smoothed over the other woman's palm, and when a pain racked her body and she gripped his fingers in a powerful squeeze, he didn't flinch.

He was gentle, kind. Just as she'd known he would be. Miranda smiled as she remembered Serena's surprised expression when Jesse walked into her bedroom. But his soft voice and matter-of-fact attitude had wiped away any trace of awkwardness. And, Miranda told herself, Serena had been so anxious to deliver the child, she was more than willing for *anyone's* help.

But how much longer could this go on? Jesse kept saying that it wouldn't be long. The pains were closer now. And harder. The last one had reduced Serena to pitiful whimpering. And every time Serena's back arched with a new spasm, Miranda cringed in sympathy. She couldn't understand why any woman would willingly go through such agony over and over. Surely the birth of one child would be enough to convince them never to do it again!

Serena moaned and Miranda knew that simply witnessing a birth was more than enough for *her*. Her wishful imaginings for a child of her own had faded with the onslaught of each new pain.

Jesse suddenly jumped up and moved to the foot of the bed. Serena's head twisted from side to side on the flat pillow and her hands clutched at her upraised knees. Miranda hurried to the other woman's side and stood helplessly, waiting for instructions.

"Jesse . . ." Serena breathed his name, inhaled sharply and groaned.

"It's all right, Serena. Everything's fine." His voice was deep, calm.

He lifted the sheet covering Serena's body from the waist down and Miranda looked away, embarrassed. Somehow she'd never really imagined everything that actually went on at a birth. And it seemed to her that the loss of one's dignity was every bit as terrible as the pain.

"I think we're about to meet your little Dexter, Serena." Jesse lowered the sheet again and smiled at her. "And whoever he is, he's got lots of black hair."

"Like her daddy." Serena smiled and licked her lips. Her back arched; she groaned and struggled to sit up, pulling at her knees.

"Don't be in such a hurry now, Serena," Jesse whispered. "Let him come in his own time." He looked over at Miranda. "Sit behind her. Prop her up. It'll make it easier for her to push this child out when it's time."

Miranda swallowed, nodded, and did as she was told. Once set, she smoothed Serena's matted hair back from her face and tried to smile. Jesse glanced up at the two women then turned back to the baby.

"He's on his way now, darlin'." He looked up, smiling. "It's almost over, Serena. Just a little ways to go now."

"Want . . . to . . . see . . . her . . ." Serena's voice was raspy, dry. She struggled up determinedly and Miranda helped her.

Jesse smiled. "Don't blame ya. After all this work, you ought to be the *first* to see him."

"*Her*."

He grinned. "We'll see who's right, won't we?" Then he pushed the plain white sheet down so that Serena's view of her baby's birth would be a clear one.

Sitting behind her friend, feeling the spasms of pain shake through her, Miranda, too, stared down at the juncture of Serena's thighs. Embarrassment forgotten, she was completely caught up in the slow emergence of a tiny head. Miranda's jaw dropped.

"Oh, Serena," she whispered, "here he comes."

Dancing candlelight flickered across Jesse's features. His hair fell over his forehead and his eyes were shining when he looked up at Serena. "All right now, darlin', you're gonna have to give him a little push out of the nest now.''

Serena obliged, the veins in her neck standing out with her effort. Awed by the strength flowing from the tiny woman, Miranda held her as gently as possible. And then it happened.

The three adults watched in fascinated silence as the baby's head appeared. Slowly, magically, while cradled in Jesse's strong fingers, the baby turned.

Miranda held her breath as Serena gave her child the final push it needed to join the world. An angry howl shattered the silence and Serena laughed gently at the healthy sound. Tears filled Miranda's eyes and she blinked frantically, trying to clear them.

The tiny, bloodied baby lay across Jesse's palms, its small legs and arms waving furiously. After setting his precious burden down on the sheets, Jesse hurriedly cut and tied the birth cord. All the while Miranda could hear him talking softly to the new baby and chuckling at the child's screams.

A swell of love and fierce envy raced through her and Miranda suddenly understood why women could endure such pain. To be able to feel such a tiny burst of life slip from your body and live on its own . . . yes, it would be worth almost anything. Well, she thought . . . *maybe.*

''Jesse?'' Serena's arms reached out for her baby. ''Is it a girl?''

Miranda watched him reluctantly pull his gaze from the screaming infant and smile at its mother. ''You lose the bet, Serena. It's a fine, big boy. You want me to keep him?''

''A boy. A son.'' Serena tipped her head back and grinned up at Miranda. ''I have a son!''

Miranda kissed her friend's forehead. "A *beautiful* son."

Jesse looked down at the baby and smiled as he lifted him from the bed. "Well, guess that means your mama wants you after all, boy!" The baby screamed even louder and Jesse laughed. "Hungry already!" He looked over at the women. "Miranda, come here and get this little squaller while I take care of his mama."

She eased out from behind Serena, laying the woman down on her pillows. A quick glance told her that the lines of strain and fatigue were already fading from Serena's features. A soft smile wreathed the woman's face as she lay perfectly still, listening to her son's indignant cries.

"I think this child needs a bath before he goes callin' on his mother." Jesse tenderly laid the baby in Miranda's arms. He seemed reluctant to let go though and ran one finger down the boy's cheek. "Ain't he somethin'?" he whispered to no one in particular.

"Yes," Miranda answered softly, "he is." Her gaze slid up to his and she wasn't the least surprised to see a sheen of dampness in his eyes. "Thank you, Jesse."

He looked down at her for a long, quiet moment. Then he reached out with one hand and touched her cheek as he had the baby's. "No, M'randa. Thank *you*."

CHAPTER 9

Shelly cuddled in closer, resting her cheek against his chest. Dave smiled and ran his hand softly up and down her arm. He glanced up at the cloudless night sky, shivered, and held Shelly tighter. Listening for a long moment to her deep, regular breathing, he counted himself a lucky man, frostbite or no. If it wasn't so durn cold, he knew Shelly would never be snuggling up next to him. Asleep or awake. At least not yet.

He grinned and laid his head back against the rocks. It was amazing how much better he felt for having told her he loved her. Oh, Dave knew it hadn't changed a damn thing. She still watched him like he was a loco dog. But still, it was good to have your cards on the table. Now she knew exactly what he had in mind.

And she could start gettin' used to the idea.

He shifted position slightly then held perfectly still when Shelly stirred. He didn't want to wake her up just yet. He wanted to enjoy holding her for a while.

Dave kissed the top of her head gently and inhaled the soft, clean scent of her. Hell, maybe she and Buck were right. Maybe he *was* crazy.

But he'd never wanted anyone or anything in his life the way he wanted Shelly Port. Almost from the minute he'd seen her in Big Pete's place, he'd made up his mind to have her. He wanted to take her home to Texas. He wanted to build a life with her. Have lots of babies together, then grow old and watch their babies' babies. There was so much he wanted to give her. To tell her.

His smile disappeared. What would she say when she knew the truth about him? Would she fear him even more than she did already?

She sighed and nestled her head against him.

A fierce, protective surge of love rushed through Dave and he just managed to keep from squeezing her in response. There was only one thing he could do. He had to make her trust him. Love him. And he had to do it quick. Before it was time for him and Buck to leave the canyon behind forever.

"What d'ya think, Birdwell?" Buck asked quietly. "They gonna hit us or not?"

Birdwell stretched his massive body and tried to find a comfortable spot on the rocks. He glanced over at the man next to him and studied him thoughtfully in the moonlight. "Hell, I don't know any more than you do," he said finally. "Them Indians are notional. Never know what they're fixin' to do. Don't believe *they* know till just before they do it."

"Maybe so." Buck nodded and stared out over the desert floor below. Between the yuccas, the ocotillo, and the Joshua trees, there were enough shadows to disguise a troop of cavalry, let alone a small raiding party. He shook his head. They'd never spot an Apache anyways, unless the Indian wanted 'em to.

He thought fleetingly of Dave and hoped the man had his eyes open to more than Shelly. Buck snorted. Who woulda thought that ol' Dave would go all doe-eyed over some woman in a bandits' holdout? Wait'll the folks back in Texas heard about it!

If they ever got back to Texas. Shit, this little job of theirs had already lasted months longer than they'd planned. They were supposed to have finished up long ago. Hell, the boys back home prob'ly figured they was dead.

"Somethin' wrong?"

Buck turned to face the big man. He'd have to be more careful about what he was thinkin'. Birdwell noticed too damn much.

"Nah." He said the first thing that popped into his head. "Just thinkin' about Dave and Shelly . . . trapped on the other side of the wash together."

Birdwell smiled. "Don't envy Dave any. That Shelly's a wildcat sometimes."

"He don't seem to mind."

"No, he don't." Birdwell shook his head. "Never can tell. He just might wear 'er down."

"Maybe." Buck didn't really want to talk about Dave. As long as he and Birdwell were stuck together on the cliff, maybe there were a few other things he could find out. Carefully he said, "What about Miranda?"

The older man's eyes snapped to Buck. "What d'ya mean?"

"Oh, nothin', nothin'." Buck held up both hands. "Just wonderin' how her and Jesse are makin' out with Serena."

"Oh." Birdwell relaxed a little, his gaze sweeping out to the desert. "All right, I s'pose."

"You ever hear of this fella before now?"

"Who, Jesse?"

"Yeah."

"No, I never."

"Don't you think that's a little peculiar?" Buck shifted uneasily under Birdwell's curious stare. "I mean most of the fellas that come here're known to *somebody*."

"S'pose that's true," Birdwell said slowly "'Course, I never heard of you and Dave neither."

Buck cleared his throat. "Yeah, but we told you that we was in prison with Sonora Mike. You knew *him*."

"Yeah, but Mike's dead. He ain't likely to up and call you two liars, now, is he?"

"Well, no . . . Birdwell, are *you* sayin' we lied?"

"No, I ain't, Buck." Birdwell stared at the man steadily. "All I'm sayin' is I don't know you two any more than I do Jesse. And at least Jesse had Jim Sully to speak for him."

Buck swallowed.

"And as long as we're talkin', Buck . . ." Birdwell rubbed one hand over his full beard. "I might's well tell ya, there's one or two things about all three of ya that don't sit right." —

"What's that supposed to mean?"

"Just that I'm keepin' my eye on all of ya." He leaned back, cradled his shotgun in his beefy arms, and closed his eyes. "Y'see, it's almighty strange to me how come none of ya find the time to bring in a little money before winter."

"But—"

"And none of ya seem too anxious to talk to the others."

"Now, that ain't so. Why, me and Dave—"

Birdwell's lips twitched. "Oh, you're willin' to drink with 'em, but whenever somebody starts layin' out a new plan, linin' men up for the job, you boys up and leave."

Buck opened his mouth then snapped it shut.

"Yep," Birdwell said as he settled in for a short nap. "I find that *real* interestin'."

Serena lay exhausted on the narrow bed, her fingers moving over her son's wrinkled flesh as if to convince herself he was real. Miranda took a step back into the shadows, not wanting to intrude on such a special moment. Helplessly her gaze flicked to Jesse.

He stood at the foot of the bed, his eyes locked on Serena and the baby. His arms were crossed over his chest and a soft smile curved his mouth. Miranda's heart thudded painfully in her breast. Her throat closed with the varied emotions swamping her. Relief that it was over and Serena and the baby were fine. Excitement and awe at what she had just witnessed, and most of all an overwhelming tenderness for the man standing only a few feet from her.

Jesse felt the power of her stare and turned to look at her. Her lips trembling, her eyes awash with unshed tears, she held herself rigidly, as though afraid to move. And he understood what it was costing her. He, too, had been struggling against the need to hold her, to feel her warmth pressed against him. To lose himself in the joy of what he'd just accomplished with the one person he'd shared it with.

With the woman who'd given him the strength to do it.

In the soft candlelight, Miranda's hair shone and sparkled. The freckles across the bridge of her nose and over her cheeks stood out sharply against her pale skin. But it was her eyes that finally touched him. The moment he looked into those shimmering pools of turquoise, he was lost. And for the first time since he'd met her, Jesse didn't try to fight it.

Slowly, half-afraid that she wouldn't come, he un-crossed his arms and opened them out toward her. Without hesitation, Miranda went to him, sliding her arms about his waist, laying her cheek against his chest. Jesse's arms closed around her, his hands smoothing over her back, pressing her close against him.

He smiled and rested his chin on top of her head. Her racing heart beat in time with his and he closed his eyes to savor the sweetness of Miranda in his arms. She took a deep, shuddering breath and leaned her head back to look up at him. Jesse opened his eyes and waited.

"It was all so amazing," she whispered. "And so . . ."

"Terrifyin'?"

She grinned. "A little. But you weren't scared, were you?"

He snorted, tightened his hold on her, and let his head fall back. "I never been so scared in all my life."

"Really?"

He raised his head again and looked down at her. "Really." For a moment his gaze shifted to Serena and her son, still totally wrapped up in each other. "What if somethin' had gone wrong? What if—"

Miranda reached up, cupped his cheek and forced him to look back at her. "But nothing went wrong. Because of you."

"No." He shook his head wearily. "Had nothin' to do with me. All I did was catch the little fella when he come out." Unconsciously he moved his fingers over her back again, caressing her, stroking her flesh with an unspoken need. Even through the heavy white fabric of her shirt, Jesse felt the warmth of her and greedily drank it in, allowing her heat to fill up all the cold, empty places inside him. "If there'd been a problem or somethin' . . ."

"You would have solved it."

Jesse shook his head, stunned at her belief in him. Why was she so sure of him? Why did she think so much more of him than he himself did? What was it she saw when she looked at him? And why did it mean so much to him?

"You were wonderful, Jesse."

He smiled self-consciously. "Serena did all the work."

"I don't mean that." She kept her voice in a whisper. "I mean, how gentle you were with her. How kind. You were able to help her when no one else could." Her gaze moved over his face. "I wouldn't have been any help to her at all."

"That ain't so, but it don't matter." His fingers moved up to the back of her head and slipped into the loose braid of her hair. His other hand moved to caress her cheek. "You helped me, Miranda. Prob'ly more than you'll ever know." He bent down and placed a soft, feather-light kiss on her forehead. His own heartbeat threatened to strangle him with its frantic pounding. Jesse read the desire in her eyes and all sensible thought fled. He forgot where he was. He forgot about the woman lying in her childbed only a few steps away. He forgot about Ezra, and Birdwell and Indians. He let go of everything in the world except the hunger in Miranda Perry's eyes.

Slowly, determinedly Jesse bent lower. Miranda

reached up, tilting her head for his kiss. Only a breath away . . . a loud crash and thud from the other room broke the spell and they almost jumped apart.

Jesse took one last look at Miranda. Her chest heaved with her effort to breathe and her erect nipples pushed against the fabric of her shirt. Groaning, he turned away, walked to the closed door, and threw it open. Jesse felt Miranda right behind him and heard her sigh heavily at the sight that greeted them.

Ezra lay on the floor, his arms and legs outstretched, his mouth hanging open and his gray hair spread out in a halo around his head. The nearest table was overturned and an empty whiskey bottle rolled noisily across the wooden floor. Even as they stood and watched the man an ungodly snore ripped from his throat, shattering what was left of the quiet, almost magical night.

Disgusted, Jesse took a step toward the fallen man, then stopped and looked over his shoulder at Miranda. "I'll take care of him. You go and see if you can get Serena to sleep some."

As the door slowly closed between them Jesse bent down, slid his hands under the other man's arms, and began to pull. "Ezra," he mumbled tightly, "I don't know whether to shoot ya or thank ya."

Jesse leaned against the porch rail and stared up into the night. His jaws hurt from smiling and he knew he must look like a fool, grinnin' at nothin', but he couldn't seem to stop. Glancing down, he looked at his outstretched hands and saw in his mind's eye the newborn baby, kicking and screaming.

And then Miranda's body cradled close against him. He shook his head and shoved his hands in his pockets. Jesse inhaled deeply, pulling the cold night air into his body, then releasing it in a rush. As long as he lived, he'd never forget that night.

A low-pitched, rumbling snore sounded out from behind him and Jesse chuckled. Poor Ezra wouldn't be forgetting it either. And after everything that had happened, Jesse found he couldn't even stay mad at the old drunk. He looked over his shoulder through the front window. The older man lay on his back, his legs dangling over one side of the old armchair, his head over the other. His mouth hung open, and when he inhaled, the rattling noise came again.

Jesse reckoned the Indians and the baby had been just too much for ol' Ezra's nerves.

Looking east, Jesse saw the first pale stirrings of dawn beginning to color the sky. Soon the men and women on the cliff would be facing who knew how many Indians. And he couldn't go to help. Even if Ezra was awake, Jesse would worry about Serena and Miranda. But with the older man sleepin' off a drunk, there was no way Jesse could leave.

Behind him, the cabin door opened slowly. Hinges screamed briefly in protest before the door was shut again.

Miranda. Jesse clenched his teeth. If it was hard *before*, keeping his eyes and hands off the woman, it was going to be far more difficult now. All he wanted to do was hold her again. Feel her snuggling close. Taste her mouth again and again until he was filled with her, then start all over.

"Jesse?" She stepped up behind him and laid one hand on his arm.

He felt her touch all the way to his soul. It took a moment for him to steady his voice before he could answer.

"Serena all right?"

"Yes."

She moved in closer. The scent of her flowery perfume teased his nostrils. He could feel the warmth of her body beckoning to him. When her head leaned against his shoulder, it was all he could do to stand still. He clenched his hands into fists to keep from reaching for her.

"She's sleeping." Miranda sighed and he saw the faint puff of breath in the cold air.

"The baby?"

"He's wonderful. Sound asleep in Serena's arms." Jesse felt her smile.

"Before she fell asleep," Miranda whispered, "Serena told me what she's going to name him."

"Pike Junior?"

"No." She leaned back and watched his face in the half-light. "His name is Jesse."

He swallowed heavily. He hadn't expected anything like that. A swell of pride filled him. He gritted his jaw and stared off at the distant horizon. In a tight voice he muttered, "She didn't have to do that."

"She wanted to."

He snorted. "Wonder what Pike'll have to say about it."

"When he hears what you did for his wife, he'll agree."

Jesse took a half step to the side. He had to escape the scent of her. She was too close. He had to keep some space between them. She followed. Pushing past his stiff arms, Miranda moved up against him and encircled his waist, her hands spread wide over his back. He didn't move. He couldn't. He wasn't even sure he could breathe.

"Jesse?"

She was looking up at him. He felt her breath, warm and soft against his neck. "What?"

Her hands moved over his back and everywhere she touched became a white-hot flame, searing his flesh with a need so strong it threatened to suffocate him.

"Jesse, don't you want to kiss me?"

He swallowed the groan before it escaped, but couldn't suppress a shiver when her fingers moved to the top button on his shirt. Jesse snatched at her hand and held it firmly in his own. "Don't, Miranda."

"Why?" Her breath fanned his cheek.

"You don't know what you're askin', woman." He looked down at her and fought against the invitation in her eyes. "If you did, you'd run like hell. Now."

She shook her head. "All I'm asking for is a kiss. The kiss you would have given me earlier if not for—"

"Ezra," he finished. "And thank God for him." Jesse struggled to talk past his constricted throat.

"One kiss, Jesse." She slipped her hand free of his and ran the flat of her palm over his broad chest. "Just a kiss. What could be the harm in that?"

Jesse's breath came in tortured gasps and he knew as well as she did that he wouldn't refuse her. That he *couldn't* refuse her any more than he could stop the sun from rising. God help him, he didn't *want* to refuse. He wanted to feel alive again. And in the last two years, the only place he'd felt alive was in Miranda's arms.

For one fleeting moment he tried desperately to remember why he shouldn't have a damn thing to do with her. He tried to remind himself that a woman had no place in the life he'd been forced to live.

Then Miranda's lips curved in a sweet, knowing smile.

His arms shot out and pulled her to him, wrapping

her body as close to his own as he could. While her lips were still parted in surprise at his sudden movement, Jesse's mouth covered them. Eagerly, hungrily his tongue explored her mouth, tasting, caressing. He leaned back against the wooden post, his arms tightened, and he lifted her from the ground, leaving her moccasined feet dangling. Jesse felt Miranda's fingers weave through his hair, but all he concentrated on was her tongue darting quickly against his.

Her fast, shallow breaths mingled with his own and he tore his mouth free of her lips suddenly and began to kiss and nuzzle the length of her throat. With one strong arm curved under her bottom, Jesse held her steady while his other hand moved around to her shirtfront and speedily undid the buttons.

As the white shirt fell open Jesse's heartbeat staggered. In the soft predawn light, the lace of her ivory chemise shone against her honey-golden flesh. He paused for a moment and looked up at her. She'd braced herself with her hands on his shoulders and now she chanced upsetting her balance by reaching to smooth a lock of hair back from his forehead. Her touch was as soft as the scent she wore and even more bewitching.

Jesse's gaze moved from her face to her elegant throat and neck and fastened on the sheer chemise that lay between him and what he sought. Slowly, tenderly his fingers moved up from her waist, over her ribs. She inhaled sharply as he skimmed the flat of his hand over her breast. Her nipples strained against the silky material, aching for his touch. Jesse gently pushed the fabric aside and cupped her breast. His thumb moved lazily over her erect nipple and his own body echoed the shudders that rippled through Miranda.

As her fingers tightened in his hair he brought her closer. Starting at the base of her throat, Jesse's lips and tongue moved over her heated flesh, leaving a trail of damp fire. His own desire mounting with every passing moment, Jesse heard Miranda moan when his mouth closed over her nipple. As his tongue moved over the small, erect bud, Miranda jumped in response and he held her even tighter. His arms were like iron bands, holding her to him as though he would never let go. Slowly, deliberately he began to suckle at her breast and the dull throbbing ache in his groin tripled in strength.

"Jesse," she called his name softly. Her head thrown back, Miranda was lost in the all-encompassing feelings rushing through her. When his mouth moved on her breast, it was as though he was drawing her soul into his.

A curling spiral of need started in the pit of her stomach and spread quickly. She'd never known anything like this before. Never even imagined that this kind of pleasure existed.

His tongue drew circles around her nipple and she felt the edges of his teeth move over the tender flesh. She arched against him, instinctively seeking more. In the very center of her, a tingling began, quickly building into a pulsing need. Miranda held his head to her breast, long past any idea of stopping him.

If she could, she knew she would keep him there forever. When he turned his attention to her other breast, slipping one hand under the chemise to caress her skin, Miranda groaned and opened her eyes wide. Above them the night sky was fading away into a parade of early-morning colors. She saw and *felt* each shade of pink and yellow and lavender. They became a part of her, swirling through her mind, mingling with the delicious sensations Jesse brought to her body.

He groaned, shifted her position slightly, and moved his free hand down over the curve of her hip. His mouth continued to tease her breasts, each in turn, but now Jesse's hand slipped between her legs and began to rub the center of her need. Through the soft, worn buckskin trousers she wore, Miranda felt the pressure of his thumb against another bud. And when he touched the throbbing, sensitive spot, she jumped in his arms.

"Hush, Miranda," he whispered, his breath cool against the dampness of her breast. "I won't hurt you. Hush now."

She eased back into his grasp and gave herself into his hands. His wonderful hands. So tender with Serena and now so strong and sure with her.

It was too much, she told herself frantically. The suckling at her breast and the hard warmth of his hand rubbing the core of her until she thought she would die with the expectation. There was more to come, she knew. She could feel it. A mounting sense of urgency filled her body. Every nerve screamed with the tension.

Cautiously she lifted her right leg higher, resting it against his hipbone. Somehow she wanted to give him more, open herself to him more.

"Yes, M'randa," he gasped, his own need to bring her pleasure blinding him to everything else. His thumb moved even more quickly over the worn buckskin.

She gasped, arched her back, and dug her fingernails into his shoulders. Something was happening. Something was going to burst. She felt it.

She opened her eyes wide. Her breath was reduced to short gasps. The colors in the sky overhead seemed to drop down and surround her. Jesse's fingers moved quickly back and forth over her sensitive flesh, seeming to draw the heat of the coming sun into her body. Spreading and growing inside, the soft colors of the dawn raced through her until there was nowhere for them to go and they split apart . . . shattering Miranda with their brightness and trembling through her with a shaking, rhythmic pleasure.

CHAPTER 10

She had no strength. Her limbs hung uselessly, and if not for Jesse's arms around her, Miranda would have fallen to the ground. Now that the astonishing throbbing had eased, she was left with a delightful contentment.

With one hand, Jesse pulled the edges of her shirt together and she was only mildly surprised that she wasn't embarrassed at all. Slowly, letting her body slide down his, Jesse lowered her until her feet were firmly on solid ground again. Immediately Miranda leaned into him, resting her head on his chest. His heartbeat pounded out frantically beneath her ear. She drew a deep, shuddering breath into her lungs and tried to think of something to say. But what was there *to* say?

Thank you?

That hardly seemed appropriate. And yet Miranda felt a need to touch him somehow. To let him know what he'd done to her. And how much she'd enjoyed it.

* * *

Jesse clenched his teeth. The ache in his groin was almost unbearable. Just having her pressed up close to him was torture. What in the hell had he gotten himself into? And how could he have let things get so far out of hand?

Deliberately he closed his arms around her, cradling her still-trembling form tenderly. Though his own body screamed for release, Jesse didn't think he would change a thing. Just watching her face as the tremors shook her had almost been enough to kill him. If he'd had to survive his own satisfaction as well, it might have been too much for him.

As it stood now, he was hard put not to touch her again. All he wanted to do was to bury himself in her. To look down at her face and watch her lips curve in pleasure. To slide his fingers in and out of her warmth and know that he and he alone held Miranda's secrets.

He groaned and slapped the back of his head against the post. She didn't seem to notice. Reluctantly Jesse grinned. She probably wouldn't notice if a buffalo stampede thundered past them right now.

What was he going to do? Like it or not, things had changed between them. Her little plan to treat each other as "friends" was a miserable failure. But was he really ready to set aside the justice he'd been seeking for two long years?

His hands moved over her back slowly and he could have sworn that she was damn near to purring. No, even for Miranda, he wouldn't stop his quest. But whatever else happened, he knew he couldn't give her up. Not now. Not yet. Maybe it was selfish of him, but Miranda Perry was the only good thing to touch him in longer than he cared to think about.

And he couldn't bear the thought of losing her.

A far-off staccato sound drifted on the morning air and Jesse stiffened.

"What?" She raised her head.

"Hush." Jesse's hand came up to cover her mouth briefly. "Listen."

They held their breaths, straining to hear more. After a long silence, another brief scattering of distant *pops* reached them.

Miranda straightened up and he reluctantly let go. They turned as one to stare at the mouth of the canyon.

"Gunshots," she whispered.

"Yeah."

He'd almost forgotten about the men and women facing a raiding party. They were so far off and the high walls of the canyon twisted and turned so that the gunshots sounded as if they came from a dream. Jesse glanced down at the woman beside him and knew that he was wrong. What he had just shared with Miranda was the dream. The other people, the canyon, the Indians . . . *they* were real.

Miranda quickly did up the buttons on her shirt, keeping her eyes fixed on the far, red rock wall. Already she was distancing herself from him. He could feel it as surely as if she'd already left him in the street alone.

"They don't appear to be doing much firing," she said finally.

"No." Jesse's gaze slid sadly away from her. "Maybe that's a good sign."

"Maybe." She turned toward the door to Serena's cabin. "I, uh, should go check on Serena and the baby."

"Yeah." He pulled his hat brim low and didn't look at her. "Reckon so."

"Jesse," she began uncertainly, "I . . ."

"You go on, Miranda." He stepped off the boardwalk into the street. "I'll keep watch."

"Jesse . . ."

"Just go in, Miranda." He kicked a pebble and watched it skitter across the road. "Please."

He held his breath until he heard her go inside and close the door behind her.

He was alone again.

"C'mon, darlin'," Dave urged, and tugged on her hand. "Somethin's wrong."

"Don't call me darlin'," Shelly muttered halfheartedly, and hurried her steps. Since the floodwaters dropped and they'd crossed the creek, Dave had been practically dragging her back to town. She hadn't heard a thing, but he swore he'd heard gunshots.

As they rounded the edge of the corral Shelly was willing to admit that *something* unusual was going on. There was no one in the street. And generally, even at dawn, there were a few early risers wandering about. Dave's grip on her hand tightened and she tried not to think about how good it felt.

"Hey!" Dave shouted.

Shelly squinted up the street. It was no use. She couldn't see who the man was yelling at. Then a figure stepped clear of the early-morning shadows. Jesse.

"Hey, Jes!"

Shelly pulled at Dave, trying to slow him down. He only shot her a quick glance and continued on. Jesse was walking toward them.

"What the hell's goin' on, Jes?"

Another short burst of firing came from the cliffs, and this time Shelly turned with the men to stare at the mouth of the canyon.

"Buck rode in last night. Said a small raidin' party was settlin' in." Jesse narrowed his gaze as though he could see the small group of defenders clustered on the rocks.

"Who all's up there?" Dave whispered, still listening for more gunshots.

"Just about ever'body." Jesse jerked his thumb toward Serena's cabin. "Miranda, Ezra, and Serena are in yonder. I stayed, just in case."

Dave nodded. "They all right?"

"Yeah. Serena's baby came last night, too."

Shelly's jaw dropped. "Did *Miranda* deliver it?"

He shook his head. "*I* did."

Dave slapped Jesse's shoulder and grinned. "Hell, you had you quite a night, old son!"

Shelly paid no attention to Dave. Instead she watched Jesse's eyes. He wasn't telling everything.

"Miss Shelly . . ."

She turned to look at the tall blond beside her.

"You best stay with Serena and Miranda. Jesse'll be here. I'm goin' on up to the rocks to help the others."

"Wait a minute," Jesse interrupted him. "I been here all night, *I'll* go. *You* stay."

Dave smiled and shook his head. "Who told you to stay put here? Birdwell?"

Jesse nodded.

"Then you best do it. Don't wanna make that man mad now, do ya?"

Jesse's teeth ground together, but he didn't argue.

Shelly was already on her way to the cabin when Dave called to her. She stopped and looked over her shoulder.

"I'll be back directly, Miss Shelly." He smiled knowingly. "You take care now, y'hear?"

Jesse looked from one to the other of them, clearly confused.

She stared at Dave for a long moment, then slowly turned away and moved for Serena's place. No point in pretendin' anything was gonna be different, she told herself. No point at all.

Grudgingly she remembered the night before. He'd held her all through the long, cold darkness and never once let his hands go roamin'. She knew it for a fact. Heaven knew, she'd waked up often enough to be sure.

But if he wasn't after her body, what was he interested in? She walked quickly across the wooden boardwalk and grabbed the doorknob. Love. That's what he'd said. Love. She snorted. It wasn't the first time she'd heard that word. Damn fools seemed to think all they had to do was say "I love you" and a woman would just curl up and die. Well, not *this* woman. She'd had to learn her lessons the hard way, but by thunder . . . she'd *learned*.

Dave Black seemed to be a nice enough man. But when all was said and done, he was still a *man*. And men seemed to use the word "love" almighty easy. Most of 'em forgot it even quicker.

She straightened her shoulders, took a deep breath, and pushed the door wide. Time to put all that nonsense behind her and get about her business.

"She seems fine." Shelly dropped the sheet back into place, glanced at the still-sleeping Serena, and whispered to Miranda. "That's a good-lookin' child. He give you much trouble?"

Miranda paled for a moment in memory of Serena's long, painful labor. But just as quickly the memory of Jesse's strength and tenderness invaded her mind. She smiled and shook her head. "No. Jesse says everything happened just as it should."

Shelly's lips quirked. "He does, does he?"

"Oh, yes. Shelly, you should have seen him!" Miranda moved around the end of the bed and stepped up beside her friend. "He was wonderful. So kind, so gentle. If he hadn't been here, I don't know what I would have done."

Shelly looked into the other woman's eyes and felt the unmistakable stirrings of jealousy. She chided herself for her foolishness. After all, for Serena's sake, Shelly should be glad that the man was here to help. For all the use Miranda and Ezra would have been, Serena would have been as good as alone. And still, it panged her to hear Miranda talk about that fella like he was some kind of storybook hero. Always, it had been *she* who Miranda'd looked up to. Come to for advice. Trusted. Now it seemed to Shelly that her friend's loyalties were shifting to a no-good outlaw who would be riding out of the canyon—and Miranda's life—as soon as it suited him.

And by the glow on Miranda's face, it was too damn late to do anything to stop it.

A sudden suspicion snaked through Shelly's mind. She recalled clearly the almost haunted look on Jesse's face earlier. And now that she took the time to notice, Shelly thought she saw the same sort of elusive shadows dancing behind Miranda's usually forthright gaze.

There was something else going on. Something beyond the birth of the baby.

Shelly cocked her head and studied Miranda as the woman bent over Serena, unnecessarily straightening the bedclothes. What else had the two people shared during that long, lonely night? Were the shadows in

Miranda's eyes a betrayal of a new knowledge of passion?

Leaving the small bedroom, Shelly glared down at Ezra, still sleeping off his drunk. He should have stayed sober. He should have kept watch.

Shelly's insides twisted. If what she suspected was true, there was nothing to be gained by pointing fingers. Besides, if there was a finger to be pointed . . . it should be aimed at her. When her friend needed her, Shelly had been sound asleep in the arms of a man who was becoming altogether too important to her.

She walked over to the tiny cookstove. She fed some kindling to the half-dead fire and watched new flames spring up and devour the fresh wood. As Shelly reached for the blackened coffeepot she told herself it was too late to protect Miranda completely . . . but she made a silent vow to keep a watchful eye on Jesse Hogan, to see that he did no more damage.

"A couple more beers ought to do it," Buck said, and looped his fingers through the handles of six glass mugs, three in each hand. He grinned and carried the drinks through the crowd, back to the table he shared with Dave, Jesse, Miranda, Shelly, and Birdwell. As he set the glasses down carefully he smiled all around and ignored the fact that his was the only smiling face.

"C'mon now," he urged. "Let's have a drink to celebrate, huh?"

"Celebrate? After a night like we all had?" Birdwell shook his bald head. "I'm too durned tired to celebrate."

"I hear ya," Dave commented. "Why, I don't believe I got more than five minutes' sleep all night." He glanced at Shelly, but she looked away.

Jesse ignored the couple and reached for his drink. Buck chuckled. "See there. Ol' Jes don't mind celebratin', and to my way of thinkin', *he* had the worst night of all of us put together!"

"Just like a man," Shelly tossed in. "Serena's the one in pain, but it's *Jesse* you feel for."

"Now don't get your back up, Miss Shelly." Buck lifted his glass and took a long drink. "I'm not takin' anything away from Serena. Lord knows, I'm right happy that the Good Lord saw fit to have women be the ones to bear children. It's only that anytime a man's got to be that close to a birthin' . . . " He shuddered and took another gulp. "Pure sets me to shiverin' just to think about it."

Jesse glanced at the other man and a halfhearted smile lifted one corner of his mouth.

"Reckon it's a good thing I left you behind, Hogan." Birdwell's calm, controlled voice cut off another of Buck's observations. "With Ezra passin' out and such . . . well, you were a help to Miranda."

Jesse's fingers toyed with his glass. He didn't look up. Birdwell's gaze shifted from the silent man to the woman he considered a daughter. Miranda seemed intent on studying the white foam riding the top of her untouched beer.

"Lucky for all of us, we didn't need him at the canyon," Buck said. "Now, Birdwell, why you think them durned Indians just up and left the way they did?"

The big man shrugged. "No way of knowin'. Just be glad they did." He pushed away from the table and stood up. "Prob'ly just some young bucks out lookin' for a little fun. Sometimes they get frisky this time of year." He yawned. "We was just lucky none of their wild hair-teasin' shots hit anybody. What with the ricochets and such, it could've been a lot worse."

The others nodded solemnly.

"You think we hit any of them?" Buck wondered aloud.

"Doubt it." Birdwell drained the last of his beer. "Them Apaches was young. Not stupid. Don't believe I actually *saw* one of 'em all night." A jaw-cracking yawn split his features. "Anyhow, I'm purely tuckered out." Birdwell looked down at Miranda. "Ever'body in town's prob'ly gonna sleep for hours. We left the Sully boys up at the canyon mouth to keep watch. Anything happens, one of them'll hightail it in and let us know. But I reckon this little 'raid' is about done. Why don't you go to your cabin and get some rest yourself?"

She looked up and smiled at him. "Maybe I will at that. It *was* a long night . . ." Her gaze slid to Jesse, then moved on. Slowly she stood up and linked her arm through Birdwell's. "Walk me home?"

As the incongruous couple left Big Pete's place Buck looked at Jesse and said thoughtfully, "That Birdwell, now. He reminds me of a big ol' blacksmith used to have a shop near my folks back home."

Jesse's fingers turned the beer mug.

"Yes, sir," Buck went on. "I get a hankerin' ever now and again to head on home . . . just to look the place over. See somethin' familiar. Know what I mean, Dave?"

Dave studied his partner for a long minute before saying, "Yeah, Buck. I sure do. Feel that way myself time to time."

"How 'bout you, Jesse?" Buck asked casually. "Where you from?"

Jesse flicked a quick glance at the man. "Texas." He lifted the mug and took a long swallow of cold beer.

Buck chuckled. "Well now, Texas is a big place. Where 'bouts is home?"

Jesse stared at the other man silently. Why all the questions? Was it possible that these men had begun to doubt him? Why? What had he done to arouse suspicion? Buck's gaze was open. Friendly. And still, Jesse hesitated.

Finally though, he told himself it wouldn't matter. Not one person in twenty would have even *heard* of his hometown. There was almost no chance at all that any of these folks would have heard about Carter and Della Hogan's death. After all, why would they care? Not only were they all outlaws . . . but what could the lives of a young couple on a small ranch in Texas mean to any of them?

He looked at Buck before saying quietly, "Coldwater." Was there a short flash of recognition in the other man's eyes? No, Jesse told himself, he was imagining things. Why the hell would anyone *here* know a little place like Coldwater?

"That there's a new one on me," Buck said on a laugh. "How 'bout you, Dave? You ever hear of it?"

Jesse looked at the blond man opposite him. Dave's features were as empty as a gambler's heart.

"No, sir, don't believe I ever have," Dave muttered.

"Not surprised," Jesse said, his lips curving involuntarily into a memory-filled smile. "Ain't much more than a spot in the road. It's about a day's ride east of El Paso."

"Good country." Dave mumbled his comment and reached for his beer.

"Yeah."

"You lived in town, did ya?"

Jesse's brow furrowed as he stared at Buck. Why was the man so damned interested all of a sudden? Even Birdwell hadn't asked all these questions. Still . . . if he was to keep on the good side of these fellas, maybe it was best to just keep his answers as close to the truth as he dared. Too many lies only made things more confusing. So he said, "No. Had me a ranch about twenty miles outside of town."

Jesse looked down at his suddenly trembling hands and missed the quick, worried look Dave and Buck exchanged.

But Shelly saw it. She didn't know quite what to make of it, either. But there were altogether too many strange things going on in Bandit's Canyon to suit her. She found herself wishing that none of these men had set foot inside her sanctuary. For three years she'd known a kind of peace she'd never hoped to find. For three years she'd lived safely in the midst of criminals and outcasts. For three years she'd been able to sleep the night through without worrying about attack.

She let her gaze move slowly over the men seated at her table. A chill crawled up her spine and she curled her fingers tight around the handle of her glass to keep from shaking. The three men, each of them wrapped in his own secrets, stared at each other, wariness battling curiosity. The other conversations in the bar faded away. The discordant noise of the untuned piano slipped into silence. Shelly heard only her own thoughts and wished she could disregard even those.

Because somehow she had the distinct feeling that the men seated at her table had brought destruction with them.

* * *

Miranda slipped quietly out of her cabin and closed the door behind her. Her fingers tightened over the handle of the big basket she carried as she shot a quick, searching gaze over the street. No one. A satisfied smile curved her lips and she stepped down off the boardwalk and hurried toward the corral.

After sitting alone in her cabin for more than an hour, she was eager to be on her way. But now she was glad she'd waited. She'd given everyone in town time to be in their beds sleeping off the long night before. Now there wouldn't be anyone around to interfere with her plans.

Clumsily she shifted the basket from one hand to the other, her body leaning to one side to offset the weight. It wasn't going to be an easy climb, hauling the basket along, but it would be worth it. Miranda bit her lip uneasily as she thought about what Birdwell's reaction to her plan would be. Hopefully, though, he wouldn't find out what she'd done. All she had to do was get back to town before anyone woke up. And they were all so tired, they should sleep for hours!

Miranda breathed deeply, drawing the sun-warmed desert air into her lungs. Strange, she thought. By all rights she, too, should be sound asleep, exhausted from a night without sleep and the worry she'd experienced.

Not to mention, her brain chided, the extraordinary encounter she'd experienced with Jesse only that morning. She'd been so weak . . . so *drained* after he'd . . . well. She stopped, switched the basket to her other hand, and tried to turn her mind to something else. Determinedly she kept climbing the familiar, narrow path winding its way up the red cliff face of the canyon. Still, it *was* strange, Miranda told herself, that the very act that had left her wobbly and languid, could, only a couple of hours later, fill her with a driving energy and a *need* to be busy!

A tingling sensation curled in her loins as though her body was ready and waiting for Jesse's knowledgeable fingers to touch her again. Her breath quickened, her heart pounded, and the palms of her hands became suddenly too damp to carry the basket another step.

Miranda set her burden down in the middle of the path and leaned back against the cliff wall. The sun-heated rock burned against her shirt and she felt the sting of it on her flesh. But she didn't move away. Deliberately she arched closer to the rock, leaning her head back and staring at the wide expanse of cloudless, blue afternoon sky above. Miranda tried desperately to concentrate on the jagged, heated boulder behind her. Instead the canyon's heat seemed to make the burning between her legs even hotter and more impossible to ignore.

What was happening to her? Her eyes wide, she searched the heavens for an answer and found nothing. Miranda flicked a quick glance toward the town below. From this distance Bandit's Canyon looked like a ghost town. Abandoned. Yet her aching body reminded her that Jesse was below. Probably sleeping like everyone else, but still, he was there.

She wasn't quite sure how it had happened, but somehow she'd gone far beyond her initial attraction to Jesse Hogan. And it was far too late now to pretend that she could still honor the vow made to her mother. Heaven knew, Miranda had never intended to care for an outlaw . . . it had simply *happened*. And now that it had, she was powerless to do anything about it. Even if she wanted to.

Inhaling sharply, Miranda turned her back on the town and Jesse Hogan. She reached down, grabbed the basket, and started climbing again. Maybe if she walked fast enough, climbed high enough, she would be able to outdistance the aching need she felt to go back and find Jesse.

He stepped out of the shadows and paused for a long moment. She'd almost spotted him. If he'd been just a hair slower, Miranda would have caught him in the act of following her.

And why shouldn't she? For God's sake, man! Why're you sneakin' around like a drunk at a teetotaler's party? He snorted. He knew good and well why he was creepin' from rock to rock, stayin' undercover. 'Cause he didn't trust himself alone with her anymore—that's why!

Jesse snatched his hat off and wiped the sweat off his brow with his forearm. This was the most damn fool thing he could ever remember doing. If he'd had the sense God gave a rock, he'd have simply waked up Birdwell and told the man what Miranda was up to. But no. No, *he* had to follow her to Lord knew where. In the heat of the day, climbing straight up the goddamn cliff!

And just what the hell did she have in the damned basket?

Disgusted, Jesse braced his palms on either side of the rock niche he'd slipped into and pushed himself clear. Then, slowly, he began his climb again. He couldn't let her take off on her own. Hell, anything might happen. Not counting Indians . . . she could fall, be snake-bit . . . with Miranda, there was just no tellin' *what* she could get herself into!

Besides, he told himself, with all the other men in

town sittin' up all night on the rocks, it was only right that *he* chase her down. All *he'd* had to do was deliver a baby!

He looked up the path and shook his head. Lord, she was a fast climber! Why hadn't she just stayed in town to sleep, like everybody else? After all they'd been through, you'd think she'd have passed out as cleanly as Ezra. Didn't she have the sense to be tired?

Jesus, if she'd done to *him* what he'd done to *her*, he'd *still* be sleepin'! Jesse groaned softly. Just the thought of Miranda's hands on his body shot liquid fire through his blood. His groin ached miserably and breathing became almost impossible.

At the rate he was goin', he wouldn't have the strength to kill the man he was searching for, even if he *did* find him!

CHAPTER
11

Jesse sighed heavily and squinted at the narrow path that stretched up before him. He shook his head and muttered a curse under his breath. The woman climbs like a mountain goat, he thought with disgust. He'd been hard put to keep up with her. He shifted position slightly and the sole of his right boot slid on the pebble-and-dirt-strewn path. Uneasily Jesse glanced over the edge of the nearest boulder and stared at the rocky ground nearly a hundred feet below. He rubbed one hand over his jaw and carefully stepped back a pace or two from the edge of the pathway.

Dammit. When he left Big Pete's place, why hadn't he just gone on back to the bunkhouse? If he had, he would never have seen Miranda sneakin' out of town, would never have followed her, and wouldn't now be danglin' over the edge of a goddamn cliff!

He grumbled again and started climbing. She'd disappeared around the top boulder almost twenty minutes ago, and the way the durn female climbed, if he didn't get movin', he'd never catch her! Of course, he reminded himself in his own defense, her moccasins were a helluva lot better for climbin' than his boots!

Pebbles skittered noisily over the path and Jesse felt drops of sweat roll down his back under the long-sleeved blue shirt he wore. She'd better have a damn good reason for all this nonsense, he told himself grimly. Imagine a woman goin' off by her lonesome into the cliffs the day after they'd had trouble with the Indians! Why, if it wasn't for the worry that the raiding party might return, Jesse would just hightail it back to town and go to sleep! Let her take her chances with all the other dangers.

He stopped suddenly, gritted his teeth, and inhaled sharply. No he wouldn't. Hell, there was no use in lyin' to himself! He'd have gone after Miranda anyway. Indians or no. It was almost as though he had no say in the matter at all. He was drawn to her warmth . . . to her smile . . . as surely as fortune hunters were drawn to a rich widow.

At the top of the rise he stopped. Jesse's mouth dropped open as he looked down into a huge water hole. The clear water was surrounded on three sides by steep rock walls. Cottonwoods and a few hardy pines straggled around the edges of the tank, making the harsh line of the rocks softer, more welcoming. On the fourth side of the water hole, a series of natural steps had formed over time. They led to the water's edge, where there was a deep cutaway into the wall. An overhang of cliff shaded the little nook from the desert sun.

It was beautiful. Just looking at the clear water below made Jesse cooler than he'd been in days. He shook his head in wonder, then suddenly dropped down to the ground.

Miranda had stepped out from under the overhang. She didn't look up. Though he knew he should say something, announce his presence, Jesse kept his silence and watched. She must have set the basket down in the shade. He didn't see it anywhere. His eyes followed her as she walked to the water's edge. She plopped down on the rocks, pulled off her moccasins, then dipped her feet into the water.

Jesse almost felt her sigh when the cool water touched her skin. His breath uneven, he swallowed nervously and waited.

She threw her head back, eyes closed, and let the sun wash over her upturned face. As she leaned back on her hands the plain white shirt pulled across her breasts and strained as she arched her back. Lazily her feet kicked in the water and the splashing echoed off the surrounding walls.

Jesse pulled air in through clenched teeth and licked his too dry lips. He stretched out full length on the clifftop, lying on his stomach and peeking out over the edge of rock.

Suddenly Miranda stood up. Moving quickly, she began to unbutton her shirt and pants. Jesse gripped the cliff edge tightly. Hungrily his gaze followed her fingers' progress. One by one her shirt buttons popped open, revealing the silky chemise he'd seen earlier and the smooth golden flesh of her shoulders and chest. His thumb and forefinger rubbed together, and in memory Jesse touched her nipples once more.

Then she slipped her hands beneath the waistband of her pants and began to smooth them down over her nicely rounded hips. Miranda's deliciously curved bottom wiggled as she pushed at the form-fitting buckskin, and Jesse's heart stopped when he realized that she wasn't wearing a damn thing under those britches of hers.

He groaned but couldn't look away. She bent over and slowly pushed her trousers down the length of first one leg then the other. As every inch of flesh was exposed Jesse's chest tightened. He felt as though he'd never be able to breathe again. And he didn't care. He only knew that he couldn't turn away if it meant his life. He wanted nothing more than to leap down the path and run his hands over her body. Feel her trembling for need of him. See his own hunger reflected in her eyes.

When she was free of her trousers, she straightened up. Jesse let his eyes travel up the length of her shapely legs to the small triangle of soft, brown curls that guarded the treasure he sought. The flat of her palms smoothed over her hips and stopped at her narrow waist. Her fingers held the hem of her chemise and she quickly pulled it off over her head.

Even from a distance Jesse saw her grin. She held her arms up toward the sun and spread wide as if welcoming a lover. Jesse's gaze moved slowly over every luscious inch of her. From the peaks of her breasts to the curve of her backside, she was a woman most men would kill for.

Miranda bent to one side slightly, swinging her long braid over one shoulder. Nimbly her fingers pulled the rawhide thong from the end of the braid and quickly pulled the long, thick hair free of its confinement.

Before Jesse'd had more than a quick look at the gold-streaked hair falling down past her waist, Miranda walked to the water's edge, positioned herself, then dived into the clear, deep water. Jesse leaned out as far as he dared and stared down into the pool. From his vantage point, he could see the rocks, ledges, and outcroppings that lined the water tank. And he could see Miranda's pale flesh slicing through the water. Her arms moving languidly, her hair streaming out behind her, and her long legs kicking her toward the surface once more.

He settled back as she climbed out of the water to repeat her dive. Tiny water droplets, capturing the sun's light, shone like crystal and rolled down her sleek body. Her hair hung straight as a lance down the center of her back, dripping water into a shallow pool at her feet.

She raised her arms, rose onto the balls of her feet, and dived in again. This time she went deeper. Jesse leaned forward again. He couldn't see exactly where she'd landed. Anxiously he scanned the tank. Seconds ticked by and still she hadn't come up. Then he saw a flash of white. It was Miranda. Floating gently in the water. Facedown, arms and legs limp, her glorious hair hanging down on either side of her face like a bed curtain. As he watched, stunned, a single bubble of air left her body, moved quickly to the surface, and popped.

Dave lit his cigarette, inhaled deeply, then exhaled the pale, bluish smoke in a rush. His eyes never leaving the door of Shelly's cabin, he took another drag of the tobacco, squinting against the coil of smoke floating upward.

"Thought I'd find you here."

Dave chuckled softly. "No wonder you're such a good Ranger. You're a helluva detective, Buck."

"Keep it down, man!" Buck twisted around nervously, letting his gaze wander over the deserted street. "You gone completely loco? What's the matter with you anyhow?"

"Me?" Dave shrugged. "Nothin's wrong with me, Buck. Not a damn thing."

Buck stepped up beside his partner. Even if he hadn't heard the sarcasm in the other man's voice, he'd have seen the disgust on Dave's face plain enough. "Yeah, I can see you're just dandy."

"Leave it be, Buck."

"Now, why in hell should I leave it be?" Buck took hold of Dave's arm and spun the man around to face him. "You're so all-fired busy starin' at that woman with your tongue hangin' out, you ain't done a thing about why we're here in the first place."

"Yeah? And what is there to do?" Dave spread his arms wide, encompassing the small town. His voice harsh and low, he went on. "You seen the fella we're lookin' for? Huh? He ride in while I was sleepin' or somethin'? 'Cause if he did, you just point me at him, Buck, and I'll go fetch him for ya!"

Buck shook his head, disgusted. "Just look at you."

"What?"

"In all the years I known you, I ain't never seen you lose your temper thataway. You're 'bout the most easygoin' man I ever knew."

Dave snorted and tossed his half-finished cigarette into the dust, where he ground it out with the toe of his boot.

"Is it the woman?"

Dave glanced at his friend and smiled halfheartedly. Hell, it wasn't Buck's fault he was in such a mess. "Yeah. It's Shelly." He leaned his shoulder against the porch post and nodded his head in the direction of her cabin. "Who'da thought this'd happen to me, huh?" He chuckled softly. "And I don't know what to do about it. She don't trust me worth a damn. Can't say as I blame her none for that, her thinkin' I'm a outlaw and such."

"You can't tell her, Dave."

He looked at his friend. "Yeah, I know." Dave shoved at Buck's shoulder. "Hell, it'll be all right. Things most times got a way of workin' out."

"I reckon." Buck's voice was quiet, hesitant. "You give any thought to how folks back home would look on Shelly?"

"What's that supposed to mean?"

Buck took a step back from the suddenly enraged man. "Simmer down, Dave. I didn't say nothin'."

"See that you don't." Dave stepped up close to his partner, his blue eyes sparking dangerously. "We been friends a long time, Buck . . . but don't you test me on this one. When we leave outta here, Shelly's gonna be travelin' with me, and as soon as we get back to Texas, we'll get married."

"That so?" Buck challenged softly. "I ain't exackly seen her out pickin' daisies for a *boo*-kay!"

"Yeah, well"—Dave grinned suddenly, his temper gone as quickly as it came—"she don't know it yet."

"Well, that explains a helluva lot!" Buck slapped his hat against his thigh. "Why in thunder are we arguin' over something that ain't happened yet? Shit, by the time you work up the gumption to ask her, we'll all be dead and buried."

"Don't you count on it."

Buck grumbled uneasily for a few minutes. Though he thought his friend was askin' for a peck of trouble, it wasn't wise to go pokin' around in things between a man and his woman . . . for now he'd let it go. "You mind if we talk a little business now?"

Dave chuckled. "Sure. Why not?"

"What'd you think about Hogan sayin' he's from Coldwater?"

"Hell, Buck. Both of us already had him figured for the brother of those Hogans that got theirselves killed. Why you actin' so surprised?"

"Well, I ain't surprised it's him, you jackass. I'm surprised 'cause he's here!"

Dave frowned.

"Why's the boy pretendin' to be an outlaw? Hell, he's no more a badman than we are."

"Reckon he's lookin' for somethin'."

"Yeah. Or *someone*. C'mon, Dave. He's got to be here for the same reason we are. To catch that man did all the killin' back home."

"How would he know to look here? Hell, we only just found out about this place a few months ago."

"Shit." Buck spat into the street. "He prob'ly heard the same talk we did." He squinted off into the distance. "'Bout our man usually turnin' up here in the canyon sooner or later. But it don't really matter *how* he found out about this place." Buck turned a flat stare on his partner. "What matters is we keep a close watch on him. If he messes this up for us, the cap'n'll have us stretched out on an anthill. Facedown!"

Dave shuddered at the thought of facing his boss with a failure. The man didn't accept defeat easily. In anyone. "Then we'll just have to see to it that Jesse Hogan stays the hell out of our way." He turned and looked back to Shelly's cabin. "I want to get this job finished so's we can go home."

Buck shook his head and looked past his partner at the tumbledown cabin across the road. This wasn't turnin' out to be the easy job he'd expected. A lovesick partner and another fella out for revenge. Hell, Buck told himself, maybe he was gettin' too old for this.

Maybe it was time to buy himself a little ranch and just sit on the porch watchin' the days die.

His whole body shuddered at the thought. Deliberately he turned away from his partner and headed for Big Pete's place. The huge man might be an outlaw, but he served the best whiskey Buck had tasted since leavin' Texas.

Jesse leaped up and started running down the sloping steps to the water below. His boots sliding on the gritty rocks, he fought for balance. On the run, he unbuckled his gun belt and tossed it aside. His gaze never left the pale, motionless figure in the water. Another bubble rose from her lips and Jesse hurried even faster. He snatched his hat off, dropped it to the ground, and dived into the water.

He paid no attention to the solid smack of the water against his chest and abdomen as he hit the pool stretched out. The cold water closed over him and he kicked his legs violently, sending himself at a rush toward the woman. Desperately his left arm coiled around Miranda's middle and flipped her over until her face was out of the water. Her hair streamed across her face and Jesse was sure he heard her gasp for air.

He didn't have time to rejoice, though. He wouldn't feel safe until he had her on dry land. His heart pounding in his chest, he kept on, grabbing at the water with his right hand, kicking his legs, and trying to hold on to a suddenly struggling Miranda.

Finally, at the steps, he put his feet down and pulled her close, pushing the long strands of hair away from her face. As he mumbled a frantic, long-forgotten prayer Jesse's fingers moved over her features anxiously. When he pushed the last of her hair aside, he stopped dead.

Miranda's eyes were wide open, staring at him with a furious intensity. "What are you doing?"

"What am *I* doing?" he shouted back, pleased to feel that his heart had started beating again. "I'm tryin' to save you from drownin', you damn fool woman!"

She pushed against his chest. Jesse released her at once and she dropped, bottom first, to the step below. She came up sputtering, shoving her hair out of her face. The cold water lapped at her belly, but she was much too angry to feel it. "*Drowning?* For heaven's sake! I wasn't *drowning*, I was floating! And I can take care of myself, thank you!"

Jesse rubbed his mouth fiercely. He stood just inches from a naked, luscious woman and all he could think was that he wanted to beat the living tar out of her! She liked to scared him to death. He glanced down at his feet and swore softly. She'd prob'ly even ruined his best boots, too.

His gaze lifted to her turquoise eyes. And did she even bother to *thank* him? *Hell* no! Well, by Harry, if she wanted to float, then he'd help her! Without any warning, he snatched her up in both his arms, turned, and tossed her into the pool. When she came up for air, he yelled, "Go ahead and float. But if you drown this time, I ain't gonna save you! You're on your own, woman!"

Miranda treaded water, her arms and legs moving lazily. Now that her initial shock and anger were over, she couldn't help wondering why he was there. He *had* to have followed her. She was fairly certain that only she and Birdwell knew about this well-hidden tank. A reluctant smile curved her lips as she watched Jesse slog over to the closest step and plop down.

From his waist down, he was still in the water, but she guessed it didn't much matter. He was already thoroughly soaked.

Clearly disgusted, he crossed one leg over the other and tugged at his boot until he got it off. Slowly he tipped the black leather boot over and watched a stream of water run out. Miranda put her mouth underwater to muffle the chuckle she couldn't squelch. He pulled off the other boot and tossed it up on the rocks beside its mate. Only then did he turn back to Miranda.

"Durn boots're prob'ly ruined."

"Shouldn't have gotten them wet."

His brows shot up. "I *thought* you was drownin'."

"I'm sorry."

He shook his head, then pushed his sodden hair off his forehead. "Just what the hell were you doin', anyway?"

"Floating. Like I told you."

Jesse inhaled then exhaled sharply. *"Why?"*

"It almost feels like you're flying. . . ." She shrugged, feeling suddenly foolish.

His eyes narrowed as he stared at her. Slowly Jesse stood up and began to pull at the buttons on his shirt.

"What are you doing?" Miranda looked at him uneasily.

"Since I'm already wet," he said, tugging the wet shirt off his body, "thought I'd try it for myself."

She looked around frantically. Trying to look *anywhere* but at his chest. "But, Jesse . . . you, uh . . . shouldn't come in. Not now."

"Why not?"

Why not. Why does he *think* why not? Because she was *naked*! For heaven's sake. How had this all happened? All she'd wanted was a little swim.

The now familiar burning and tingling began deep within her and she fought against it, knowing that if she gave in now, there would be no turning back. Ever.

"Uh, Jesse," she said shakily, still moving her arms and legs, "before you come in, would you mind just handing me my clothes and turning your back for a moment or two?"

He took one step down further into the pool, letting the water level reach his abdomen. His hands, below the clear water, pulled at his trouser buttons.

Miranda pulled her gaze up immediately, but staring at his well-muscled chest, covered with a mat of curly black hair, was no easier. Unwillingly her eyes raked over his body, and as he bent down to pull his pants off, Miranda spun around, her back to him. Blood rushed to her cheeks and the sound of her own heartbeat almost drowned out Jesse's answer to her plea.

"Don't think that's a wise idea, M'randa," he said softly.

"Why . . ." She cleared her throat. "Why not?"

"Well, for one thing, I ain't got my pants on."

"Oh, Lord," she whispered, and blew a stream of bubbles into the water.

"So, if I go get you your clothes, why . . . you'd see me naked!" She heard what sounded like a chuckle, then he added, "Couldn't stand that, M'randa. Why, the shame'd prob'ly kill me."

"I promise not to look," she offered.

"Oh, I don't know . . . how can I trust a woman that won't look me in the eye when she's talkin' to me?"

Something warm and luscious spread through her veins and Miranda fought to slow it down. Every inch of her body felt as though it were on fire. The cold water had no effect on her anymore and she was only surprised that she couldn't see steam rising up around her. Jesse was teasing her, she knew. It was most likely an effort to pay her back for his "rescue" attempt.

But if facing him now was the only way she could get out of this situation, she would have to do it. She only hoped the flush in her cheeks had died away sufficiently that he wouldn't be able to see her embarrassment.

"All right, Jesse." She began a slow turn to face him. "Once I look you in the eye, you'll get me my clothes?"

"If that's what you want . . ." His voice seemed deeper.

She'd kept her eyes closed during her turn and now she took one long, deep breath to steel herself, then opened her eyes to meet his. Miranda sucked in her breath and knew she was lost.

He stood on the step, confident, proud. Hands on his hips, his dark brown eyes watching her, Jesse waited for her reaction. With the sun at his back, he was outlined in the brightest of lights. Her gaze moved over his broad shoulders, strong arms, brown, muscled chest, and narrow waist. Cautiously she followed the trail of black hairs down over the paler flesh of his belly to where it disappeared below the water.

"M'randa?"

"Hmmm?" She forced the sound out. The sight of him had made her mouth and throat dry.

"M'randa."

She shook her head and looked up into his eyes. "What?"

"You want me to go get your clothes for ya?"

There it was. Her chance. He would climb out of the water, walk to the underhang, and get her clothes. Then he would turn around, she would get dressed, and then she would leave the pool. And him.

Somehow Miranda knew that if they walked away from this time together, it might never come again. And could she bear that?

The aching, trembling sensation coursing through her body grew until it throbbed in time with her pounding heart. Miranda parted her mouth slightly and ran her tongue over suddenly too dry lips. She saw his gaze narrow. Saw his chest rise and fall with the struggle to breathe evenly. Even his relaxed pose was just that. A pose. At his sides, Jesse's fists were clenched tightly and she knew that he felt the same aching need that she did.

She knew, too, that there would be no turning back for either of them.

"Is that what you want?" he asked again quietly.

She shook her head. "No, Jesse."

"What *do* you want, Miranda?"

Miranda's gaze held his for a long, silent moment. "I'm not . . . sure."

He took one step further into the pool. The muscles in his jaw twitched slightly before he asked again, "What do you want, Miranda?"

Miranda swallowed heavily. Her arms and legs were tired and she began to sink lower into the water. She knew what he wanted her to say. A deep, shuddering breath racked her body and she struggled to keep her voice steady.

"You, Jesse. I want you."

CHAPTER 12

He didn't smile.

He didn't speak.

He moved slowly into the water, and when he was deep enough, he pushed away from the rocks and swam toward her.

Miranda couldn't look away from his eyes. The shining green depths seemed to hold her captive. In them she read his desire, his need . . . and something else. Something she couldn't quite name. And then his arms snaked around her and all thought ended.

The moment he had her in his arms, Jesse released the breath he'd been holding. If she'd said no—if she'd refused him—he'd watched her eyes and though he'd seen the desire there, he'd also seen hesitation. And in the few moments it had taken for her to decide, he'd aged twenty years.

Cradling her head in the crook of his left arm, Jesse wrapped his right arm around her waist and pressed

her close. Together their legs moved slowly, languor-
ously, just enough to keep them afloat while at the
same time rubbing and stroking each other's flesh.

He looked down into her face and felt his heart race.
Her eyes closed, a half smile on her lips, she ran one
hand down his naked back, her short nails dragging a
tender trail over his skin. Jesse's gaze dipped lower,
following the line of her throat, smoothing over the
pale gold vee of skin where her shirt always lay open
to the sun. Her pale, ivory breasts pressed against his
bronzed chest and he slowly, deliberately moved her
body back and forth, creating small sparks of delight
that shuddered over both of them.

Her eyes opened and he read her pleasure in the soft
turquoise gaze she fixed on him. The cold water
lapping around them gently, Jesse lowered his head
and traced kisses across her brow, down over her
temple, and along her jaw. When his lips finally
claimed hers, she parted her mouth to him, welcoming
his tongue with an eagerness he'd dreamed of.

He felt her hands on his body. His back and chest.
His arms and shoulders. Frantic touching as though
she was afraid he might disappear. And Miranda's
excitement fed the flames of the fire building inside
him.

With a muffled groan, Jesse locked his body around
hers and allowed the cold water to swallow them.
Spiraling together, they drifted for a few seconds of
eternity, their tongues and hands alive with the need
to touch and be touched. Jesse opened his eyes briefly,
and in the clear water he saw Miranda's long hair
billowing out around them like a protective cloud of
darkness.

Then suddenly, with quick, determined strokes, his
powerful legs propelled them to the surface. Miranda

took a deep gulp of the warm air and smiled at him as she wound her arms around his shoulders. Flipping over onto his back, Jesse swam for the rocky edge of the pool, with Miranda lying full length atop him. When he reached the bank, he stood up, helping Miranda to her feet.

Her gaze swept over him and Jesse waited, sure that the sight of him, fully aroused, would make her hesitate again. Maybe even frighten her.

He needn't have worried.

She took a step closer and pressed herself against him, her arms around his neck. Looking up into his eyes, she said softly, "You, Jesse. I want you."

Jesse groaned, bent down, and scooped her off her feet. Hurriedly he stepped out of the pool and crossed the few feet of space to the overhang. As he walked his fingers moved over her flesh as if reassuring himself that she was really there with him.

The basket lay where she'd left it when she'd arrived. Right on top was an old quilt. He looked from the blanket to her and grinned. "Now *that* was thoughtful."

"I sometimes take a nap after a swim," she said, a soft smile on her face.

"And maybe we will." He snatched the quilt with one hand and deftly shook it, still managing to hold on to Miranda tightly. "Later."

No sooner had the blanket hit the ground than Jesse laid her down atop it, smoothing out the edges of the frayed, flowered quilt with his free hand. He reached for her shirt, balled it up, and put it beneath her head, then cupped her cheek gently. His thumb moved lazily over the curve of her eyebrow. He couldn't stop looking at her. Her eyes, her hair, the feel of her skin, the sound of her voice, he needed to have all of her. To touch her so deeply that separation would be impossible. To be a part of her.

He bent his head and kissed her lips, gently at first. A feather-light brush against the softness of her mouth. His tongue traced the outline of her lips while his hand smoothed over her breasts, each in turn. Her nipples sprang into life under his palm and she shivered as she tried to deepen their kiss. But Jesse wasn't to be hurried. He'd waited too long. Thought about this too often. Prayed too hard.

His breath warm against her flesh, his lips trailed down her neck and his tongue licked gently at the hollow of her throat. Miranda's pulse throbbed wildly and Jesse struggled for air. She sighed and threaded her fingers through his hair, shifting her body anxiously.

Jesse's fingers toyed with one rigid nipple and he smiled when he heard the groan from deep in her throat. Her hands now on his face, she tried to pull him up to her for a kiss, but instead he lowered his mouth to the taut peak that waited for him. At first his tongue drew warm, lazy circles around the sensitive flesh and he smiled with each tremor of delight that shook her. But soon his own need to taste her overcame his desire to go slowly and he closed his lips over her nipple and suckled her. She gasped aloud, feeding the fever that gripped him. He felt her fingers in his hair again, but this time she held him to her breast.

He looked up at her and found her watching him through softly glazed eyes. She licked at her lips and whispered, "Don't stop, Jesse. Please, don't stop."

"Never," he assured her, and ran the edges of his teeth over her nipple. She arched her back and murmured his name in a breathless hush. Quickly he shifted his attentions to her other breast and allowed his hand to slide down the smooth skin of her belly, past the small, dark triangle and down to the center of the heat that was consuming her.

Slowly, teasingly his fingertips touched the small bud he'd caressed earlier that day and Miranda's eyes flew open. So much the same and yet so different. When there was no fabric, no buckskin to separate them . . . only the magic of his hands.

Miranda's body twisted and stretched, searching for the profound release she'd experienced before. But now she wanted more. Seemed to realize that *this* time it would be different. More shattering. More complete.

His mouth locked down on her nipple, and as he sucked at her breast Miranda felt the drawing pull of it snake through her body. Each time his tongue flicked against her skin, she wanted to capture it. Hold it there. Feel that way forever. He drew his head back and blew a short puff of breath onto her damp breast. The gooseflesh spread over her and even the heat of the afternoon sun wasn't enough to warm her. She let the wave of pleasure course through her, willingly giving over to him control of her body.

His long, supple fingers left the bud of her desire and she wanted to cry out at him to come back. Not to leave her. But she couldn't find her voice. And then she realized that he hadn't stopped. He'd simply gone further. His fingers slid down the damp, warm folds of her sex, and when she arched her back and briefly, instinctively, tried to close her legs, he pushed them apart again.

"Just feel, Miranda. Don't think. Feel," he soothed her, his voice as soft as his touch.

Immediately she relaxed again, parting her thighs

for him. His fingers smoothed over the dampness between her legs, and she didn't think. Didn't care that she should be embarrassed . . . and wasn't.

Jesse propped himself up on his right arm and stared down into her face. She licked her lips, but they were immediately dry again, in the face of the short, panting gasps of air she dragged into her lungs. The shirt beneath her head had long since become useless as a pillow and she twisted her head from side to side, trying to reach . . . something.

Suddenly, without warning, Jesse's fingers slipped inside her. Strong, hard, he dipped in and out of her body like a bee in a flower garden. Her eyes wide, she stared up at him, her mouth parted in surprise and an exquisite delight. He was going beyond the pleasure he'd shown her earlier, and Miranda shuddered and lifted her hips to meet his questing fingers, loving the feel of him inside her. It was as if he had *become* her. And when his thumb moved to caress the too sensitive nub of flesh, Miranda jumped against him, startled by the incredible feelings shaking through her.

"Jesse. Jesse, I . . ."

He lowered his head and covered her mouth with his, ending her attempt to speak. Her hips pushed against his hand and he dipped his fingers inside her warmth once more. The slick dampness welcomed him and every caress of his thumb against her core sent her body into rocking, jerking spasms of pleasure.

Her mouth opened to him as eagerly as her legs and their tongues met and danced in warm abandon. Jesse's breathing strained, he struggled for control, wanting to prolong this first time of joining, for both of them. But the sweet pain of waiting was becoming too much to bear and he didn't think he'd be able to withstand it much longer.

Deliberately slowing down, Jesse moved his tongue over the inside of her mouth and pulled his fingers free of the damp heat that surrounded them. He felt her disappointment, tasted her sigh of regret, and shared it.

Lifting his head, he looked down at her. The turquoise eyes were glazed, hazy with unfulfilled passion. Hunger. Her hips rocked slightly, she licked her lips and whispered, "Jesse, I need—"

"I know, darlin'. I know." He kissed her lips gently and smoothed her hair back from her brow. Then he left her side. In only a moment he was kneeling between her thighs and watching the expectation on her face.

His forefinger skimmed over her sex and Miranda's body jerked in response. Deliberately Jesse dipped his fingers inside her once more, smoothing the damp heat to prepare her for his body's entry. She raised her hips and groaned softly, her eyes locking onto his.

His hands moved to cup her behind and he rose up off his haunches, his sex brushing against the warmth of her gateway. Miranda's hips moved again and Jesse couldn't stand it any longer. As gently, as easily as possible, he slid into her warmth. His head fell back on his neck and a moan escaped his throat. So tight. So hot. So right. Somewhere in the back of his mind, a small voice reminded him that there might be pain for her. To go carefully.

And he wanted to. But Miranda's hands reached down to hold his thighs and any rational thought left him. With one quick thrust, he pushed himself home. She tightened and gasped in surprise, but when he looked at her in concern, she only whispered huskily, "Again, Jesse. Again."

He was undone and thrust again into Miranda's warmth. Her nails dug into the flesh of his thighs and he saw her head twisting and turning, her lips dry, her breath coming in short, hard gasps. He slipped his hand between their bodies and teased the swollen bud of her womanhood.

Faster and harder he moved, Miranda's body matching him as though they'd loved together many times. Jesse kissed her hard, his tongue imitating the heated thrusts of his hips. In response, her fingers clutched at his legs, the nails biting deep.

And when he didn't think his flagging control could last another moment, Miranda cried out his name. At the sound Jesse's own release claimed him, and together they tumbled into oblivion.

The man poured a little more water from his canteen into the upturned crown of his hat and offered it to his horse. While the tired gray drank, the blond let his gaze travel swiftly over the surrounding area.

Rocks, dirt, sand, and the straggly clumps of desert plants, mostly brown in the near-winter sun. He squinted off into the distance and saw a vague outline of the far canyon. Almost there. He threw his horse a worried glance. Damn good thing he was so close to the canyon. The gray needed a rest as bad as he did.

The animal lifted its big, well-shaped head and shook it fiercely.

"Yeah, I know, boy." The blond patted the animal's neck reassuringly. "Only another day or so now. 'Sides, if I recollect right, there's a small tank not far from here."

The animal snorted as if he understood completely.

"Get you all the water you can carry." The man jammed his hat back on his head, enjoying the cool damp against his skin. "Then, when we get to the canyon, I'll see to it you get some of those oats Birdwell's always got set aside."

He stepped into the stirrup and swung his right leg over the animal's broad back. "Me"—he laughed under his breath—"I'll take a little of somethin' else Birdwell's been holdin' out." He wrapped the reins loosely in his hands. "C'mon, boy. You and me are goin' callin'."

A touch of spurs sent the big animal into a determined, mile-eating trot.

"Miranda?" Shelly knocked on the cabin door again. "Miranda?" She turned the latch and opened the door just wide enough to peer in. Maybe she was still sleeping.

Moving softly, Shelly walked into the cabin and headed for the small bedroom in the back. She didn't even glance at the familiar, painfully neat furnishings. She just wanted to get in, pick up what she needed, and get out again before disturbing Miranda. She should have realized that her friend would still be resting up. She should have told Serena to wait.

It was so quiet. And not just in Miranda's place. The whole damn town was still sleeping. Well, everyone except Serena. Shelly smiled, shook her head, and went on. Childbirth hadn't been enough to make Serena rest. Not once she'd convinced herself that Pike would be riding in soon. Oh, no. Serena wanted to look pretty when her husband arrived. She wanted everything to be perfect. And so she'd talked Shelly into getting the dress Miranda was making for her so

Serena could finish up the sleeves and collar while she lay in bed.

But it could have waited another hour or two. She stepped up to the makeshift wall that separated Miranda's bedroom from the rest of the cabin. Carefully Shelly lifted the edge of the green-and-yellow fabric hanging from hooks pounded into the ceiling and slipped under it. Thankfully she spotted Serena's new dress, draped across a battered, ladder-back chair in the corner. As she snatched it up she threw a quick look over her shoulder at the bed. It was empty.

Puzzled, Shelly walked closer, staring down at the pale blue quilt as if waiting for an explanation. Pillows plumped, blankets straight and unwrinkled, the bed was obviously untouched. Miranda hadn't been to sleep at all. Or if she had, she was up and gone already. But where?

Shelly turned to look out the back window toward the convenience. But the slat door hung open, swaying back and forth in the canyon wind.

Gripping the dress in one hand, Shelly swung around quickly, swept the fabric wall aside, and walked to the middle of the tiny cabin.

Now she took the time to look around her. Everything was as it should be. Tidy, clean. Absently she noted the new curtains hanging across the window over the small, round kitchen table. The Sullys must have brought Miranda some new fabric. Then her gaze locked on the tabletop. Half a loaf of fresh bread was gone, the knife and crumbs standing evidence. Also, a small jar of preserves always kept on a shelf beside the table was missing. Quickly Shelly's gaze moved over the rest of the room. Now that she was paying attention, she noticed that the old quilt, usually folded up on a chair, was gone and Miranda's pistol and holster weren't hanging on the peg beside the front door.

Shelly grumbled under her breath. Miranda'd taken off on one of her jaunts. By the looks of the supplies she'd taken with her, she was meaning to be gone for a few hours at least. Shelly's fingers curled tightly around Serena's dress. Dammit, she shouldn't have gone. Not right after an Indian scare. And not with the whole damn town asleep. What if she needed help? What if she got into trouble? All alone out there . . . Shelly stopped.

Alone? She remembered the look on Miranda's face earlier. And, Shelly told herself, hadn't she noticed Jesse actin' a little peculiar, too? She took a long, deep breath and stared blankly at the opposite wall. It had to be. Somehow Jesse had managed to get around Miranda's usual good judgment and had wormed himself into her favor. And Shelly knew just what he was after. What all men were after when it came down to it. Even Dave, with all his talk of love.

And dammit, she wasn't going to see Miranda hurt. Not for the likes of Jesse Hogan. But first she had to be sure. Shelly marched across the cabin floor, threw the door open, and stalked off down the boardwalk toward the bunkhouse.

"M'randa?"

She mumbled something in her sleep and cuddled in closer to the warm man beside her.

A low rumble of gentle laughter rattled through the chest beneath her cheek. "M'randa? Wake up, darlin'."

"Hmmm?" Her hand smoothed the tickling, dark, curly hairs away from the end of her nose. She tried to ignore the voice and slide back into her dream. But it was much too bright. The shade of the overhang no longer covered them. Sunlight poured against her closed eyelids, refusing to be ignored.

Grudgingly she opened her eyes and tilted her head back to meet Jesse's amused gaze.

"Woman, you sure can *sleep!*"

She smiled and stretched her limbs like a contented house cat. Then Miranda reached out one hand and caressed his beard-stubbled cheek. It wasn't a dream then. They really had done everything she'd been reliving in her sleep.

She searched his eyes, looking for reassurance, and found something else besides. For the first time since the night she'd met him, there were no shadows in Jesse's green eyes. Instead there was a spark of amusement. A good-humored smile curved his lips and the perpetual frown lines between his brows were gone.

Miranda traced one finger along the contours of his mouth, feeling his breath warm against her hand. His eyes darkened slightly but not with the shadows of pain that she'd come to know so well.

He grabbed her hand in one of his and turned the palm toward him. Gently he placed a single kiss there and smiled at her again.

"You're smiling," she whispered.

"Ain't surprised."

"I like it." Miranda laid her head down on his breast again.

"Well, I'm glad. But if we don't get outta this sun damn fast, you ain't gonna be seein' a smile on my face again for days."

She rose up and cocked one eyebrow at him.

He grinned. "You been sleepin' for a couple of hours and that durned sun's been beatin' down on parts of me that ain't seen so much sunshine since I was a bare-ass boy back in Texas!"

A bubble of laughter burst from her and Miranda's head dropped to Jesse's chest. Immediately she straightened up, surprised to find that he was right. His skin felt as though it was on fire. And, she realized with a start, her left side was just as hot!

As if reading her mind, Jesse pushed himself to his feet then drew her up, too. "C'mon, M'randa. Let's cool you off some."

A canyon breeze ruffled past, sliding over her too warm body with delicate, cool fingers. A glance overhead told Miranda that their short time at the tank was nearly over. Soon they would have to head back to Bandit's Canyon. And try to pretend that none of this had happened.

Instinctively she knew how it would be. Once he was among the others, the shadows would return to Jesse's eyes and his smile would fade. He would be polite but distant. He would stay clear of her. Just as he'd always tried to do. She sighed and reminded herself that he'd made no promises. That he'd said nothing about love or forever. That nothing real had changed.

Miranda looked into his eyes and saw the same sad knowledge there. He shared her regret that their time together would be so brief. A secret, private time, enjoyed only by the two of them.

She had a sudden, overwhelming urge to wrap her arms around him and hold him tightly. To somehow make time stand still and allow them to remain in that afternoon always.

"Miranda?"

She looked up to his fathomless, shimmering, grass-green eyes.

"Miranda, don't. Remember what I said before?" His hand squeezed hers gently. "Don't think. Just feel." Jesse's thumb moved over her knuckles with bewitching slowness. "For today, Miranda. Just feel."

Her fingers curled around his and her heartbeat faltered, then quickened again when his lips curved in a tender smile. Together, they crossed the few feet of scarred rock separating them from the clear, cold pool. They moved carefully down the slanted steps into the water and she gasped at the icy shock against her heated flesh. His arm encircled her waist to steady her and she leaned into his strength gratefully.

It seemed the most natural thing in the world to swim naked in the afternoon sun with Jesse holding her tightly. His whispered voice in her ear as gentle as his hands against her back, her breasts pressed close to his chest, the touch of his lips, the sunshine on his dark, wavy hair, the restrained strength of his arms and hands.

Even the shadows that haunted him were as familiar to her as breathing.

And Miranda didn't know how she would live without him.

CHAPTER
13

Serena chatted happily while she worked on her new dress. The woman was so pleased with herself, her new son, and her husband's imminent return, she didn't even notice that Shelly had almost nothing to say.

The afternoon seemed to be crawling by. It was all Shelly could do to sit still. Not even the sweet weight of baby Jesse in her arms as she rocked him was enough to get her mind off Miranda. And Jesse Hogan.

Little Jesse fidgeted and rubbed his tiny fist across his face. Absently Shelly patted his bottom and began to hum softly. She couldn't very well just go off and leave Serena and the baby to fend for themselves. But the minute the town started stirring, Shelly would get someone in to sit with Serena. Then she'd be free to go and look for the missing couple. And Lord help Jesse Hogan when she found them.

She stopped rocking suddenly. Why should *she* do the looking? Wouldn't it be better if she just told

Birdwell of her suspicions? A slow smile curved her
lips as she remembered the *last* time some passin'-
through outlaw tried to get close to Miranda. The man
had been laid up for near a month in the bunkhouse.
But as soon as he healed, he climbed aboard his horse
and nobody'd seen him since.

The baby whimpered and Shelly started rocking
again. That's just what she would do. Once they were
rid of Jesse Hogan, things would get back to normal
around town.

Serena said something and Shelly shook herself.
Now that she had a plan, she could relax and pay
more attention to what she was doing. She smiled at
Serena and said, "What?"

Swimming would never be the same again.

Miranda watched as Jesse dived from the rock ledge
into the tank. His strong, lean body knifed through the
water, barely making a splash. He stayed underwater
for what seemed forever and Miranda understood
how he must have felt when he'd seen her "drowning."

Her gaze moved over the still surface of the water as
she watched for his appearance. When he finally came
up for air, she released a pent-up breath as he made
his way straight to her at the tank's edge.

She went into his arms without a word, and when
his lips touched her neck, Miranda tilted her head
eagerly, hungry for his touch. It seemed as though she
couldn't get enough of him. Every time he moved
away, she wanted to call him back. She wanted to feel
the hard strength of his broad back beneath her palms.
She wanted his mouth at her breast, wanted to hold
him deep inside her.

The cold water lapped gently around them as Jesse

pulled her close. His hands moved over her behind, up the swell of her hips, along her rib cage to her breasts. As his thumbs moved gently over her nipples, Jesse's lips and tongue teased the sensitive skin at the side of her neck.

Miranda sighed, letting her fingers trail down his back. She lifted her legs and wrapped them around his waist, then bent her head to kiss his sun-warmed shoulders. Jesse's hands moved over her body slowly, gently, as if he was memorizing every curve, and then he covered her mouth with his own. His tongue swept the inside of her mouth and Miranda melted against him, tightening her legs around his waist even as her tongue moved to match his stroke for stroke.

She heard him groan, and as his hands moved to cup her behind she felt his readiness hard against her belly. He shifted position on the wide rock step, bracing his legs far apart, and then moved one hand to let his index finger skim lightly over her sex. Miranda's body jerked in response to the delicate touch, and instinctively she tried to get closer.

Instead Jesse moved his hands to her waist and gently pulled away from her. He ignored her protests and determinedly lifted her up until she was sitting on the rock ledge.

"Jesse," she whispered, and reached down for him.

"It's all right, M'randa." He stepped closer to her and looked up at her face as he gently stroked the soft, smooth skin of her abdomen.

"What . . . ?"

"Let me show you, M'randa," Jesse whispered, and kissed the inside of her thigh. The muscles in her legs tightened, but he didn't stop. He ran his tongue over her flesh, and when she squirmed, the edges of his teeth stroked her tender skin.

Miranda bent low, trying to join him in the water. She'd had enough of the gentle teasing and wanted to feel his body slide into hers. But Jesse wasn't finished.

"Just lean back, Miranda." He smiled up at her and planted a kiss just inches from the aching center of her.

"Lean back?"

"Yes, darlin'. Lean back. Relax now." His voice was low, and she recognized the desire in his eyes.

Slowly she laid her palms flat on the rocks and leaned her weight on them. Miranda stared up at the late-afternoon sky, and when she felt Jesse tug at her legs, she scooted forward a little. His lips and tongue again began to move over the sensitive flesh of her thighs. No sooner had he begun on one leg than he switched and lavished his attention on the other. His fingers moved over the juncture of her legs, and her hips moved with every touch.

Then she felt his breath, warm and close on the tender skin his fingers had been toying with. She straightened and looked down at him. Her breath caught and she fought down a sudden urge to run and wrap a blanket around herself. Instead, helplessly, Miranda watched as his long, tanned fingers gently held her damp folds open, and before she could say anything, Jesse's mouth covered her.

She gasped. Her entire body stiffened with shock and pleasure. There was no escaping the warmth of his tongue as he explored the secrets of her body. Deliberately, teasingly he licked at the center of her until she thought she would go mad. It was luscious, warm, and embarrassing and she never wanted him to stop. Miranda groaned and threaded her fingers through his hair. She opened her thighs wider, urging him on silently.

Unable to help herself, she looked down and

watched his mouth move over her with tantalizing slowness. Her breathing ragged, Miranda emptied her mind of everything but the sensations Jesse brought to her. The now familiar ache swelled in her body and she welcomed it. Eagerly she felt it build and she gave the ache free rein, knowing that a pounding, throbbing release would not be far behind.

Jesse's arms snaked out of the water, wrapped around her buttocks, and pulled her closer to the edge. His tongue flicked, darting caresses at the bud of her desire as his fingers slipped inside her warmth. Miranda jumped, then braced her hands on his shoulders. There was too much to feel at once. His mouth, his fingers, then his other hand slid to her behind and Miranda knew she would die.

Her body tormented by far too many delicious feelings at once, she tried desperately to race to the pulsing completion waiting for her. Jesse was relentless. His mouth and tongue stroked at her center and suckled her more gently than she'd thought possible.

The ache in her grew and grew until it spiraled out of control, sweeping her along with dizzying speed. And when she finally reached the edge of completion, Miranda groaned and rode the crashing wave of pleasure tearing through her.

Eternity passed in a heartbeat and everything was still. Stunned, Miranda hardly knew what was happening when Jesse lifted her down into the water, set her on the step, and pushed himself into her body. But once he'd entered her, she welcomed him and held him until he found the pleasure he'd given her.

Only an hour later it was time to go back. They dressed in silence, as if each of them wanted to ignore the fact that their time together was over.

Miranda, suddenly, unreasonably shy, kept her back to Jesse. The magic of the afternoon had vanished, leaving only the silence of the rock canyon in its wake. But in the span of a few short hours, all of her carefully laid plans had been shattered.

Her dreams of what Bandit's Canyon could be someday dissolved in the face of what she'd experienced here in the secret tank. She let her gaze move over the familiar scene. No matter what happened in the future, Miranda knew that sooner or later she would have to leave the canyon. She couldn't live her life surrounded by the memories of Jesse. And she realized that long after he'd gone, the canyon would echo with his voice. From that day on, every time she dived into the water, she would feel Jesse's hands on her body. Every time she laid the old flowered quilt over her bed, she would remember lying atop it in the sun with Jesse.

"Miranda?"

She froze. Her fingers tightened over her belt buckle and she held her breath, bracing herself for whatever might come.

"Miranda, we have to talk before we go back down."

"No." She shook her head. She'd rather leave the afternoon as it was. She didn't want to tear it apart now with questions and discussion. "You don't have to say anything, Jesse."

He stepped up behind her. "Yes, I do." His fingers curled around her upper arms. "Miranda."

"Jesse," she cut in, "please. Don't say you're sorry." Don't let the day end with one or both of us making excuses or giving promises we have no intention of keeping, she thought. Her head dropped back on her neck and Miranda wanted to curse and shout. Why couldn't he just leave it alone? Let their time together be what it was . . . stolen hours. She pulled a deep, shaky breath into her lungs. "Don't tell me it was all a mistake."

"Miranda." His fingers tightened, he bent his head down and whispered in her ear. "If that was a mistake, then God help me. Because I can't be sorry."

Her eyes squeezed shut, and even when he turned her around to face him, she didn't open them again. She felt him cup her face in his hands and noticed that his fingers were trembling.

"Jesus, Miranda," he continued. "I don't know what to say to you."

Relief in her voice, she said softly, "I already told you. You don't have to say anything."

His thumbs moved gently over her features. He went on as though she hadn't spoken. "I never expected to . . ."

"To what?" Her eyes opened and she stared at him, captivated by the confusion in his gaze.

"I don't know." He exhaled in a rush and pulled her close. Her head on his chest, his arms wrapped around her, Jesse said softly, "I only know that as long as I live, I'll carry you . . . and today, in my heart. No matter what else happens, Miranda"—he tilted her head back and forced her to look at him—"I'll never be sorry. I only hope you won't be." A sudden, clear image of Miranda, soft and rounded with his child, flashed through his mind. Jesse was momentarily stunned as he realized for the first time what he might have done. Intuitively he knew that the chance of a pregnancy hadn't occurred to Miranda yet. Just as he knew that he would now *have* to stay in Bandit's Canyon. At least until he knew if she carried his child or not.

Surprisingly that thought didn't bother him in the least.

Miranda reached up and stroked one finger along his clenched jaw. "No, Jesse, I'll never be sorry. No matter what."

He studied her face for a long, breathless moment, then nodded, seemingly satisfied. His hands moved up and down her arms slowly and there was a sad good-bye in his touch. When she opened her mouth to speak, Jesse inhaled sharply.

"Gettin' late," he said. "We'd best head back."

He released her and went to pick up the basket and Miranda knew that he was already putting their time together behind him. Trying to distance himself from her before the people in town did it for him. She glanced up at the darkening sky overhead and rubbed her arms as a sudden, cold breeze shot through the hideaway.

The magic was gone.

"Whoa there, Miss Shelly." Dave reached out and grabbed her arm as she hurried past. "Where you off to in such a bother?"

She yanked at her arm, but Dave held her fast. "Let go," she warned.

"Here now." Dave grinned. "You look like you're off to do some scalpin'. Anybody I know?"

Shelly's lips twisted mutinously, but she said nothing.

"Just simmer down a bit, Miss Shelly." His grip on her arm loosened slightly and she pulled away. "I just woke up, y'know. I ain't up to a whole lot of shenanigans till after at least *one* cup of coffee."

"I didn't ask for your help," Shelly pointed out,

then continued on down the boardwalk, her heels clicking furiously.

He caught up in a few easy strides and walked briskly beside her. "You gonna tell me where you're goin'?"

"No."

"Hmmm." He glanced at her curiously and asked, "Serena all right?"

She shot him a look. "Serena's fine. Ezra's sittin' with her."

"Ezra?"

"What's wrong with Ezra?"

"Nothin'. Just a unusual choice for a nursemaid."

"I won't be gone long."

"That brings us back where we started." Dave grabbed her elbow again to slow her down some. "Where we goin'?"

Shelly drew a deep breath, looked pointedly at his hand until he pulled it away, then answered, "*I'm* goin' to see Birdwell."

"He ain't at his place." Dave grinned slowly. "He's down to Big Pete's havin' a wake-up shot."

Her shoulders slumped, but she did a quick about-face and began to back up the way she'd come. She should have known the big man wouldn't still be abed. More wasted time now. Hurrying toward the saloon at the end of the street, Shelly tried to ignore Dave's presence. It wasn't easy.

"What you want with Birdwell?"

"I need him to do somethin' for me."

"Well, what is it?" Dave stepped out in front of her and stopped dead, forcing her to a halt. "Maybe I could help. Save you a trip."

"No. It has to be Birdwell."

He sighed and shook his head. "Miss Shelly, I been

tryin' real hard to convince you to trust me some."
Her eyes narrowed and he hurried on. "I ain't
askin' for a lot . . . just a little bit of faith, now and
again." He cocked his head and smiled at her teasingly. "Kinda try me out. Give me a chance."

She tried to step around him, but he was too quick.

"Why don't you tell me what's got you so het up?"

Concern flashed in his blue eyes and Shelly was
sorely tempted to confide in him. Memories of the
long night spent safely in his arms rushed back, but
she pushed them away. One night was not enough to
convince her.

"Let me try to help?" he wheedled. "Huh? What
d'ya say?"

"You can't help," she said finally, her decision
made. "You'd be on *his* side."

His eyebrows shot straight up. "Well, now I *got* to
know what's goin' on. C'mon with me." Dave took
her arm firmly, allowing for no arguments, and pulled
her toward the restaurant. "You can tell me over
coffee."

Shelly cast one last look over her shoulder toward
Big Pete's place before Dave hustled her inside the
restaurant.

"You seen Miranda?" Birdwell looked up when Buck
passed the table.

"No, sir, I ain't." Buck lifted his glass sheepishly.
"But I ain't hardly left the saloon since we all come
back, didn't even go to bed yet. So it ain't likely I'd see
her, is it?"

Birdwell frowned. His black gaze moved over the
small barroom, barely stopping at any one, familiar
figure. Something wasn't right. Oh, Miranda'd gone
off on her own before, been doin' it since she was a

child. Didn't usually stay gone this long, though. And there *had* been that Indian scare just the night before.

Besides, this time Jesse Hogan was gone, too.

Birdwell shook his shaggy head and snorted. Most times Miranda could take care of herself as well as any man. Hadn't he seen to that himself? But, he thought, now that she was grown, there was a different sort of danger. One that Birdwell didn't feel capable of saving her from.

He stared down into the dregs of his beer. Hell, he couldn't whip *every* man that came buzzin' 'round her. It'd be natural to miss one or two. A man couldn't be everywhere at once. And he had the feelin' that Jesse Hogan had managed somehow to get around him to Miranda.

If the two of them were off together somewhere right now, there wasn't a damn thing Birdwell could do about it. There was so many nooks and crannies and caves and the like in the canyon, the two of them could be just about anywhere. Shit, a man could walk right past their hidey-hole and not even see it.

Solemnly Birdwell lifted the mug and tossed the last of his beer down his throat. He signaled to Pete for another, then leaned back in his chair.

And if they were together? If Miranda was in love with Hogan? Then what?

Hell.

Jesse Hogan. Birdwell rubbed his bearded jaw and propped one boot on the chair next to him. What was it about Hogan that didn't ring true? Nothin' for certain. Nothin' that Birdwell could put a name to. It was more of a feelin' than anything else. He'd spent years livin' on the outside of the law. Trustin' to his own judgment of people had saved his bacon time and again over the years. And every gut instinct he had

was tellin' Birdwell that somethin' about Jesse Hogan
wasn't right.

That man was no outlaw. Birdwell's jaw clenched
and he stared blankly into the smoky air of the saloon.
For some reason, Hogan was bound and determined
to pretend to be a badman. But he had no more claim
to the name than Birdwell did to bein' a solid citizen.

Pete brought another beer to the table and took
away the empty glass. A burst of laughter from the
corner drew Birdwell's gaze. He watched Buck Farley,
his arm looped over Fat Alice's shoulders. That's
another one, Birdwell told himself. Buck and his ridin'
partner, Dave. Them two was all wrong, just as much
as Jesse.

What the hell was goin' on?

Sighing, the big man lifted his glass, tilted his head
back, and chugged down the beer. He slapped the
mug back onto the table and pushed himself to his
feet. He was just gettin' too damn old for all of this. He
should have gotten out of the canyon two years ago
when Judd died. He should have *forced* Miranda to
leave. Hell, she deserved better than this! Outlaws and
whores wasn't the kind of folks she could build a
decent life with. He wanted her to have a home.
Maybe a husband. A family.

Grumbling softly, he told himself that he should
have taken all the money he'd saved over the years
and bought himself and Miranda a place. A ranch
maybe, near some nice little town where she could go
to church socials and meet a good man whose face
she'd never see on a wanted poster.

But he'd let himself be talked into stayin'. A reluctant smile curved his lips momentarily. Miranda
wouldn't hear of "deserting" Bandit's Canyon and the
folks she thought of as family. Her soft heart kept

askin' what would happen to Ezra and Pete, Shelly, Alice and Wilma? Where would the others go for the winter? Who would take care of 'em?

And now he'd waited too long. If she had feelin's for Hogan, he'd never get her to leave. Miranda was a good woman, but she had a head as hard as the rocks in the canyon.

If he could have Judd Perry in front of him for just five minutes, Birdwell knew that he'd give his old friend what for. Between the two of them, they'd managed to wedge Miranda into a corner that she might not be able to get out of.

Disgusted, Birdwell turned and left the saloon. He stood on the boardwalk, his gaze fixed on the far rock wall. It was almost sunset, and the canyon walls seemed to glow with the captured heat of the desert sun. A lavender sky hung over the craggy peaks and Birdwell fancied he could see Miranda making her way down the narrow path toward home.

He stroked his full beard thoughtfully. If she truly cared for Jesse Hogan, there might be a way out of this situation after all. Birdwell smiled softly. Hogan was no outlaw, he felt it in his bones. But the man *might* make a good husband.

Jesse stretched out his hand to help her over the last patch of loose pebbles scattered over the trail. Even as he felt her fingers wrap around his, he knew that she didn't need his help. He knew that her reason for taking his hand was the same as his for offering it.

The need to touch again.

And Lord, he needed to touch her again. To hold her. To hear her voice, soft and low in his ear. How would he ever be able to leave her? Since Miranda, the cold that had enveloped him for the last two years had disappeared. How could he ever go back to the loneliness he'd known before? How would he survive?

His fingers tightened over hers as if her hand was a rope tossed to a drowning man. A rope he never wanted to let go of. Jesse even found himself hoping that he'd given her a baby that afternoon.

"Jesse?"

Miranda's voice shattered his wayward thoughts. "Yeah?"

"Tell me about Texas—about Coldwater."

He flinched and hoped she didn't notice. Coldwater. All of the memories he'd tried to bury for the last two years rushed back at him, smothering the new, bittersweet images in his brain. In a sea of emotion, he moved his thumb across her knuckles, smoothing over her comforting warmth. His right hand, though, tightened convulsively over the handle of the basket he carried.

Portraits of his brother and sister-in-law swam before his eyes. The ranch they'd worked so hard for, abandoned now and neglected. Miles and miles of open country. Cottonwood trees and the flower bed with Della's prized roses. The barn he and Carter had finished just before the first big snow. And the corral where they'd had their last fight.

Jesse wished suddenly that Miranda had been able to see his home before it had all changed forever. He wished that he could take her now to meet Carter and Della.

Della would have liked Miranda. The two of them would have gotten on well together. One corner of his mouth lifted in a sad parody of a smile. He and Carter wouldn't have stood a chance around two such strong-minded females!

What a time the four of them could have had!

"Jesse?"

His jaw clenched, Jesse tried to steady his breathing. He fought to separate the painful memories from the good. He didn't *want* to concentrate solely on his brother and sister-in-law's deaths anymore. The images of them laughing and loving each other were so much more important. In this long quest for revenge-justice, he didn't want to lose sight of the people they were. And until he'd come to the canyon and found Miranda, Jesse realized that he'd almost forgotten the living, breathing family he'd lost in the face of their terrible, senseless deaths.

"Jesse?" she said again, more hesitantly this time.

He stopped and turned to look at her. Miranda's shining blue-green eyes held him and wouldn't let go. Without saying a word, she seemed to urge him to speak. To invite her into his pain and let her share and understand it.

She gave him an uncertain smile and Jesse felt a loosening of the last iron band of loneliness that had held him prisoner so long.

CHAPTER 14

"Jesse?" Miranda laid her hand on his forearm. "Are you all right?"

"Yeah." She watched him as he set the basket down, then reached up to pull off his hat. He stepped closer to the cliff edge of the path and squinted down at the town below. Miranda followed his gaze and, for the first time, realized just how small her home looked, nestled deep in the canyon. A wispy tendril of smoke lifted and coiled above the restaurant chimney. From the far end of the street came muted bits of piano music. The town was waking up again.

Jesse pointed down at the cluster of false-fronted buildings and said on a half chuckle, "Coldwater ain't a helluva lot bigger than that." His hand dropped to his side. "Got a few more folks than you do here, but that's about it."

"Did you live in town?"

He shook his head. "No. Had a ranch about twenty miles outside of town."

"*Had?*" she asked quietly.

Jesse looked over his shoulder at her and shrugged, but his pain-racked gaze gave the lie to his seeming indifference. "Have, I guess. Didn't sell it or nothin'. The place is prob'ly a tumbledown mess by now, though."

Miranda took a step closer to him, but kept a watchful eye on the edge of the rock. "Tell me about it. What's your ranch like?"

He stared off into the distance. "Now? Who knows?" He inhaled and blew it out in a rush. "Couple of years ago it was a nice place. Trees, plenty of water, miles of grazing land."

"The house?"

"The house, well . . ." He pushed one hand through his hair and snorted. "She wasn't much. Me and—" He broke off, swallowed convulsively, and started again differently. "*I* was so busy tryin' to get the barn and the corral up, the house kinda got short shrift. It's small. Not hardly room to turn around in, but we built it so's it'd be easy to add on extra rooms."

Miranda looked at him steadily. He'd said "we." She knew it had slipped out. That he hadn't meant to say it at all. But somehow she thought that he *needed* to say it. "We?" she asked. "You didn't build it alone?"

She waited what seemed forever. Jesse's eyes closed to slits as he squinted into the setting sun. She could almost *see* him thinking, mentally weighing whether or not to speak. His jaw worked feverishly as he battled whatever demons haunted him. Her hand moved to grasp his in silent support and Jesse's fingers squeezed hers gently, acknowledging her concern.

"No." His voice was harsh and Miranda knew he was forcing himself to speak. "I didn't build the place alone." He inhaled and sighed heavily, the words tumbling out. "My brother, Carter, and me built it. Him and his wife, Della, did all the plannin'. Carter was the smart one in the family. Knew just how to do things. Always could figure out any sort of problem. Me"—he shrugged and smiled softly—"well, I could swing a hammer."

Miranda held his hand in both of hers and let him talk.

"Had lots of plans for that place." He glanced down at her, then turned his watery gaze back to the canyon. Jesse snorted. "Hell, listenin' to Carter tell it, the Hogan ranch was gonna be the biggest, best ranch in Texas." He nodded slowly. "Yeah, Carter was quite a talker." Jesse rubbed his jaw and added quickly, "But that man could *work*! I've known him to go sixteen, seventeen hours at a stretch, eat somethin', sleep for a hour or two, and be right back at it. 'Course, he expected everybody else to work like that, too."

Miranda's fingers moved over his hand slowly and she watched his changing expressions as he talked about his family.

"The fights we used to have over that." He shook his head and smiled fondly. "Lord, we had some knock-down-drag-out, root-hog-or-die fights in our time! They were fights I'd've traveled ten miles just to watch." His voice softened and his jaw worked again as he fought for control. "But Della didn't like fightin'. She was such a softhearted woman, she just couldn't bear it. Upset her somethin' fierce when me and Carter would go at it." He swallowed and looked down at Miranda. "She wasn't no weak sister, though. Don't think that. That head of hers was as hard as yours!"

Miranda smiled and leaned into him.

"You'd have liked her fine, M'randa. She didn't take no guff from me nor Carter neither when it come down to it." Jesse dropped her hand and wrapped his arms around her, resting his chin on top of her head. "Nope. No matter what Carter liked to think, *Della* was in charge of the Hogan ranch."

A long silence followed his last statement and Miranda knew he was letting himself enjoy his memories. There was more, she knew. He'd only talked about good things. Nothing to explain the sadness always lurking just behind his smile. And she wanted to understand, to *know* what it was that caused Jesse to keep such a distance from people. And for some reason, Miranda was convinced that Jesse needed to tell her.

A man as loving and gentle as Jesse Hogan was not a lone wolf by nature. She had to know why he'd chosen such a life.

Finally she asked quietly, "You keep saying 'was,' Jesse. What happened? Did Carter and Della leave the ranch?"

His arms tightened convulsively and Miranda wished fervently she hadn't spoken. They had to be dead. That was the only explanation for his strong reaction. His family was gone and she'd forced him to remember it.

"No. They didn't leave," he said, confirming her thoughts. "They're buried there. Side by side."

"I'm sorry, Jesse." Miranda tilted her head back to look at him. She wasn't surprised to see the pain in his eyes, only saddened that she had caused it. "I shouldn't have asked."

"It's all right." He didn't meet her gaze. "You got a right to know."

"What do you mean?"

"I mean, you got a right to know why I ain't the kind of man you should have." His hand smoothed over her hair, then he pushed himself away from her and shoved his hands into his pockets.

"I know what kind of man you are," Miranda argued, and took a step toward him. "And I think it's up to me to decide what kind of man I want."

"No, it ain't up to you. And no, you don't know me." He backed up. "You don't know that Carter, Della, and her unborn baby are dead because of me."

She stopped and looked at him, more confused than ever. How could he possibly mean what he was saying?

"That's right. Me." He pulled his hands from his pockets and slammed one balled fist into the rock wall behind him. "If not for me, Carter and Della would be alive right now. And Della would've had that baby she wanted so bad."

"What are you saying, Jesse? This makes no sense." She stood directly in front of him and stared at him until he finally gave in and met her gaze squarely. "Are you really trying to make me believe that you *killed* a woman? *And* your own brother? Well, I don't. It's impossible."

He snorted and shook his head. "Oh, maybe I didn't *kill* 'em. Not directly."

"What?"

"Shit, Miranda. I might as well have pulled the trigger! It's 'cause of me, they got killed. If I'da been home . . . like Carter wanted me to be . . . things would've been different."

"What are you talking about?" She felt him getting farther and farther away from her, though he hadn't moved a step.

His head fell back on his neck, he breathed deeply and sighed it out again. A twisted, mocking smile curved his lips and he directed his rage-filled voice to the sky above. "I'm talkin' about me leavin' the ranch. Carter and me had a big ol' fight—one of our worst—he wanted me to stay put on the ranch—help him fix up the corral and such before winter." He reached up and ran a hand over his eyes as if he could wipe away the images in front of him. "But I hadn't left the place in months. I was itchin' to be out and about. Have some fun, maybe. Carter was a devil for work—and I was plain tuckered. Told him I was headin' for San Antone for a while. See me some new faces. Told him I was sick of lookin' at his."

"There's nothing wrong with that," Miranda cut in. "Why shouldn't you be able to come and go as you please? You were entitled to a rest."

He glanced down at her and smirked. "That's what I said. And even when Della asked me to stay, I said no. Figured it was just cause o' the baby she was fretful—and it wasn't due for a couple months. Knew I'd be back by then." Jesse looked away, rested the back of his head against the canyon wall, and propped one foot up behind him. "Carter was mad as all get out. Told me I was a good-for-nothin' fool, lightin' out when there was still work to be done. I told him what to do with his damn ranch and took off."

"What happened?" Her throat dry, Miranda waited anxiously for the end of the story.

"After a couple weeks I cooled down and went home. Figured Carter was some worried. What with winter comin' on and a new baby and all. Hell, we'd all been pretty fractious." His eyes screwed tightly shut, he pulled in a deep, shuddering breath and told the rest of his story in a rush. "I rode up to the ranch and there wasn't nobody around. Everything was quiet. Scared me. Figured maybe Della had some trouble and they'd gone to town. I walked into the house and tripped on Carter. He was layin' on the floor, cold as a stone, his eyes wide open. Two bullet holes dead center in his breast pocket. Della was in the bedroom. She, uh . . . she . . . was dead, too.''

"Oh, God," Miranda murmured helplessly. The image he created was too strong. She felt as though she'd stepped into that empty cabin along with him. And now she was as caught as he.

"After I buried 'em, I found out all I could about who done it. Folks in town and a couple of neighbors saw a stranger hangin' around who all of a sudden wasn't around anymore. Couldn't tell me much, though. Then I left home to find him." Jesse opened his eyes and looked down at her. She saw the shadows of the deserted cabin in his eyes. "And I ain't about to stop till I *do* find him. I owe them that much."

"Jesse." Miranda moved close to him and wrapped her arms around his waist. She laid her head on his chest and listened to the steady thumping of his heart. Through her touch, she tried to bring him back to her. "It wasn't your fault." She swallowed and tried to steady her voice. "How can you blame yourself?"

He made no move to touch her. "How can I not? If I'da stayed home like I should, it wouldn'ta happened."

"You can't know that."

"One more man might've made all the difference."

"Maybe." She held him tighter. "And maybe you would have died, too."

He snorted. "I *did* die the day I found them. Part of me is still back on that hillside. With them."

"But you're *here*. With me."

Jesse's mouth quirked slightly. "Yeah. And I ain't done you no favors, neither, Miranda."

"Jesse . . ."

He shook his head. "No. Just let it go, M'randa. I can't let anything stop me from findin' that man. Not even you."

"How can you find him?" She ignored that statement, tilted her head back, and stared up at him. "He could be anywhere. You said yourself you couldn't find out much about the man."

"True." He set her aside gently, put his hat on, then picked up the basket. "Alls I know is he's a blond and he's got a Indian-lance tattoo on his back. Last I heard, he was ridin' a big gray horse."

"There're *three* grays in our corral right now! And how many blond men have you seen in the last couple of years?" She talked quickly, trying to break through that stubborn look in his eyes. And even as she spoke she knew it wasn't working. "How do you plan on looking for that tattoo? Do you make every outlaw you meet take his shirt off?"

He shook his head and turned away. "We best get goin'."

"Jesse!" She grabbed his arm and held on. "Can't you see how impossible it's going to be to find this man?" A slow, burning anger began to grow inside Miranda. "What happened to Carter and Della wasn't your fault! Do you really think they'd want you to spend the rest of your life looking for a vicious killer who will probably be hanged sometime anyway?" One palm flat against his chest, she added, "If that's what they would want for you, then you were wrong. I wouldn't have cared for them at all."

He gave her a patient, tolerant smile that only served to feed her anger. "Someone, somewhere will catch the man. A man who kills like that will keep on doing it until he's finally caught. And hanged."

"I know. That's why I mean to catch him."

"That's not up to you," Miranda argued. "That's for the law." Why wouldn't he *listen*?

"The law ain't done much in two years."

"How do you know?" she said quickly. A sudden gust of wind whipped past her and she pushed her hair out of her eyes. "Maybe they've already caught him. You'd have no way of finding out."

"I know that a couple months after he killed Carter and Della, he came here. To Bandit's Canyon."

Miranda's jaw dropped. Her first instinct was to deny it. After all, the most important rule about the canyon was that no killers were allowed. She looked up at him and saw the truth in his eyes. He was sure of his facts. And that meant only two things. The killer was here. In her town two years ago. She knew him. She'd cooked for him, and most likely she'd talked and laughed with him, too.

And it meant that the only reason Jesse'd come to the canyon was to find his man and kill him.

Miranda turned from Jesse, moved back to the edge of the cliff, and stared down at her home. For the first time in her life, the canyon didn't feel safe.

"Why in the hell would you want to do that?" Dave slammed his coffee cup down on the kitchen table. He looked over at Shelly and noted that her determined expression hadn't altered a bit.

"Because I don't trust Jesse Hogan, that's why."

Dave snorted. "Shit, woman! You don't trust *no-body*!"

"Not true. I don't trust *men*!"

"Fine. Men. Jesse. Me. But you ought to at *least* trust Miranda."

"Oh, I do." Shelly straightened her shoulders, lifted her chin, and looked at Dave steadily. "Miranda's a

fine woman. None finer. But what she don't know
about men could fill this canyon."

"That right?"

"Yeah, that's right."

"Seems to me," Dave said, and walked around the
edge of the table toward Shelly, "that Miranda was
raised around more men than most females see in a
lifetime. All kinds of men."

"That's different." Shelly backed up a step, but kept
her gaze fixed on Dave.

"Why?"

"'Cause she's always been protected. First her pa,
then Birdwell." He was getting too close. She took
another step and felt the back doorknob press into her
spine. "And now Jesse Hogan is out there somewhere,
fillin' her head full of pretty lies and empty promises."

"Jesse don't seem that sort to me." Dave stepped up
next to her and ran one hand up her arm lightly.

She pulled away and tried to breathe. "That's 'cause
you're not a female. All of you men treat each other
fairly decent. It's us women you lead up the garden
path till we're so full of sunshine and roses we don't
even notice we're headed for a cliff until it's too late to
turn back."

"You talkin' about Miranda here?" he asked. "Or
you?"

"Miranda, of course." She edged sideways, but he
followed. "I won't be strollin' in no gardens again. Not
for anybody."

"That so?"

"Yeah." Shelly felt his breath on her temple and
swallowed heavily. If she turned her head the slightest
bit, their lips would be only a hairbreadth apart. She
closed her eyes and gritted her teeth. She'd seen that
"garden path" too many times in the past to be

tempted into taking the trip again. Even for someone who'd been as kind to her as Dave Black.

"What if," he asked in a whisper that tickled her ear, "somebody was to ask you to try again? To trust again?"

"He'd be whistlin' in the wind." Shelly kept her face averted from his. The fresh clean scent of him surrounded her and she felt her determination weakening, despite her best efforts.

"Even if he loved you?"

She laughed suddenly. A short, harsh laugh that shattered every tender feeling that had been growing inside her. "Love? It'd take a sight more than that!" Shelly risked a glance at him and saw that she'd surprised him. She didn't want to talk about this anymore. She didn't want to talk about herself.

She had to save Miranda.

Quickly she grabbed the doorknob, turned, and tried to leave.

Dave stopped her, one strong hand holding the door shut. "Where you goin'?"

"Told you. To see Birdwell."

"Leave it be, Shelly. Leave Miranda and Jesse be."

"No."

He grabbed her shoulders and held tight. "Dammit, Shelly. Miranda's a big girl. She don't need you to take care of her." She looked away, but he took her chin in his hands and turned her back to face him. "And no matter what *you* think . . . Jesse Hogan ain't a bad sort." His fingers smoothed down the line of her throat. "And neither am I."

"Don't, Dave." She reached up and brushed his hand aside.

"Shelly, I got somethin' to say to you and I want you to listen careful."

"No. I heard all this before." Shoving past him, she walked around the edge of the table until she was a safe distance from him.

"What? What'd you hear?" His palms flat on the table, he cocked his head, grinned, and waited.

Shelly shook her head and smiled grimly. "All right. You gonna tell me how pretty I am. How sweet. You're gonna promise to buy me fancy dresses and take me to the big city. We'll go to fine restaurants and ride in shiny carriages." She bit her lip, gulped in air, and continued. "You're gonna fix it so's I never have to do no work again. We'll see plays and meet fine people. We'll . . ." She covered her mouth with her fingertips and stared at him.

Dave watched her silently for a long moment. Then he slowly walked around the table until he stood beside her. Shaking his head, he smiled ruefully. "Shelly, darlin'. *Now* can *I* talk?"

She didn't move.

His right hand moved to cup her cheek and his thumb wiped away a solitary tear. "I wasn't gonna say none of that."

She looked up, surprised but quiet.

"I ain't got much money. So I can't promise you no fancy dresses. Nor shiny carriages nor fine restaurants. I can't even promise you'll never have to work again." Dave's other hand moved to her hair and smoothed it back over her shoulder. "I *can* tell you how pretty you are, though. And you surely are, Shelly." He sighed softly. "And I *can* tell you that I'll always stay with you."

She looked away, but he tilted her chin up determinedly. "Shelly, I love you." Her doubt must have shown on her face, because he gave her a sad smile. "I know you got no reason to believe me. But I'll prove it to you in twenty or thirty years if you'll let me."

Her brows drew together in confusion.

"I'm askin' you to marry me, Shelly."

Her jaw dropped.

"I'm askin' you to let me love you. To help me build a home. To have my babies and then to get old with me." He grinned. "I want to be a crotchety old bastard and watch the lines of a long life of lovin' fill your face. I want us to give each other looks that other folks will be jealous over. And I want our children's children to point to us and say, 'That's the kinda life *I* want. That's the kinda *love* I want.'"

Unshed tears shimmered in Shelly's eyes and she blinked them back. She couldn't believe he was serious. No one had *ever* wanted her to be a wife. A mother. Carefully she searched his gaze, looking for some small sign of deception. But she saw only the same gentleness she'd always seen in his eyes.

Married? For one brief moment Shelly let herself entertain the notion. A husband and a family was all she'd ever really wanted. And if she was honest with herself, she'd have to admit that Dave Black stirred feelings and desires in her that she'd thought long buried. But an *outlaw?* As a husband?

She remembered Serena's worried face during her pregnancy. All the time wondering about Pike and if he was safe. No. If she married Dave, she'd still be in the fryin' pan . . . only this time she'd have him to worry about as well as herself. The three years she'd spent in Bandit's Canyon had taught her that she *liked* being safe. She enjoyed not being on the run or lookin' over her shoulder all the time.

Shelly touched Dave's cheek gently. Rising up onto

her toes, she gave him a kiss for the first and last time and tried to ignore the rush of pleasure it brought.

"Thank you, Dave." She stepped back and half turned toward the door. "I thought to never be asked and I'm grateful to you. But I can't marry an outlaw. I can't live like that no more."

"Shelly . . ."

She shook her head and hurried to the backdoor. Dave grabbed her before she could slip outside.

Dave turned her around to face him, then, his fingers under her chin, he forced her to look up at him. Tenderly he wiped away the tears rolling down her cheeks, took a deep breath, and said softly, "Shelly, I'm gonna tell you somethin' I got no business tellin'. If word of this gets out, I'm as good as dead. So's Buck."

"What . . . ?" Her eyes narrowed in confusion.

"Only reason I'm tellin' you is so's you'll see you got nothin' to fear from me. I love you. And now I'm fixin' to trust you with my life." His hands cupped her face gently. "I ain't no outlaw, Shelly. Neither's Buck. We're Texas Rangers. Sent here after one fella did some killin' back home."

Her eyes wide, she stared at him. His voice was almost lost under the roaring in her ears.

Dave grinned at her stunned expression. "Y'see now, Shelly? I ain't lyin'. And I wasn't lyin' before when I asked you to marry me. Come home to Texas with me, Shelly."

Hand over her mouth, Shelly stared at him silently. Her eyes filled and streams of tears rolled down her cheeks.

The uneasy silence between them lasted until they reached the edge of town. Close to the corral, Jesse stopped suddenly and without a word handed the basket to Miranda.

"Jesse," she said quietly as she tried one last time to make him listen to reason, "can't you see that this 'hunt' you're on isn't right? You're giving up your whole life to make up for something that wasn't your fault."

"You don't understand, Miranda."

"Yes, I do." Anger flared up. "My father died two years ago, too. I *know* what grief is. I know how hard it is to accept."

"It ain't just the grief, Miranda." Jesse snatched his hat off and stared at her, desperate to make her see. "Hell, folks die. I know that. But a huntin' accident and cold-blooded murder ain't the same thing. And grief passes." His hands came up, then dropped. "Guilt don't."

"But . . ."

He shook his head firmly. "No matter what you say, I know. It's my fault. I should've been there." Twisting his hat brim in his hands, he mumbled, "Thought for a while maybe . . ."

Thought what? she asked herself furiously. That she would smile and say go on ahead, Jesse. Waste your life and mine. Miranda bit down hard on her bottom lip. Her fingers curled tightly over the handle of the basket. She pulled a deep breath into her body and deliberately pushed away any further attempt at tender sympathy. Maybe he'd had enough of that already. From himself.

She couldn't believe it. All her life she'd managed to avoid having any special feelings for the men riding through her life. When she finally did find the one man she wanted, despite everything, he set her aside.

"So what you're saying is, you're just going to walk away from me . . . from everything."

His gaze snapped up to hers. "I never said I was gonna stay, Miranda. And as for walkin' away, well." He pulled a deep breath into his lungs and said gruffly, "Don't you worry about that. I'll stay around long enough to make sure you ain't carryin' a child."

"*What?*"

"You heard me." He shoved his hat on and pulled it low over his ears. Squinting at her, he continued. "Maybe you ain't thought of it yet, but you *could* be carryin'."

Eyes narrowed, Miranda nodded her head slowly and listened to him in silent astonishment.

"And you don't have to worry 'bout that. If you are, I'll take care of ya. And the baby. It's all my fault. I ain't the kind to walk away from my, uh . . ."

"Mistakes?" she offered, her voice dripping with sarcasm he didn't notice.

"Well, yeah. I wouldn't have called it that, but you know . . ."

"Yes." Miranda's mouth twisted in an effort to contain all the curse words trying to get out. "I *do* know." She took a step closer and poked his chest with one finger. "You don't want me enough to stop what you're doing, but you're willing to marry me anyway for the sake of a child you *might* have created?"

"Well . . ."

"Don't bother." Miranda glared at him. "I don't want your help. Or your guilt. You don't owe me a damn thing, Jesse Hogan."

"Just a damn minute!"

"No!" Miranda couldn't believe this. "If I *am* expecting, I'll take care of the baby myself. No child needs a father who considers him a 'mistake.'"

"That ain't what I meant."

"It's what you said." She whirled away from him, took a few steps, then stopped again. "And I don't want a man who's determined to stay only half-alive until he can get himself killed." Miranda shook her head sadly and pulled in a shaky breath. "Let's just pretend today never happened, Jesse." She glanced at him over her shoulder. "You go back to avoiding me. You keep on snapping and snarling at anyone who gets too close. And when you don't find your man here, you just leave and go on hunting him."

Jesse straightened and clenched his jaw, but he kept silent under her tirade.

"And when you're an old, lonely man with nothing more to show for the years gone and missed except a saddle and a few memories that will be more smoke than substance, you remember today."

Her eyes raked over him slowly, as if taking his measure and finding him wanting. He shifted position uneasily under her stare.

"Remember what you gave up. And try to wonder what might have been." She turned away again. "See, Jesse, you had a choice to make today. You had to choose between the dead and the living. Revenge or love." As she started to walk toward her cabin she added, "I hope you can live with the choice you made."

CHAPTER 15

Jesse stood in the lowering shadows by the corral and watched Miranda walk away from him. He snatched his hat off and slapped it against his thighs. He opened his mouth to call her back, then closed it again. Right now Jesse didn't trust himself to talk to her.

What the hell was wrong with her anyway? All he'd done was offer to do the right thing! Lord, he didn't even want to *think* about what she would have done if he *hadn't* offered to marry her! And just who did she think she was, tellin' him that he had no right to his own child?

His gaze followed her stiff-backed progress until she disappeared around the corner of the bunkhouse. He slammed his hat back on his head and cursed under his breath. Damn female! She talked so durn fast, he could hardly keep up with what she was sayin', let alone think of somethin' to say back!

Why, she'd as much as called him a fool outright for wantin' justice for his murdered brother! What kind of man, he wanted to know, did she *want* him to be? The kind that shrugged off violence visited on his family?

He squinted into the distance. Sounded to him like she didn't want him to go and she didn't want him to stay. Hell, he couldn't *win*.

Slowly Jesse walked to the corral fence and leaned his forearms on the top rail. Digging the makings out of his shirt pocket, he rolled a cigarette, lit a match, and dragged the hot smoke into his lungs. As he blew it out in a rush he watched the pale, blue-gray smoke dip, twist, then vanish in the wind. As if it had never been.

And for two years, that's just what Jesse'd been. No more than smoke in the wind. Abruptly he dropped the cigarette into the dirt and stubbed it out with the toe of his boot. He was tired of living like that. But he wasn't sure how to stop.

Of course, if Miranda turned up pregnant . . . *that* would change everything. No matter what she said, they would be married. And they'd go back to the Hogan ranch to live. He found himself smiling at the hazy mental images floating through his mind.

And what about the man you've been searching for for two years? his conscience chided. Jesse shook his head. That wouldn't change. He'd still find the man. He'd just have to do it faster. Try harder. Then, he'd have Miranda and their baby to go home to.

Jesse slapped his hand down on the fence post. This was all supposing Miranda was pregnant. What if she wasn't? They'd know soon enough. What then? He flicked a quick glance toward town and came to a sudden decision.

Baby or no, he *would* marry her. Everything he'd said to her earlier in the day came back to haunt him and he was almost as angry as she'd been. For God's sake, he loved her. That was all that *really* mattered.

The rest could be ironed out. All that hogwash he'd spouted about not bein' right for her . . . well, she could forget it. 'Cause right or not, he was the *only* man she was gonna have.

He wanted to follow her now. Find her and tell her he loved her. Make her listen. Even now, the irony of the whole thing hit him. If not for the man he hunted, Jesse'd never have known Miranda. Just the thought of going through life without her was enough to give him a chill colder and deeper than anything he'd ever felt before.

Every sound, every scent seemed to bear down on him. A puff of wind carried the smell of bacon frying and the tinny sound of Big Pete's piano was unnaturally loud in the otherwise still afternoon. A sudden burst of laughter from the nearby bunkhouse echoed out and Jesse smiled ruefully. It was as if admitting he loved Miranda had allowed all the sights and sounds he'd missed to touch him again. He almost felt . . . alive again.

He deliberately conjured up the images of his brother and sister-in-law. Their faces were becoming blurred in his memory and it seemed that he had to try harder and harder each time just to remember. And maybe that was as it should be. Maybe the forgetting was God's gift to us to ease the pain.

One thing he knew for certain. For the first time in two years his quest was not the most important thing on his mind.

But maybe it would be wise to let Miranda cool off some before telling her about his decision.

He pushed away from the fence and walked toward the stable. His horse could probably use a good brushing. Besides, it would give Jesse something else to do besides think. With one last look over his shoulder, he stepped into the darkened building.

As he got near, the huge horse stamped its feet and whinnied a greeting. Gently Jesse ran his hand over the big animal's neck.

"At least *you're* glad to see me," he said, and chuckled when the animal's nose pushed at his shoulder. Jesse stroked the animal's jaw and said softly, "She *loves* me. How 'bout that, horse? Who'da thought a woman like that could love somebody like me, huh?" The horse snorted. Jesse reached for the currycomb and added, "Y'know somethin' else? I love her, too. Helluva thing to happen, ain't it?" He stared down at the comb in his hands and went on. "Somebody somewhere must be havin' quite a laugh over this. Sendin' me a woman like that at a time like this." Jesse stroked the horse's nose softly and said, "But you know what? Like it or not, that woman's goin' to marry me. After what happened today, she's got no choice anyhow."

Two giant hands came down on his shoulders. Jesse's eyes widened as his feet left the floor. Before he knew what was happening, he was flying through the air and then his body slammed into the stable wall, knocking down the newly mended bridles hanging there. When he landed with a crash on the ground below, he heard Birdwell thunder, "After *what* happened?"

"Shelly?" Dave said softly. "Did you hear me? I said me and Buck are Tex—"

She laid her fingers over his mouth and looked around uneasily. "Don't say it again. Someone might hear."

He kissed her fingertips and smiled. "You sayin' you would care if somebody shot me?"

Shelly lowered her gaze and let her hand fall to her side. She still couldn't believe it. Texas Rangers? In the canyon?

"Shelly?"

She looked up at him again and read the truth in his eyes. Good God. A *Ranger*. Her arms crossed over her chest, she took a step back, but Dave followed.

Marry a Ranger? Impossible. He didn't know. He *couldn't* know what she was. What kind of life she'd led. If he did, he'd never be sayin' all this.

"Shelly," he said, his voice strained. "You're commencin' to worry me. Say something."

Her mouth moved, but no words came out. How could she tell him? How could she not? Shelly's brain raced frantically as she tried to find a way out. Lord, if she accepted and said nothing about her past, what would happen the first time a man recognized her? What would Dave do then?

Accepted? her mind asked. Did she *want* to accept? She glanced up at his pale blue eyes, fringed with golden lashes. She studied the stray lock of blond hair that fell over his wide forehead. The soft smile she'd come to associate with him curved his lips and she noted his nervousness in his unusually stiff stance.

Yes. She wanted to accept. She wanted everything he'd said to her to be true. She wanted babies and to grow old with a man who would always love her. She wanted it all. But did she dare to risk it by telling him the truth about herself?

"Shelly?" He laid his hands on her shoulders and his thumbs moved in a slow reassurance, stroking her skin through the fabric of her blouse.

She took a deep breath, and before she could lose her nerve, Shelly started talking.

The man stopped, dismounted, and poured water from his canteen into his hat for the big gray to drink. The animal was tired. Nearly beat with the fast traveling of the last couple of weeks. But the man was determined to reach the canyon as quickly as he could. It had been too long already since he'd seen Miranda.

Two years ago he'd left her behind. But this time, when he left the bandit stronghold, he'd be taking Miranda with him.

Whether Birdwell liked it or not.

Jesse shook his head violently, blinked his eyes, and pushed himself to his feet. He pulled at the fallen reins and bridles draped over him until they lay on the floor in a heap, then he straightened up and faced the big, bearded man in the corner.

"I don't want to fight you, Birdwell."

The big man snorted. "Ain't surprised. Not many do." He took a step closer to Jesse.

"No." Jesse shook his head and took a step to the side. "It ain't your size. Not even that you'd prob'ly kill me."

"Then why?"

Jesse shrugged. "Guess it's cause you're only tryin' to protect Miranda. Can't fault you for that."

Birdwell stopped suddenly. Planting his feet wide apart, he cocked his head to one side and said much too quietly, "I saw you and Miranda outside. Couldn't hear ya, but I figure you're causin' her grief. I don't often see her that mad."

"That's between me and her," Jesse said just as quietly.

"That's where you're wrong, mister." Birdwell lifted his bearded chin and glared at the younger man. "You bring her grief, you deal with me. Now, are you gonna tell me just what the hell happened or ain't you?"

"Nope."

Birdwell pulled air into his massive chest and nodded abruptly. "Reckon we'll have to go a few rounds then, till you change your mind."

"Won't happen, Birdwell." Jesse met the big man's gaze squarely. "I'll talk to Miranda. Later. After she's cooled down some. But I ain't tellin' you a damn thing."

A long, quiet, tension-filled minute passed before Birdwell relaxed his stance and crossed his arms over his chest. "All right. Then you just listen while I tell *you* something."

Jesse waited.

"I seen the way you two been circlin' 'round each other. You been givin' her looks that should've curled her hair since the day you first come here. And she's been lookin' back. *And* I know you was together today." He looked steadily at Jesse. "You was prob'ly at the tank. Miranda always heads there. *And* I'm bettin' that what with you two bein' young and healthy, somethin' went on up there that I wouldn't care to know about."

Jesse tried to keep his expression blank. He wasn't about to talk to Birdwell before he told Miranda.

"So I'm here to tell you, boy." Birdwell unfolded his arms and pointed one finger at the younger man opposite him. "You're about to be a married man."

"What?" It was one thing for Jesse to decide on his own, but it was quite another to be told what to do.

"You heard me. You ain't no outlaw, boy. I don't

know just who the hell you are, or why you're
here . . . but I *do* know you don't belong here."
Birdwell paused another moment, then added, "And
Miranda don't belong here no more neither."

"And you think she'll marry me just cause you say
so?"

"I do."

Jesse laughed. He bent over, put his hands on his
knees, and laughed until his sides hurt. Leaning back
against the stable wall, he looked up at the con-
founded big man and laughed even harder.

"What's so damn funny?" Birdwell walked closer to
him.

Gulping in air, Jesse fought for control. It wasn't
easy, though. The idea of that hardheaded woman
doin' what *anybody* told her to do was just too funny.
Finally he managed to look up at the man next to him
and say, "I already told her I'd marry her if she was
pregnant and she as much as told me to go to hell." He
straightened up. "And you think she'll just up and
marry me on your say-so." Jesse shook his head
slowly in disbelief.

"Pregnant?" Birdwell murmured.

Jesse glanced at the other man and didn't like what
he saw. He tried to duck, but he was too late.
Birdwell's fist caught him on the left cheek and he
spun around and dropped to the ground. Lying in the
dirt, Jesse looked up at the big man.

Birdwell rubbed his knuckles. "I *told* you. I didn't
want to know what happened at the tank."

By the time she finished talking, Shelly couldn't bring
herself to look Dave in the eye. Most of what she'd
told him she'd never mentioned to another living soul.
It was hard enough to admit to yourself that you'd

been a fool, let alone owning up to it to someone else.

But she'd done it. Told him all about Slick Stephens and how he'd forced her to "work" for him. About how coming to the canyon had saved her life because Birdwell rescued her from Slick and warned the man never to bother her again. She'd even reminded Dave that he just might run into some of her former "customers" one day.

Her fingers twisted together nervously as she waited for some sign from the tall blond man. She wished heartily that the restaurant floor would open up and swallow her. Then she'd never have to look into his eyes and see the disgust she was expecting.

"You finished now?" His voice was soft, caressing. She nodded, but didn't look up.

Dave's hand cupped her cheek and turned her face up to his. Resolutely Shelly kept her eyes closed. She heard his quiet chuckle and then felt his lips brush against her mouth with a feather-light touch. Startled, her eyes flew open and the warmth in his eyes disarmed her.

"You're really somethin', Shelly. You know that?" She shook her head.

"Yep." His other hand moved to smooth her hair back from her face. "You're so busy tellin' me why you're no good, you don't even notice that a 'bad' woman wouldn't have bothered to open her mouth."

Shelly bit the inside of her lip and blinked frantically at the tears filling her eyes. She held her breath and waited.

"I love you, Shelly. Nothin' you can say or do is gonna change that." He bent down and kissed her forehead. "As for your past"—he smiled gently— "hell, I've had quite a time myself." He planted a small kiss on the tip of her nose. "And if I ever run into one of your 'gentleman friends,' well, they'll just know that *I'm* the lucky one. Because I'll have you for always." His mouth touched hers again and she tasted her own tears. "Isn't that right?"

Tentatively Shelly raised her hand and stroked the line of his stubbly jaw. Then she smoothed that errant lock of hair off his brow. His smile warmed her soul, and for the first time in more years than she cared to think about, Shelly knew she was loved. Slowly she stepped into the circle of his arms and gratefully felt his strength close around her.

"That's right, Dave," she whispered, and laid her head on his chest.

Pike Dexter leaned over his smiling wife and gave her a careful kiss. Then, under Serena's proud gaze, the outlaw picked up his son and stared down into the little face so much like his own.

Miranda and Shelly tiptoed out of the room and closed the door after them.

"When did Pike get here?" Miranda asked.

"Just a couple of minutes before you." Shelly crossed to the front door, opened it, and stepped out onto the boardwalk. When Miranda joined her, Shelly asked quietly, "Where'd you go for so long today?"

"The tank."

Shelly nodded absently and looked off toward the restaurant, a half smile on her face.

"Shelly?" Miranda waited until her friend turned to look at her. "Are you all right?"

"Yeah. Yeah, Miranda. I'm fine." The same secretive half smile curved her lips again. "Why?"

"Well . . ." Miranda shrugged helplessly. "I don't know. You just seem . . . different."

Shelly chuckled and stepped down off the board-walk. "Maybe I am different."

"Shelly, what's going on?"

Instead of answering the question, Shelly asked one of her own. "Was Jesse with you today?"

Miranda's jaw snapped shut, but she felt the incriminating rush of blood to her cheeks.

"I thought so." Shelly grinned and turned toward the restaurant.

Miranda stepped into the street, confusion written plainly on her features. "No lectures or warnings this time? Are you *sure* you're all right?"

Shelly looked over her shoulder and grinned. "I'm *fine*. And no more warnings. You're not a little girl, Miranda. I'm sorry if I treated you like one."

"No, you didn't."

"Yeah, I did." Suddenly Shelly turned, came back to Miranda, and took both her friend's hands in hers. "But today I found something that I thought was gone forever."

"What?"

"I found *me* again." Shelly's dark brown eyes seemed lit from within and her cheeks were flushed a lovely pink. "The *old* me. The one before Slick came along."

"I don't understand, Shelly."

"You don't have to." She squeezed Miranda's hands. "I'm just tryin' to tell you to go ahead after what it is you want. If it's Jesse, then I hope you get him."

"Don't even *talk* about Jesse. . . ."

"What's wrong?"

Concern and worry replaced the happiness in the other woman's face and Miranda immediately regretted speaking. "Nothing. He just made me angry."

Shelly nodded, convinced. "It'll be all right, Miranda. He loves you. Anybody could see it in his face when he looks at you."

Miranda knew better, but she didn't want to upset Shelly again.

"I have to go now," the dark-haired woman said quickly. "But I have something important to tell you later, all right?"

Miranda nodded and smiled hesitantly as she watched Shelly hurry off down the street. Glancing toward the corral where she'd last seen Jesse, Miranda felt a sudden, overwhelming urge to go down there and finish telling him exactly what she thought of him.

Instead she turned and walked back to her darkened cabin alone.

CHAPTER
16

Birdwell stood just outside the stable and silently congratulated himself.

Just as he'd thought, Jesse Hogan was no outlaw.

Birdwell rubbed his sore knuckles and snorted. It hadn't been very difficult to convince the boy that he should do the right thing by Miranda. In fact, Birdwell was fairly sure that Hogan had about already made up his mind to marry her. He'd just needed a little extra "push" in the right direction.

The big man slowly straightened his blue-and-red-checked flannel shirt and tucked it into his well-worn, baggy black pants. He'd settled things with Hogan; now all that was left was to deal with Miranda. Birdwell grimaced and smoothed his full beard thoughtfully.

He looked down the length of the narrow street and squinted toward Miranda's cabin. Overhead, ribbons of clouds scuttled across the moon, leaving uncertain, dappled patches of light across the false-fronted, weathered buildings of the tired old town. Birdwell's gaze fastened on the flickering lamplight showing between the folds of Miranda's curtains.

He wasn't looking forward to the coming scene. Miranda could be downright stubborn when she wanted to be. And besides, he didn't relish talking to her about her and Jesse and what they'd been up to that afternoon. Birdwell shuddered. Just the *thought* of his little Miranda and some fella . . . Deliberately he emptied his mind of the disturbing images.

He stiffened his spine and inhaled deeply. Squaring his broad shoulders, the older man marched steadily down the boardwalk, straight into the teeth of the most important battle he would ever fight.

"I will not!"

"Miranda . . ." Birdwell's thunderous roar made Miranda's ears ring.

"It doesn't matter what you say, Birdwell. I will not marry a man simply because I *might* be carrying his child!"

Birdwell flinched and rubbed one beefy hand across his mouth. "Like I already told him, I don't want to know about any of that."

"Then why are you here?" She pulled the belt of her pink silk robe tighter, crossed her arms, and waited, tapping her foot. For over an hour she'd listened to the man she considered a second father spout the most ridiculous notions. And he had the nerve to tell her that Jesse not only agreed with him, but had actually planned most of this on his own.

If *that* were true, why wasn't Jesse here himself to propose? She *knew* why. He was probably lying unconscious somewhere. She'd seen Birdwell "talk" to suitors before.

"I already told you that, too." He walked to the

nearest chair and dropped into it. "The boy figured you'd take it easier—I mean, we figured you'd want to know that this here idea was all right with me."

"Uh-huh." She nodded abruptly and walked to his side. "Well, it's not all right with me."

"Miranda."

"No." She shook one finger at the seated giant. "Oh, I'll admit to you that I love him. And ordinarily I would have been happy to marry the man."

He smiled.

"*But,*" she went on, as his smile faded, "he was ready to leave me behind and go on with his search for . . ." Miranda glanced at Birdwell. "Did he tell you about . . ."

"His folks? Yeah."

"Good." She walked to the window, lifted the curtain, and stared out at the night. "Did he also tell you he said very plainly that he couldn't let anything, even *me,* stop him from searching?"

"Yeah."

"And that when he suddenly realized that he might have left me with child, he decided that he would be willing to pay for his 'mistakes'?"

Birdwell cleared his throat uneasily. "That ain't how he put it."

"It doesn't matter."

"Yeah, it does," Birdwell said quietly, firmly.

He pushed himself up from the chair and leaned toward her. Miranda tilted her head back to look him in the eye. She wasn't at all happy with what she saw in those black depths.

"Miranda, honey," he said softly, "we been goin' around and around for more'n an hour. And we're all done now."

"Finally."

"That's right." He took her stubborn chin in his fingers and held her still. "And sometime this week you *are* gonna marry Jesse Hogan. Even if I have to snatch a parson myself!"

"I—"

"No!" He shook his head. "I heard all I'm gonna hear about it. Now *you* listen. It ain't right anymore, you stayin' in the canyon." She opened her mouth, but he went on quickly. "Things're different. It ain't like it used to be. And if your pa was here, he'd tell you the same. Now, Hogan's got hisself a ranch in Texas and you two could build yourselves a nice place. Have the kind of life you *should* have."

"But, Birdwell—"

"Don't Birdwell me in that sweet tone, either. Won't do no good." He smiled halfheartedly. "I'm gettin' on now, Miranda, and—"

"You'll *never* be old, Birdwell."

He snorted. "Hell, with any luck, we *all* get old sooner or later! But what I'm tryin' to say is, with me gettin' on in years and all . . . well, I'm not gonna be around to look out for you forever." Birdwell leaned down and kissed her forehead. "And I want to know for sure that you're safe and taken care of."

"There must be some other way—"

"No, honey. There *ain't* no other way. You best get used to the idea." He smoothed his big hand over her cheek gently. "You already said you love him. It won't be no hardship to live with him."

In spite of herself, Miranda had a brief, clear vision of her and Jesse together. That afternoon she'd had a sample of what that could be like. And to be with him all the time would only make things better. If she were completely honest, she would have to admit that she'd like nothing better than to be Jesse's wife and live with him on his ranch. She'd like to help him banish the haunting memories that surrounded him and his home.

And deep inside she knew that Birdwell was right about something else, too. It *was* time to leave her little town behind. So much had changed since she was a child. And even *she* could see that Bandit's Canyon would never be the *real* town she'd always hoped it would be. If she wasn't there to make a home for her outlaws, they would, no doubt, find some other way to survive. They'd done it long before she was born.

But it would be so much better if the man she married actually *wanted* her for a wife.

"He doesn't want to be married, Birdwell," she said on a sigh.

The big man drew her close and held her in an enveloping hug. Softly he told her, "Hell, honey. No man *wants* to get married. Leastways, not till some female convinces him he does." He pulled back, tilted her chin up, and grinned. "And Miranda, I don't think you're gonna have much trouble 'convincin'' Jesse Hogan."

She leaned into his strength and listened to the steady beat of his heart. Everything was happening so quickly. How could she be *sure* that Birdwell hadn't already done the "convincing" necessary to get Jesse to agree with this plan? Maybe she should talk to Jesse. See how he *really* felt about all of this.

And no matter what Birdwell said or did, if Jesse wanted no part of this marriage, she wouldn't go through with it. She didn't want the man she loved to hate her for forcing him into a wedding that never should have happened.

"You Jesse Hogan?"

Jesse spun around to face the man behind the deep

voice. A man he'd never seen before stood just inside the bunkhouse, his hat in his hands. In a split second Jesse noted the man's slicked-down, light brown, almost blond hair. He wore a clean shirt still wrinkled from the bedroll it had been packed in and a pair of faded black pants. Around his hips was a well-worn pistol and holster. Blue eyes narrowed and watched Jesse steadily.

"Well?" the man asked again.

"Yeah. I'm Hogan." Jesse took a step closer to his holster and pistol, lying on the bed beside him. A big man, he told himself. Almost blond. It could be.

The man noticed his move and smiled in approval. "No need to be nervous."

"Who're you?" Jesse asked quietly.

"Dexter. Pike Dexter."

Serena's husband. The notorious Arizona Pike. Somehow Jesse wasn't reassured. He took another step toward the pistol. He'd heard enough stories about Pike to warrant caution.

Pike laughed. His blue eyes softened and the tired lines in his face stretched into a long-unused smile. "Hell. Get your damn gun on if it makes you feel better."

Curious, Jesse watched the other man. From everything he'd heard about Arizona Pike, laughter was not what he'd expected. Of course, Jesse reminded himself, Miranda had told him about how Pike had been before his brother was killed. Still, there was no point in taking chances. Jesse reached for his gun belt, swung it around his narrow hips, and buckled it. He *did* feel better with his gun on. "Thanks," he said.

Pike nodded and took a step closer. "Look, Hogan, I only come here to thank you for what you did for my wife." He leaned in for a better look at Jesse, whistled, and said softly, "Man, you look like you come out on the wrong end of a fight. What happened?"

Jesse's hand flew to his left eye and cheek. Gingerly he ran his fingers over the swelling. Not for the first time he told himself how lucky he was that Birdwell had only hit him the one time. "Nothin'," he answered. It was nobody's business where he picked up his black eye.

"Up to you." Pike nodded. "Like I said, I only wanted to thank you for helpin' Serena."

Jesse shrugged and waited. He was sure there was more.

"See." Pike stepped over to one of the bunks and sat down. He stared at the worn hat in his hands and spoke, almost to himself. "I don't know what I'da done if anything happened to Serena." His fingers tightened on the brim. "Scared me somethin' awful when she told me she was gonna have a baby." He shook his head, snorted a laugh, and glanced at Jesse. "'Magine that? *Me* scared of a little thing like a baby?"

Remembering his own fear during that long night, Jesse smiled at the other man. "Yeah. I can imagine."

Pike studied him for a long minute, then nodded. "I think maybe you do know what I'm talkin' about." He sighed heavily. "Anyhow, I know I shoulda been here with her when it come." He looked up at Jesse sheepishly. "Reckon I was just too scared to stay, though."

Jesse sank down to his own bed, across from the outlaw. No longer leery of the man, he relaxed and listened.

"Hell." Pike laughed again self-consciously. "I been so skittish lately I ain't even stole anything in a month."

"But Serena said—"

"Oh, sure," Pike continued, smiling, "I left outta here plannin' on robbin' a bank. The boys was all set and ready. Plans all made. Figured it was perfect."

"*Was?*"

"Yeah." The outlaw shook his head and shrugged. "When it come down to it, I just pulled back. Kept seein' myself shot up or in jail and Serena all alone, takin' care of a baby that'd never know his pa." He took a deep breath and blew it out. "I lit out and the boys went ahead with the job anyhow."

"What happened?" He knew for a fact that Pike's bunch hadn't *all* come to the canyon. Jesse would have heard that many men arrive.

Pike frowned. "Few days later I heard that the town marshal caught 'em in a cross fire with some of the townsfolk. Shot 'em to doll rags."

A sudden, too clear image of the fallen bandits littering the street of some unknown town leaped into Jesse's brain.

"Don't know why I'm tellin' you all this"—Pike glanced at Jesse and shook his head—"but seein' as how my boy carries your name . . ."

Jesse grinned wryly. "Was wonderin' how you was gonna take that news."

Pike laughed. "Hell, for my money . . . you *earned* it! Serena couldn't say enough about you. Shit, even Ezra stopped me a while ago and told me how good you done." He leaned forward and winked. "And I hear Ezra was passed out in a chair! Anyhow, thought you'd like to know that I'm hangin' up my gun. Takin' Serena and little Jesse back home to Arkansas. Got a nice little place there just waitin' on us." He pushed himself to his feet and held out his hand to Jesse. When the other man stood and grabbed his outstretched hand, Pike added, "I'm tired of the runnin' and hidin'. I want to sit on a porch with Serena. Maybe teach little Jesse how to fish . . ." As if overcome by too much sudden emotion, he suddenly released Jesse's hand and put his hat on. Turning toward the door, Pike stopped in midstride, looked over his shoulder, and said softly, "I owe you, mister. You ever need *anything*, you get word to me. I'll come runnin'."

Jesse only nodded and watched the famed outlaw leave the room and quietly shut the door behind him. He sank back down onto his bunk and stared at the clapboard wall across from him. Pike Dexter hanging up his guns. Going home with his wife and baby. Maybe, Jesse told himself, if Dexter could walk away, maybe *he* could, too.

Miranda reached for another cookie and took a sip of her hot tea. But it was no use. Not even time alone in the middle of the night could calm her racing mind. She looked around her at the empty restaurant. Wild shadows danced and jumped on the walls to the silent tune played by the dipping flame of her lamp. The wind whispered outside, teasing the ancient wooden shingles and rattling the windowpanes.

She sighed and idly crumbled the cookie into dust on her plate. Pushing at the crumbs with her index finger, Miranda tried to guess where Jesse'd been hiding all night. After Birdwell left her cabin, she'd gone straight to the stables to look for him. But he wasn't there. In fact, she'd spent the better part of an hour poking her nose in and out of the buildings in town searching for him.

In fact, it seemed to Miranda that Jesse was deliberately trying to avoid her. A fine way for a marriage to start. She set her teacup down with a clatter. The longer she thought about the whole situation, the

madder she got. Oh, at first she'd felt badly for Jesse.
After all, no woman wants to believe a man had to be
forced into marrying her. But as the hours passed and
he continued to stay out of sight, the first stirrings of
anger had spread through Miranda.

For heaven's sake! It wasn't as if she was the one
hog-tying him! Her spine stiffened and she lifted her
chin. And he hadn't seemed to mind bedding her at
the tank! Was she not *good* enough to marry? Was that
it? She crossed her arms over her chest and narrowed
her eyes in thought. Because he's not an outlaw and
her family and friends are? Or was it much simpler
than that? Did he not want soiled goods even though
he himself was the soiler?

She pushed up from the table suddenly and walked
to the window overlooking the canyon wall. There
was absolutely no excuse for this! Miranda bit at her
bottom lip and leaned her forehead against the cold
glass. He could have *talked* to her.

The restaurant door creaked as it opened and Miranda stiffened. So. He'd finally come. Well, she
wouldn't make it easy for him. He would have to
explain why he'd been avoiding her and apologize.
Maybe *then* she'd forgive him.

The door closed again and she heard boots moving
quietly across the floor. She straightened up and
watched the windowpane for his reflection. As he
stepped into view and took off his hat, Miranda
gasped. Tom Forbes.

"Hey, M'randa," he said, and moved up beside her.
"Soon as I saw that light in the window, I knew it was
you. You always did favor comin' in for a snack late at
night."

She clutched at the edges of her robe and wished
frantically that she hadn't worn the pink silk. At that

moment she'd have given anything to be wrapped in a smelly horse blanket. Anything that would help keep Tom Forbes at a distance.

"Hello, Tom," she finally managed to say as she took a quick step to the side.

"Hello, Tom?" he said softly. "That all you got to say?"

Miranda glanced up at him quickly. His sandy blond hair fell over his forehead, lying just above his cold, gray eyes. She suppressed a shudder and tried once more to move away. "It's, uh . . . been a long time." Two long, wonderful years, she added mentally.

"Yeah. *Too* long." He reached out and ran his fingers down the length of her arm. "But that's all over now. I'm back."

"Well, you're probably tired. I'll find Birdwell. He can get you settled at the bunkhouse." Miranda turned and took a step before his hand shot out and grabbed her.

"No hurry, M'randa." His voice came low and soft. "Plenty of time for that. Let's you and me visit for a while, huh?"

She smiled nervously. "I'd like to, Tom, I really would. But it's late and—"

His fingers curled around her upper arm and squeezed. "It ain't that late, honey. 'Sides, you ain't give me a proper welcome yet."

Miranda's gaze flashed to his. "What do you mean?"

He smiled lazily and ran his tongue over his lips. "I mean, I liked to rode my horse to death gettin' here to you." His hands cupped her shoulders and drew her closer. "I figure that should at least earn me one little kiss." He grinned and winked. "For starters."

"Miranda?"

Jesse. Miranda almost laughed her relief out loud as Jesse walked into the restaurant. Tom made no move to release her, though, so she stood completely still and waited.

"Hell, honey!" Jesse came up behind her, wrapped one arm around her waist, and lifted her away from Forbes before the man could react. Before he set her down behind him, Jesse gave her a quick, hard kiss. "Been lookin' all over for you. You should be in bed!"

"I was just going back to my cabin when you came," she answered, and raised her hand to touch his discolored, swollen eye and cheek. Jesse shook his head slightly, warning her to be quiet. She risked a glance at Tom. If looks alone could have killed, Jesse would be dead. She'd never seen such anger in Forbes.

"And this nice fella was helpin' you along, huh?" Jesse looked at Tom and challenged him silently to disagree.

"Who're you, mister?" Tom glared at the other man.

"Name's Hogan. Jesse Hogan." He didn't bother to offer his hand.

Miranda saw the warring gleams shining in both men's eyes and didn't want to risk any more trouble. Deliberately she stepped between them, wrapping one arm around Jesse's waist.

"Would you take me home now, Jesse?"

"Sure, honey." He laid his arm across her shoulders and rubbed his hand familiarly over her upper arm. Miranda couldn't help leaning into him. She'd never been so happy to see someone in her life.

Jesse slowly began to move toward the door, somehow managing to keep from turning his back on Tom Forbes.

Just before they stepped outside, Jesse stopped.

Miranda felt the tension in him and tried to keep him moving. Threads of anger stretched tightly between the two men and Miranda knew that they could snap at any moment. But Jesse wouldn't be moved.

Glancing at Forbes, Jesse said much too softly, "I'd appreciate it if you'd stay clear of Miranda from now on."

"Yeah? Why should I?"

"Because we're gettin' married. And I don't much care for other men layin' hands on my wife."

CHAPTER 17

"What the hell was goin' on in there?" Jesse's grip on Miranda's arm tightened as he hustled her down the boardwalk toward her cabin.

She didn't say anything and he didn't push for an answer. Plenty of time for that once he got her inside and off the street. Besides, he was still too mad to talk. Their heels clicking on the wooden walk were the only sounds in the still night. Bandit's Canyon was asleep.

At her cabin, Jesse ushered Miranda inside, stepped in behind her, and closed the door after them.

The fire in the hearth had burned down to a few smoldering ashes. Jesse watched impatiently as Miranda crossed the room, picked up a medium-sized branch from the woodpile, and laid it across the hot embers. Then she began poking at the ashes until flames licked up the sides of the fresh wood.

Soft, wavy brown hair tumbled down her back and over her shoulders as she studiously ignored him.

Jesse clenched his teeth and pulled in a deep, shaky breath.

"Well?" He couldn't stand it any longer. "Who is he?"

"Tom Forbes." Miranda stood up and brushed her palms together.

Jesse deliberately kept his gaze from straying to her breasts, outlined nicely by the silk robe. All he really wanted to do was tug at the belt of that robe and let it slide to the floor. Mentally he shook himself. If he let himself be distracted now, he'd never find out a damn thing. "Yeah? And?"

"And what?"

"And what were you doin' in the restaurant in the middle of the night *with him*?"

Astonishment crossed her face and Jesse was as surprised as she was. He'd never felt like this before. He'd never in his life wanted to punch a man the way he wanted to hit the man who'd touched Miranda. Ever since he'd glanced in the restaurant window and seen the two of them together . . . Jesse shook his head and pulled his hat off.

Hell, he knew it was none of her doing. He'd seen her face when that fella got too close. She was afraid. Jesse'd never seen her afraid before and he found he didn't much like the notion of Miranda being scared. Indians, babies, a boy dyin' of a gunshot wound . . . none of that had bothered her. But Tom Forbes did. He wanted to know why.

Tall and straight, she stood quietly, just watching him. When he'd stormed into that restaurant after her, Jesse'd seen the relief on her face. The welcome in her eyes. Now that welcome was gone. Replaced by a wary disappointment that made him ashamed.

But she just didn't understand what it had been like to stand on the outside watching another man touch her.

"I wasn't with him," she said, and Jesse winced at the calm formality in her voice. "He came in just a minute or two before you arrived."

"Yeah." He blew out a rush of air. "I guess I knew that." He dropped onto the closest chair and leaned forward, his forearms on his thighs. "Hell, I'm sorry, M'randa. Guess I lost my head when I saw you and him."

"I was surely glad to see you," Miranda said quietly, and took the chair beside him.

He cocked his head at her. "What would you have done if I hadn't come by?"

"Well, I would have . . ."

"Uh-huh." She didn't know. Jesse shook his head and stared down at the hat in his hands. "That's what I figured."

"I'd have thought of something."

"Why should you have to?"

"What do you mean?"

"I *mean* when I first got here, everybody was always tellin' me to stay away from you." He looked up at her and smiled ruefully. "They said that was the one rule everbody had to obey. Leave Miranda alone."

"Yes." Her hands gripped each other tightly in her lap.

"So how come this fella don't pay any attention to that rule? How come he thinks he can do whatever he likes?"

Miranda wasn't sure how to answer him. It was difficult to explain about a man like Tom Forbes. There was something strange about Forbes. Something elusive that she couldn't quite name. Oh, over the years, other men had tried to flirt with her. Some had even tried for more. But Forbes . . . he acted as though it was his *right* to touch her.

She looked at the man opposite her for a moment, then lowered her gaze again. How could she explain what was really no more than a *feeling*? Finally she simply said, "I don't know."

Jesse looked over at her again, head down, her voice so soft he had to strain to hear it.

"He's been coming here for about ten years. I never much liked him," she began, "but he never bothered me until the last time, two years ago." Her gaze lifted to meet Jesse's and he saw that flash of fear in her eyes again. "Oh, he never actually *touched* me, it was more the way he looked at me." She shivered. "And he always seemed to be right behind me, no matter where I went." She rubbed her hands together as if for warmth. "My father and Birdwell looked out for me, but there wasn't any way they could make him leave as long as he followed the rules." She shrugged. "Anyway, he left right after my father died and I was beginning to hope that he wasn't coming back. Until tonight."

"Well, it don't much matter what he does," Jesse said, though he knew if Forbes tried anything again, he'd kill him. "After we're married, I reckon he'll keep his distance."

"Married."

"Yeah." She didn't sound any too pleased with the idea, Jesse told himself. But then memories of their day together came rushing back and he knew that come hell or high water, they were going to get married. Whether she liked the idea or not.

He couldn't live with the thought of some other man touching her. Holding her. No matter what else happened, Miranda would be his.

"We don't have to get married, Jesse."

"Oh yeah, we do," he snorted. "I ain't about to be the one to tell Birdwell the weddin's off." Her face fell, but there was nothing to be done about it. He wouldn't start talkin' about love and such now. She probably wouldn't believe him anyway after he'd made such a jackass of himself only a few hours ago.

"He did that to you, didn't he?" She pointed at his swollen cheek.

He winced and touched his face gingerly. "This? Nah. I, uh . . ." Dammit. Jesse'd spent all night avoiding her, hoping the swelling would go down before she saw him.

"Oh, yes, he did." She nodded firmly. "And I'm sorry. He shouldn't have. I don't even know how he found out about, uh . . ."

"He heard us talkin' when we got back to town."

"Oh." Her brow furrowed and Jesse knew she was trying to remember exactly what she said. Then she shook her head.

"Well, don't worry, Jesse. It doesn't matter what Birdwell told you. I won't marry a man who had to be beaten into it."

"What?"

"You heard me." Miranda stood up and walked to the tiny kitchen. The pump handle groaned and clanked as she filled the coffeepot with water.

When she'd set the pot down near the fire, Jesse stood and walked up behind her. "He didn't beat me into nothin'."

"Jesse." She sighed. "I've seen your eye, remember?"

"That's nothin'. Hell, I had worse black eyes than this from Carter!"

"That's not the point."

Grabbing her shoulders, Jesse spun her around to face him. "You're right. That ain't the point. Just forget about my eye. Birdwell figured I had it comin', and maybe I did."

She opened her mouth to argue, but Jesse laid one hand across her mouth to keep her quiet.

"I mean it. I knew damn well I shouldn't have laid a hand on you today." His fingers moved over her lips and slid down the length of her throat. His gaze followed the movement as if hypnotized. "But I couldn't help myself."

"It wasn't only you at the tank, Jesse."

"Yeah, I remember." He chuckled softly. "Lord, do I remember. That's all I been thinkin' of since we got back." Miranda's eyes closed and Jesse pulled her up against him.

"And what about the man you're looking for?" she asked, her voice muffled against his chest.

"I'll find him. I'll just have to find him quicker." He squeezed her tightly and whispered, "I know you don't want me to, but you're gonna have to understand. I've *got* to do it."

He waited, but she didn't answer him. Finally he said, "I ain't sayin' I'm the best choice for a husband, M'randa. But I'm the only choice you're gonna get." Jesse smiled inwardly. He was going to make her understand that they *were* getting married if it took all night. Doing right by her had become terribly important to him. But it wasn't only that, he knew. Jesse wanted Miranda more than he'd wanted anything or anyone before in his life. And the longer he played with the idea of marriage, the better he liked it. Even the terrible image of Carter and Della that he'd carried with him the last two years had begun to fade.

She pulled back and stared up at him, startled by the steely determination in his tone.

"'Cause so help me God, woman . . ." He kissed her cheek. "It about kills me to think of you"—another kiss on the tip of her nose—"with anybody else." Jesse leaned down and covered her mouth with his. His hands moved over her back, down the curve of her behind, and back again.

A flare of hope ignited in Miranda's heart at Jesse's words. She knew that desire, not love, was driving him, but she didn't care. She loved him. And if he wanted her enough, maybe his passion would grow into something real, something lasting. Like love.

She moaned softly, and when Jesse's arms locked around her, holding her so tightly she thought her ribs would break, she gave herself up to the exquisite pleasure of being so close to him. Her lips parted for him and Miranda gasped when his tongue dipped into her mouth and she heard him groan like a dying man.

Outside, Tom Forbes stood quietly on the empty boardwalk. Peering through the folds of Miranda's curtains, he watched as she ran her fingers through the other man's hair. As the other man slowly pulled at the belt of her silk robe, Forbes gritted his teeth, rubbed his thumbs and index fingers together, and imagined the feel of the soft fabric beneath his hands. The pale pink dressing gown hung open, revealing a tantalizingly sheer white bed gown with more lace and ribbons than material. Tom stared hungrily at the rise and fall of Miranda's full breasts and licked his lips slowly when Jesse's hands moved to cup them, his thumbs toying with her erect nipples.

Hogan pushed the robe and then the sheer gown over Miranda's shoulders until they dropped to the floor. Forbes sucked in air through tightly clenched teeth and looked his fill of the smooth ivory flesh that had been denied him for so long.

Through the closed window, he heard the woman groan her pleasure and saw her arch into Hogan's touch. When Jesse bent, scooped her up in his arms, and carried her back to the bed, Tom Forbes turned away from the window at last.

Stepping down into the street, he turned toward Big Pete's place. Fat Alice or Wilma was bound to be awake. If not, he'd wake 'em. *Somebody* had to pay for that no-good, lyin' whore!

She was supposed to be his! She *knew* it as well as he did. Why was she with Hogan? Why would she *marry* him?

He glanced over his shoulder at the dark cabin where a man was even now leaning over *his* woman. An ugly smile curved his lips.

He'd be back.

He'd show them both.

"Still can't see why it's so all-fired important to ride all the way into town!"

Shelly smiled at Dave and shook his head. "There's a few things Miranda and me want to get. We'll be back this afternoon."

Miranda sat on the buckboard seat and looked up at Buck on his horse. Buck rolled his eyes and Miranda just managed to smother a chuckle. Dave and Shelly had been saying good-bye now for five full minutes.

"Well," Dave asked for the third time, "I don't see why I can't go with ya. Why the hell do ya want *him*"—he jerked his head at Buck—"instead of me?"

"Shit." Buck pulled off his hat and wiped his shirt sleeve across his forehead. "She already told ya that. She don't want you seein' what's she's buyin'. Now, will you get the hell outta the way so's we can get goin'?"

Miranda laughed quietly but was glad Buck had spoken. Honestly, if they didn't start soon, they wouldn't be back till after supper. She glanced up at the clear blue morning sky and told herself the long trip to town would be worth it. Hat Creek might not be San Francisco, but surely the store would have *something* nice she could wear to be married in.

She wanted to look beautiful for Jesse when she married him. This was her wedding she was preparing for, and no matter what the circumstances that made her and Jesse man and wife, she wanted everything to be perfect.

Shelly's shining face told her that the other woman didn't care in the least about wedding dresses or anything else. She already had everything she wanted. Miranda'd never seen Shelly so happy and that happiness made her own even stronger.

Dave frowned at his partner, bent down, and kissed Shelly briefly. Then he helped her onto the wagon seat. The other two people shifted restlessly.

"All right, all right," Dave muttered. "Go on and go then. But you best be careful, Buck. Anything happens to Shelly and I'm huntin' your hide!"

"Aw, for chrissakes!"

"And you don't even want to *think* about what Jesse would do to ya if Miranda comes to harm."

Buck shot his friend a disgusted look, then gave his horse a little kick to start it moving. Miranda couldn't quite catch what the man said, and judging from his expression, she was pleased about that.

"Hey, son!" Jim Sully grinned, stepped forward, and held out his hand toward Jesse. "Congratulations! Birdwell told us you and Miranda was gettin' hitched."

Jesse smiled back at the friendly blond and shook the outstretched hand. Bill Sully leaned on a corral post just a few feet behind his brother. Jesse nodded to him.

"What I can't figure is how the hell'd you find a way to get past Birdwell to do your courtin'?" Jim pulled off his hat and scratched his head. His cheeks dimpled when he added, "Most of the boys that come through here been tryin' to do that for *years*!"

"Guess I just got lucky," Jesse answered softly. He silently prayed that his luck would hold. Now that everything was settled, he found the thought of anything going wrong too much to bear. Then he deliberately pushed all his dark thoughts away. *Nothing* was going to happen.

"I'd say so." Jim slapped the other man's shoulder. "That Miranda is really somethin' special."

"Yeah."

They walked to the corral fence and leaned their forearms on the top rail. "Birdwell says you'll be takin' her back to your place in Texas?"

Jesse squinted into the late-morning sun. "That's right."

"Sure am gonna miss her around here."

"Hell yes," Bill tossed in. "That girl can *cook*!"

Jim frowned at his younger brother. "I swear, all you ever think about is that damn stomach of yours!"

"Shit, somebody's got to!" Bill grinned and headed for the restaurant. "Reckon I'll see what ol' Birdwell's cookin' up for dinner."

Jesse only half listened to the Sully boys' banter. His brain was already busy tryin' to plan what to do about Miranda. He smiled to himself. Even thinkin' about her did things to him that he hadn't dreamed possible. He let the memory of the night before come up before his eyes and it was all he could do to breathe. It was amazin' what you could do on a real bed! And it was a helluva lot more comfortable than those damn rocks in the canyon. Although he'd always have a soft spot for that rocky outcropping on the tank.

His horse trotted up to Jesse and butted his nose into Jesse's shoulder. Shaken out of his daydreams, Jesse tried again to decide what to do. Should they spend the winter here in the canyon or go on back to the ranch now? And if they did, would Miranda be safe at the ranch alone while he went after his brother's killer?

That thought brought another. Why would Birdwell stay here in the canyon? Hell, he was Miranda's only family! Maybe the big man could be talked into returning to Texas with them. Lord knew, Jesse was going to need all the help he could get in rebuilding the ranch. Maybe he could even talk the Sullys into goin' back to bein' workin' cowhands. Even *they* must realize they weren't very good outlaws!

And there was another good side to that idea. When he *did* leave on his search again, Miranda would have people with her. People they both trusted.

"Hey, Jes!" Jim shoved him hard and Jesse scrambled to keep his footing.

"What are you doin'?"

"Tryin' to wake you up!" Jim laughed. "Hell, the way you're just a standin' there all quiet like, I'd swear you was already married and afraid to talk!"

Jesse shook his head and laughed.

"Now, ain't them some fine pieces of horse flesh!" Jim sighed enviously and stared into the corral.

Jesse followed his gaze and saw three new horses in the paddock. One bay and two big grays. His breath caught and his stomach tightened for a moment before relaxing again. Damn. Miranda was right. He'd been on the hunt too long. Just 'cause there was a couple of gray horses in the corral didn't mean his man was in town. Shit. Half the people in the territory rode gray horses.

"Who do they belong to?"

Jim glanced at him. "Two of 'em are Pike's." He frowned slightly when he added, "One belongs to Tom Forbes."

"Forbes."

"Yeah," Jim said disgustedly. "He blew into town last night. Hear tell he woke up Wilma and about wore her out. Started gettin' rough with her and Big Pete had to throw him out of the place."

"She hurt?"

"Nah." Jim spat into the dirt. "Not bad. But I got no likin' for a man that hits a woman."

A cold chill crawled down Jesse's spine. Its icy fingers spread through his body until he had to force himself not to shake. "Me neither," he said softly. "This Forbes fella. What do ya know about him?"

"He's a bad one. Nobody messes with him, Jesse."

Jim looked at his friend steadily, his blue eyes filled with a silent warning. "I mean nobody. Only ones I ever saw stand up to the bastard was Judd Perry and Birdwell."

"Judd?"

"Yeah. Last time Tom was in town, he was hangin' around Miranda, gettin' her real skittish. Judd warned him off." Jim rubbed his chin thoughtfully. "I remember at the time it some surprised me that Forbes backed down. I thought sure he'd kill Judd." He shrugged. "But he didn't."

"This was two years ago?"

"Yeah." He nodded. "Yeah, two years."

Jesse stared at the horses moving lazily around the paddock. Forbes's size and coloring was right. He rode a gray horse. And he sure as hell had the character of a killer. But the time was wrong. If he was here in the canyon two years ago, how could he have been in Texas?

"Does Forbes usually come here about the same time of year?"

"What the hell do you care?"

Jesse ignored the question in his friend's eyes and demanded, "Just tell me, Jim. Same time? Every time?"

"Well, lemme think a minute." Jim's eyes screwed shut and his brow wrinkled. It seemed to take forever, but it was really only a few seconds before his eyes opened again and he said, "Y'know, now that you say that . . . he always did show up around the same time. Until two years ago . . ."

Jesse's chest tightened. He could hardly breathe. His mouth dry, his palms sweaty, he waited.

"Usually most of us don't come in till close on to

winter. Forbes, too. But two years ago he beat us all here." Jim nodded thoughtfully and spoke as if to himself. "I remember thinkin' at the time that he'd prob'ly got himself into a tighter spot than he was used to."

Jesse drew a shuddering breath. He forced himself to calm down. To think. None of this was proof. He didn't *know* anything for sure.

"'Course, it all evened out anyway," Jim went on. "Forbes left early that year, too. Right after ol' Judd died in that huntin' accident."

Hunting accident. Why did that suddenly sound wrong? Jesse mumbled under his breath, listing everything he knew. It wasn't much, but he was beginning to think it was more than enough. At least it was enough for him to face the man and find out. Even if he had to hog-tie the man, Jesse would check to see if Forbes had the knife scar and the tattoo that would prove him guilty.

"Where's Forbes now?"

Jim drew back a bit. "Shit, I don't know. His horse is here. So he must be, too. *Somewhere.*"

Jesse turned on his heel and marched off toward the center of town.

"What the hell's goin' on, Jess?"

Jesse ignored him and kept walking. His brain raced with the unexpected information. After all this time, was it possible that he would just *stumble* across the man he'd searched under every rock in the country for? And if it *was* him?

Jesse stopped dead. He looked down the street toward the main bunkhouse where Forbes was bedding down. A memory of the man's face as he watched Miranda flashed into his brain. Forbes wanted her.

But Miranda was safe. She, Shelly, and Buck had left for town a couple of hours ago. So whatever happened now, she would be safely out of it.

And if Forbes *was* the man he sought, Jesse promised himself as he started walking again, *he* wouldn't be safe anywhere.

CHAPTER 18

By the time Jesse reached the bunkhouse, his temper was on the rise. He burst through the door, ignored the startled expressions on the few men inside, and quickly glanced over the room. Forbes wasn't there.

Muttering under his breath, he went back outside and stood in the middle of the street. Looking first one way then the other, he tried to decide where to search next. The sun shone down from a clear sky and the ever-present wind shot a blast of cold that seemed to go right through him.

He took a long, deep breath and rubbed one hand over his whisker-stubbled jaw. His brain refused to calm down. Instead it raced with possibilities. Though he had no proof of his suspicions, his thoughts leaped from one clue to the next, building on what little information he had.

Two years. Forbes had been early getting to the canyon two years ago. Carter and Della were killed in the middle of summer. Miranda's father had warned the blond man to stay away from his daughter two years ago and Forbes had backed down unexpectedly. Then Judd Perry was killed in a hunting accident. And right after Judd's death, Forbes left the canyon. Much earlier than usual.

Jesse shook his head. There was still no proof. But if his hunch was right, Forbes had killed Judd Perry to get to Miranda. And if he was willing to do that, what might he do now that he knew Miranda would soon be marrying somebody else? Jesse *had* to find Forbes.

Now it wasn't only the past calling out for him to find and settle with Tom Forbes. It was his future. His future with Miranda.

But how was he to know for sure? He reached up and tugged the brim of his hat down lower over his eyes, blocking the sun's glare. He squinted, his gaze moving once more over the lonely street as if searching for an answer. Suddenly he stopped. Of course.

Big Pete's place stood silently at the end of the narrow road. He started toward the saloon, picking up speed with every step. He had to talk to Wilma. She might be the only one who could help him.

"What do *you* want?" Wilma frowned at Jesse then turned and walked back to her rumpled bed.

He stood uncertainly in the open doorway and looked around her room. It looked as though a Texas twister had set down smack in the middle of it. The mattress was cockeyed on the bed, a lamp lay broken on the floor, and there were clothes tossed everywhere. Even the paintings on the stained walls were hanging at odd angles. The smell of cheap whiskey and stale sweat hung over the whole mess like a heavy cloud. What the place needed was an open window and the canyon wind sweeping the air clean.

He wrinkled his nose slightly and turned to look at

the woman. Wilma was probably never what a body would call a *pretty* woman. Her dark eyes were too close together and her nose a touch too long for that. Still, Jesse'd seen her all done up and she usually turned herself out nicely.

But no amount of makeup or perfume was going to help her today. Jesse's gaze swept over the woman perched on the edge of the bed. Her bare feet swung back and forth, inches above the floor. A plain, blue cotton wrapper was knotted around a once lush figure now thickened and destroyed by years of rough living, bad whiskey, and late hours. Wilma's dyed black hair frizzed out around her head like a spill of ink and made the purpling bruise on the side of her face stand out even sharper. Her bottom lip was split and there was a small, bloody cut on her wide forehead.

"Damn, Wilma." Jesse winced just looking at her injuries. "You all right?"

She cocked her head and smirked at him. "That what you woke me up to ask?"

"Sorry." He stepped inside and took off his hat. "Didn't stop to think is all."

She waved one hand at him. "Don't matter. I got all day to sleep, I guess." Wilma chuckled then gasped at the accompanying pain. "I sure as hell won't be *entertainin'* till this here mess clears up some." She wagged one finger at him. "I've about had my fill of outlaws, though, I'll tell you that. You give me a preacher lookin' for some sinnin' or a good man runnin' from his wife every time!"

Her speech was slurred slightly and Jesse hated to have to make her talk more, but he didn't have any choice.

"Tom Forbes do that to you?"

Her small black eyes narrowed dangerously. "You damn right he did, that no-good son of a bitch!" She looked up at Jesse and shook her fist at him. "He caught me when I wasn't lookin', or I swear to you I'd've dropped him where he stood." Her hand slid under a flat pillow and pulled out an old army pistol.

Jesse's eyes widened as the woman stroked the gun barrel lovingly. Watching her, he didn't have any doubt that she would have killed the man if given a chance.

"I ever see him again though"—Wilma gave a half smile—"and I will put a hole in him so big you could drive a damn wagon through it."

Jesse stayed quiet and didn't breathe easy again until she slid the gun back into its hiding place.

"So what'dya want, Jesse?"

"I want you to tell me somethin' about Forbes."

"Huh!" She pushed her flyaway hair back out of her face with one thin hand and grimaced. "Yeah, what?"

"Before he hit you, did he, I mean, was he undressed?"

Her narrow, plucked eyebrows shot straight up into her hairline. "*What?*"

"I want to know, did he have his shirt off at all?"

"Shit, yes." Wilma scooted back farther onto the bed, reached around for another pillow, and leaned against it. She crossed her dirty feet at the ankles and gave him a parody of a leer. "I like my men naked, mister." She winked her good eye. "Before he commenced to slappin' me around, he was doin' fine."

"Good."

She gave him another odd look.

Jesse ignored it and took another step toward the bed. He was almost afraid to ask. What if she didn't say what he wanted to hear? What if he was no closer to the end of his search after all? But he *had* to know. "Wilma, did Forbes have a tattoo on his back? A Indian-lance tattoo?"

"How the hell'd *you* know? You sleep with him, too?" She cackled delightedly at her own joke, then groaned and clapped one hand to her cheek.

"He did?"

"Yeah." She worked her jaw tenderly and touched her tongue to her lip. "Said he got it put on to remind him how he got that knife scar on his arm."

The room spun wildly. Jesse heard her voice, but as if from a great distance. Images blurred until Wilma's messy room at Big Pete's disappeared and he was back at the ranch in Texas.

Covering Della's body with the quilt she'd made for her marriage bed. Burying Carter on the hillside where he'd planned one day to build a fine house for him and his wife.

Jesse's heart pounded and a sharp, fierce pain behind his eyes nearly blinded him. His throat closed and he gasped for air that was suddenly too thick to breathe.

"Jesse?" Wilma crawled out of bed and walked to his side. She laid her hand on his arm but got no response.

"What's going on?" Fat Alice stepped inside, carrying a breakfast tray for Wilma.

"I don't know," the injured woman answered quietly. "He just went kinda strange. Maybe you best get Miranda up here."

Miranda!

Her name hit Jesse like a bucket of frigid water. He shook his head, looked at the two worried women like they were strangers, then turned and bolted for the door.

* * *

"What is it you two are lookin' to buy anyhow?"

"We don't know yet, Buck," Miranda called back. "We haven't had a chance to look around the store."

"Women!" Buck reined his horse in slightly and waited for the buckboard to catch up. Riding even with the two women, he went on. "Womenfolks is the onliest ones I know who go shoppin' not havin' any idea what they're gonna buy!"

"Don't you like women much, Buck?" Shelly laughed and tightened her hold on the edge of the seat as the wagon hit a rock in the road.

"Now, I didn't say that." He grinned. "I like women fine. Just don't care to go to stores with 'em is all."

"It won't take long." Miranda slapped the reins over the pair of horses' backs. "We want to get home before suppertime if we can."

The man tilted his hat brim up and looked at the sky. "Well, then, you best pick things up a bit." He turned his gaze back to the women. "Got a late start already with all that kissin' and such!" Buck gave Shelly a wry glance and continued. "Still got quite a ways to go to town, too." With that, he spurred his horse ahead a few feet and cantered down the middle of the trail.

"Is Buck going to be living near you and Dave?"

"I don't know," Shelly answered hesitantly. In fact, she didn't have the vaguest notion of where they would all be living when they got back to Texas. But, she reminded herself, as long as Buck and Dave were Rangers, she had no doubt she'd be seeing plenty of Buck Farley.

She gave her best friend an uneasy glance. It didn't feel right, not telling Miranda about Dave and Buck. Shelly turned and looked off at the distant mountains.

She'd always been able to talk to Miranda about *anything*. But this . . . it wasn't that she didn't *trust* her friend. She did. But Shelly was simply too afraid for Dave's safety to take the risk of the wrong people finding out.

As easygoing as the folks in the bandit stronghold were, they wouldn't take kindly to knowing that two Texas Rangers had been living with them. Pretending to be something they weren't in order to track down one of the outlaws' own.

No. She shook her head and told herself that as soon as it was safe—when they were all out of the canyon— she would tell Miranda everything. Until then, Dave and Buck's lives demanded her secrecy.

Determinedly she changed the subject. ''Enough about Buck. Miranda, I'm gettin' *married*! What in *hell* am I gonna wear?''

Miranda's laughter floated out to Buck, who shook his head disgustedly. He hoped Dave and Jesse knew what they was getting into.

Jesse marched down the street like a man possessed. He stopped at every building, checking through rooms, closets, wherever a man might hide. Despite the voice in the back of his mind screaming at him to hurry, he went through the town thoroughly. Carefully. He had to make sure. He had to look everywhere.

He had to find the bastard.

Tom Forbes. Jesse's insides twisted. He'd had the man he'd been looking for so long right in the palm of his hand and let him get away!

He darted around the few people littering the street, his gaze continually searching for the big man with sandy-blond hair. Forbes *had* to be in town.

But when he'd searched every building, Jesse was no closer to finding the elusive man. There *had* to be an explanation. The man's horse was in the corral.

At the end of the street he stopped suddenly, his chest heaving in an effort to catch his breath. At least, he told himself, the horse *was* there a while ago.

An ominous fear gripped him and Jesse sprinted to the corral fence. Stepping onto the bottom rung, he carefully looked over the dozen or more horses in the paddock. His breath caught. In grim disbelief, he looked again.

One of the grays was gone.

"What's goin' on, Jes?"

Jesse spun around. "You seen Forbes?"

"Shit. You on about him again?"

"Goddammit, Jim!" Jesse leaped off the fence and ran to the blond. "Did you see him?"

Jim took a step back and answered warily, "Sure. Sure I seen him. He saddled up and rode out about a half hour ago."

"Sonovabitch!"

Jesse turned on a run and raced for the stable. He'd thought Miranda safely out of Forbes's reach, at least temporarily. He should have *known*. He should have checked the corral *first*. His brain churned with dire possibilities.

He kept seeing Miranda as she was the night before. Cradled in his arms, a soft, satisfied smile on her lips as they lay together in quiet contentment. A rush of fear swamped him, obliterating the sweet memory. He *couldn't* lose her.

Not now.

Not ever.

Jesse knew, as surely as he knew his own name, that Tom Forbes had set out after Miranda. His only hope now was to catch up to him before Forbes reached the others. In a few brief minutes that seemed to last forever, Jesse had his horse saddled and ready.

He left the animal standing in front of the stable and ran back to the small bunkhouse. Hurriedly he grabbed up his saddlebags and rifle and raced out again.

Jim Sully was still standing in the shadow of the corral when Jesse spurred his horse into a gallop and left Bandit's Canyon behind him.

A small group of people stood at the end of the street an hour later, watching a wagon roll off down a long-unused trail.

"Why's he takin' *that* road?" Ezra asked of no one in particular.

Birdwell turned to look at the much smaller man. "Pike don't want to take any chances. Now that he's headin' home, he don't want to run into any lawman that might be wanderin' around loose." He glanced back to the slow-moving wagon, stubbornly rolling over the uneven, rocky road. "Wants to get Serena and that baby home safe."

Ezra nodded and left abruptly, headed for Big Pete's. Every leave-taking affected the older man, but he always found consolation in the bottom of a bottle.

Birdwell's gaze fixed on the little wagon, now barely in sight. Pike had gotten out. Barring something going wrong, he'd have his family safely out of Bandit's Canyon forever. No more runnin'. No more hidin'. Pike Dexter the outlaw would disappear forever.

Birdwell pulled in a great gulp of air and nodded to himself.

He was doin' the right thing. No matter how much

he missed the girl, it was good and proper for Miranda to get the hell out of her desert home. And Jesse would be good to her. He felt sure of it. Besides, if he ever heard different, Birdwell would just go and have a "talk" with the man.

Turning away from the dwindling farewell group, Birdwell started walking back to the restaurant. It was his turn to cook again and he'd best get started. What with Miranda and Shelly off to town, he'd most likely get no help at all with dinner *or* supper. But, he thought, smiling halfheartedly, he'd best get used to doin' for himself anyway.

"Pike already gone?"

The big man's black eyes snapped up to Jim Sully as the young man hurried toward him. "Yeah. A few minutes ago."

"Durn it." Jim slid to a stop and rested both fists on his hips. "Wanted another look at that youngster before they went." He grinned up at Birdwell. "Been a long time since I seen a baby close up."

Birdwell nodded and kept walking. Jim fast-walked to match the bigger man's strides.

"So," Jim asked, smiling, "how're you holdin' up, Birdwell?"

"What'dya mean?"

"Why the weddin' of course!" He gave the man's broad back a playful slap. "I swear the way Miranda and Jesse are carryin' on, you'd think nobody ever done this before."

"Hmm?" Birdwell looked at him. "What?"

"Well, first Miranda and Shelly take off for town draggin' Buck along practically kickin' and screamin'!" Jim chuckled and shook his head. "Them two women about *never* go off to town, even though it's the *one* place most of us can go without worryin'."

"They got to get some female things." Birdwell shook his head. Sometimes Jim Sully talked just to hear the sound of his own voice. "Nothin' strange about that."

"Maybe. But ol' Jesse's actin' like he's one bullet shy of a full load."

"What the hell are you talkin' about!" Jim frowned.

Birdwell knew the man disliked having his stories interrupted, but enough was enough!

"Well . . ." Jim took a deep breath. "He was runnin' all over town like a band of Apaches was hot on his heels."

"Why?"

"Shit, who knows?" Jim scratched his head. "Kept askin' me all kinds of questions about Forbes. Then he ups and goes off to talk to Wilma." He snorted. "When he come back from there, he was pokin' into everything, lookin' everywhere like a hound who couldn't sniff. Then he charges over to the stable, sees ol' Forbes's horse is gone, and saddles up himself."

Birdwell stopped and cocked his head.

"Why?"

Jim shrugged. "When I told him that Forbes left town already, he got all hot under the collar, started racin' here and there . . . you'd think he'd have the sense to be pleased the bastard left. *I* sure as hell was!"

"What'd he do?"

"Who?" Jim's brow furrowed. "Forbes?"

"No, damn you anyhow! Jesse!"

"Oh." The blond scratched his head for a long moment, and just as Birdwell was getting set to reach for his throat, he continued. "Kept mutterin' 'Miranda' over and over, grabbed his war bags and rifle, and took off outta here like his seat was on fire!"

"When?" Birdwell fought down a spiral of uneasiness and somehow kept his voice calm. "When did he go?"

"I don't rightly know exactly."

"Guess!" he shouted, his patience spent.

Jim's eyes popped open. "'Bout an hour, I reckon."

Forbes. It always came back to Tom Forbes. The man had been nothin' but trouble for years. But what was it now? What was it Jesse knew that he, Birdwell, didn't? The big man tried to draw a deep breath, but found his chest tight with an unnamed dread.

Suddenly then, Birdwell took off at a fast trot toward the stable. He wasn't sure why Jesse was actin' so peculiar. But it didn't feel right. Something was wrong. Something that Jesse might not be able to handle alone. And if the younger man was worried about Miranda . . . then Birdwell figured *he* ought to be, too.

Buck was singing again. Miranda rolled her eyes and tried to close her ears to the hideous sounds coming from the man's mouth. It was a wonder his horse didn't buck him to the ground just to shut him up.

Shelly laughed quietly beside her and Miranda glanced at her friend. "How can you even *laugh* at that?"

"At least he's not complaining," Shelly answered from behind her hand.

Miranda shrugged and nodded. It was true. She'd never heard a man kick up such a fuss over going shopping!

"I talked to Wilma last night," Shelly said in a suddenly serious tone.

"About what?"

"One of the men got a little rough with her and—"

"Is she all right?" Miranda snapped a quick look at the other woman.

"She will be." Shelly's lips twisted sardonically. "But right now she's fed up with outlaws, or so she says."

Miranda's gaze went back to the road stretching out ahead of her.

"Anyhow," Shelly went on, "I thought you should know that Pete, Wilma, and Alice are gonna be movin' on."

"What? Moving on? Where? When?"

"They don't know." Shelly shrugged and straightened her skirt.

"Because of this man?"

"No. Leastways not completely." Shelly pulled in a deep breath and said, "Pete says he's stayed in one place too long already. And Fat Alice'll go wherever *he* goes . . . and Wilma"—Shelly snorted—"hell, she'd be happy anywhere. Long as she's got a bed and some cowboy to . . ." She glanced at Miranda and let her voice trail off.

A twinge of sadness at the prospect of the end of the life she'd always known touched Miranda briefly then faded away. Everything was changing so quickly. For years Bandit's Canyon had been the one thing she could count on. Its familiar rock walls and ancient buildings. The same people coming and going like visiting family. And now it was over. She shook her head slightly. Oh, right now it was only Pete and his girls. But soon the others would leave, too. She herself would be leaving the canyon behind and finding a new life. It was only right the others should, too. It was probably for the best, she knew.

And still, the thought of her home, abandoned to

the desert wind and the blowing sand, brought a chill she had to fight to be rid of.

"Miranda?" Shelly touched her friend's arm gently. "You all right?"

"Yes." Miranda nodded firmly and tightened her grip on the reins. "Yes, I'm fine." She turned a weak smile on Shelly. "At least I *will* be."

"Yeah, I know. Kinda scares me, too." Shelly looked away, her gaze moving over the wide expanse of desert on either side of the buckboard. "Goin' somewheres else . . . meetin' new folks . . ." She shook her head. "What about Birdwell? What's he gonna do when you're gone?"

As soon as the question was asked, Miranda knew the answer. In fact, she'd probably known all along, she just hadn't put it into words before. "He'll go with us. With Jesse and me."

"He will?"

"Of course. It makes perfect sense. We'll need help with Jesse's ranch in Texas anyway." She turned and smiled sheepishly at her friend. "And besides, I couldn't bear to be separated from him. He's as much my father as Judd Perry is."

Shelly nodded firmly. "Think Jesse will go along?"

Miranda thought for a long moment before answering. "Yes. Yes, I do." Memories of Jesse's hands moving over her body in the moonlight, his soft voice whispering to her about Texas, and the steady beat of his heart beneath her cheek filled her. She knew as sure as she was breathing that Jesse wouldn't deny her her family. "In fact," she added on a sudden impulse, "I think we'll try to talk the Sullys into coming along as well." She laughed shortly. "Lord knows they're terrible outlaws . . . maybe it's time they went back to being working ranch hands!"

"You're braver than me, Miranda," Shelly said with a shake of her head.

"What do you mean?"

She shivered. "The very idea of havin' to cook for Jesse, Birdwell, *and* the Sullys! Lord. Makes me tired just thinkin' about it."

Miranda laughed and the sound floated out to Buck, who broke off his singing. He turned in his saddle to glare at the women. "If you two don't quit your yammerin' and get them durn horses movin', we're gonna be at this here trip forever!"

"For heaven's sake!" Miranda called back. "You'd think somebody held a gun at your back and *forced* you to come along!"

"You best believe it!" Buck tipped his hat back on his head and grinned. "It'd *take* a bullet to make me go shoppin' with jabber-mouthed females!"

Suddenly he grabbed at his chest, his mouth dropping in shock. A split second later Miranda and Shelly heard the accompanying shot. The women watched in horror as a bright blossom of red appeared and spread with terrifying speed across Buck's white shirt. Slowly the man bent over and slumped from his perch on the horse's back to the rocky ground below.

CHAPTER 19

"Son of a . . ." If he hadn't seen it with his own eyes, Jim would never have believed a man as big as Birdwell could run that fast.

"What's goin' on, Jim?"

The blond man turned and watched as Dave Black approached. Shaking his head, Jim said disgustedly, "Hell, *I* don't know! Seems like everybody's just bustin' outta their britches today!"

Dave stood beside the other man and looked in the direction Jim was pointing. A few hundred yards away Birdwell, astride a huge black horse, thundered out of the stable yard and down the main road out of the canyon.

"Where's he goin'?"

"Shit." Jim pulled his hat off and slapped it against his thighs. "Could be anywhere! First Forbes, then Jesse, now Birdwell."

"What?" Dave grabbed the outlaw's arm and spun him around. "What are you talkin' about? Jesse? Forbes?"

Jim pulled back a bit. "Yeah."

"Tell me. All of it." Dave's eyes narrowed meaningfully. "Now."

"Sure thing, Dave," Jim said quickly, and launched into the story of the morning's odd goings-on. Almost before he finished speaking, Dave cursed viciously, then sprinted toward the stable and his own horse. "Well goddamn," Jim muttered, and jammed his hat back on his head.

"Who you goddamning, big brother?"

Jim barely glanced at Bill. Instead his gaze followed Dave Black, astride his lean brown gelding, as he raced out of the stable on the same trail Birdwell had taken only moments before.

"Jim?" Bill asked.

But Jim didn't answer. Shaking his head and muttering, the blond started toward the stable yard, where a cloud of dust still hung in the unusually still morning air.

"Jim? Where the hell you goin'?"

Without turning around, Jim shouted, "I'm goin' after the rest of 'em. I'm durn tired of bein' left standin' here by my lonesome." He glanced back at Bill. "I'm fixin' to find out what the blue blazes is goin' on! And durn it, *somebody* is gonna tell me!"

Bill grinned. Always ready for an adventure, he trotted after his brother calling, "Well, wait for me, son!"

Miranda jerked back on the reins, pitting her own strength against that of the agitated horses. The hitched pair tossed their heads at the insistent pressure, but finally gave way and came to a stop. She pushed the brake handle forward, wrapped the reins around it, and jumped to the ground only a moment after Shelly.

Buck lay where he fell, his eyes closed and the patch of blood still growing at a terrifying rate. Shelly reached him first and dropped to her knees beside him.

Miranda moved more slowly, her gaze sweeping over the open countryside, searching for the source of the gunshot. Her first thought had been Indians. But she dismissed that idea almost as quickly as it had come. If there were Indians about, they'd already be swooping down on them. Carefully she looked toward the long, low line of rocks sprinkled along one side of the road. One man or many might hide among the jagged boulders in safety, and though the road was too far away for a pistol shot, a good man with a rifle wouldn't have any trouble picking them off one by one.

Her stomach tightened in fear and she cursed herself. There was no gun on the buckboard. How could she have been so stupid? She couldn't remember the last time she'd left the canyon without her rifle. Somehow she'd allowed Jesse Hogan to so fill her thoughts, she'd forgotten the most important rule of survival Birdwell and her father had ever taught her. *Never* go anywhere unarmed.

Jesse. She drew in a shaky breath and squinted into the sunlight. What she wouldn't give to see Jesse ride up right now.

Her mouth dry, she lifted the hem of her skirt and stepped off the packed-dirt road into the desert sand. Miranda's feet shifted unsteadily as she made her way to Shelly and Buck.

If she'd only brought her rifle. Or even a shotgun. *Something*. Of course! Suddenly she stopped and looked frantically for Buck's horse. His rifle would still be in the saddle scabbard. "Dammit." Her shoulders slumped and the last ray of hope died in her breast. Buck's horse, frightened by the gunshot and his rider's collapse, had taken off at a dead run. Miranda held her hand up to her forehead to shade her eyes from the sun. She was barely able to make out the animal, still running back toward the canyon.

Miranda bit at her lip and blinked back the useless tears beginning to fill her eyes. No time for crying now. They needed help. Quick.

There was still no sign of life from the rocks and Miranda couldn't help wishing that whoever was there would make his presence known and be done with it. The waiting was worse by far.

She walked to Buck's side and dropped to the ground beside Shelly. Her friend's fingers flew down the line of buttons on Buck's shirt until his bare chest was lying open to the sunlight.

Miranda sucked in air through clenched teeth. It looked bad. High on the right side of his chest, blood still poured from the open wound at an alarming rate. Shelly gave the hem of her blue cotton skirt a vicious yank and tore off a long strip of fabric. Folding it over and over several times, she placed the pad over the wound and pressed down firmly. Then she looked up and met Miranda's gaze.

"He needs a doctor."

"I know." Miranda turned and once more scanned the rocks. "We'll have to get him in the wagon somehow and get him to town."

Shelly nodded grimly. It wouldn't be easy. Buck wasn't a small man by any means. But they didn't have much choice, either.

"No, you ain't."

Both women turned startled gazes on Buck.

His eyes open and glazed with pain, the man looked at each of them in turn. "You got to get outta here. Now."

"We're not going to leave you here, Buck," Miranda told him. "You'll die if we do."

"Hell, we'll all die if you don't." He winced, licked his dry lips, and said softly, "Whoever done this ain't gonna just leave. Get my rifle, Miranda."

She shook her head. "It's gone. The horse ran off."

"Sorry son of a mule. Shoulda shot him years ago." Buck grimaced and drew in a shaky breath. "Then take my pistol. You two climb up on that blasted wagon and hightail it back to the canyon. You can send somebody back for me."

Miranda glanced at Shelly then reached for Buck's pistol. She held the revolver for a long moment, balancing its weight in her hand, then shoved the barrel down beneath the waistband of her skirt. She didn't bother to look at Buck again, she simply said quietly, "All right, Shelly. I'll move the wagon closer, then we'll drag him aboard."

Shelly nodded and Buck muttered something about "damn blasted females." Miranda pushed herself to her feet and took a step toward the buckboard when she noticed something out of the corner of her eye.

Turning her head slowly, she searched the rocks one more time. Her breath caught and her stomach plummeted to her toes. A lone rider had emerged from behind the rocks and was headed directly toward them at a gallop.

No time now for the wagon. She went back to Shelly and Buck and dropped to one knee. Coolly, deliberately she drew out Buck's pistol. Thumbing back the hammer, Miranda lifted her right arm level with her shoulder, took careful aim, and fired.

The rider kept coming.

She'd known even before she took the shot that there wasn't much chance of her hitting the man. Not with him in motion and the limited range of a handgun. But she wanted him, whoever he was, to know that she was armed and not afraid to shoot.

As the rider closed the distance between them Miranda saw him raise his arms. An instant later sand spat up into the air in front of them and was immediately followed by the sound of a rifle shot. Reluctantly Miranda lowered the pistol. Whoever it was, he'd made his point. Even astride a running horse, the man was able to make the shot he wanted. And next time he might not be satisfied with spraying sand at them.

"Miranda . . ."

She took Shelly's reaching hand in hers and gave it a reassuring squeeze before standing up. From the corner of her eye, Miranda saw the other woman scoot around Buck until she was blocking his body with her own.

"Dammit, get outta the way, woman!" Buck's voice was weaker. "I ain't never hid behind a woman before and I ain't about to start now."

"Shut up, Buck Farley," Shelly whispered over her shoulder, "or so help me, I'll shoot you myself!"

"Hmmph!"

Miranda ignored them. Narrowing her gaze, she studied the rider who was almost upon them. He was familiar. His shape, the way he sat a horse . . . but who? She held her breath as the man's face finally came into view.

Tom Forbes.

Fear coiled in her stomach and shot out shaky tentacles that reached for every nerve in her body.

Leaning low across his horse's neck, Jesse raced down the open road. How long ago had Forbes left town? How big a head start did the man have on him?

The horse's labored breathing and the pounding of its hooves against the dirt road thundered in Jesse's brain. Over and over the hollow, empty sound echoed through him, teasing his raw nerves into a spiral of panic. If he was too late . . . if Miranda and the others were dead when he found them . . .

Two years he'd chased Tom Forbes. Every waking thought bent on justice. Revenge.

Now nothing mattered except Miranda. He grasped the reins tighter, and for the first time in years Jesse Hogan found himself praying.

"Well, now," Forbes said, and drew his horse to a stop right in front of the little knot of people. "'Bout time you folks got here. Swear I been waitin' on you bunch forever!"

Miranda kept her eyes on the big blond with the cold gray eyes and took a step closer to Shelly.

Forbes tilted his hat back and grinned easily. "You know that wagon don't make good time atall. All I had to do was ride off the trail and set here to wait!"

"What'dya want, you son of a—"

Shelly reached back and laid a warning hand on Buck's arm.

"You shut your mouth, mister." Tom Forbes's easy grin faded and he tried to look through the women to the man behind them. "You're lucky you ain't dead now. Can't understand why not, myself. Don't believe I've ever missed a shot that easy."

"You didn't miss." Miranda spoke up and was rewarded when Forbes's gaze shifted back to her. "He's hurt bad. He needs a doctor."

"I don't think so," Tom answered, and reached for his holster.

"You can't just shoot him!"

"I already did, Miranda. Now I'm just fixin' to finish the job."

"No." Shelly and Miranda spoke as one.

"Get the hell outta the way," Buck groaned. "I don't need your durned help!"

"Listen to the man, Miranda." Tom stared at her. One corner of his mouth lifted in a parody of a smile. "As soon as I'm finished, you and me'll be goin'."

"Going where?" Miranda swallowed heavily and tried to keep her voice from shaking.

"Mexico first, I figure. After that . . ." He shrugged. "I been waitin' on you a long time now, M'randa. You didn't really think I'd let you marry that Hogan fella, did ya?"

She watched as his long fingers smoothed over the steel-barreled pistol. His thumb moved to draw back the hammer and Miranda wondered wildly if she would be able to swing her own gun up and shoot him before he had the time to kill her friends. He must have read her thoughts in her eyes because he said quietly, "Drop that pistol, M'randa."

She didn't move.

He cocked his pistol and waved it negligently toward Shelly. "Drop it now, woman."

She hesitated and Tom Forbes could see the wild thoughts running behind her eyes. He swallowed back a grunt of admiration. She was a hard scare. Slowly, deliberately Forbes pointed the barrel of his pistol at

Shelly's breast, then turned his stony gaze on Miranda.

He watched as the light of defiance dimmed in her blue-green eyes and the pistol dropped from her hand.

"That's better." He motioned to her and added, "C'mon over here now."

"What about them?" She nodded at her friends.

He flicked a casual glance at the two other people and shrugged. "I got nothin' against Shelly. And as for *him*, hell, he's as good as dead now. Only thing to save him is a doctor . . . and he ain't about to get one."

"You won't do anything to them?"

He studied the worried look on her face and knew he could make good use of her concern. "That depends on you, darlin'."

"What?"

"You come with me . . . don't give me no trouble"—his eyes narrowed meaningfully—"and I'll leave 'em here."

"Miranda, don't." Shelly grabbed at Miranda, but she pulled free.

"Don't you listen to that no-good—"

"You close your mouth, mister!" Forbes glared at the man almost hidden by the width of Shelly's skirt. "I said I ain't got nothin' against Shelly, but if you try me any more, I swear I'll shoot right through her to hit you."

Buck cursed softly, but otherwise kept quiet.

"If I don't?" Miranda asked quietly. "If I don't go with you?"

Tom Forbes's eyes widened in surprise. "Well 'course you're goin' with me, M'randa. You and me's gettin' married. Just like I told your pa two years ago." He chuckled and let his eyes rest on Miranda's heaving breasts. His tongue touched his lips before he added, "I been waitin' on you for too long to let you go now, honey. 'Sides, you know as well as me, we was meant to be together."

She pulled in a deep breath and Forbes almost shuddered at the sight. His fingers itched to touch the white flesh of her breasts. His body burned to have finally what he'd dreamed of for so long.

"Tom," Miranda said, her voice a throaty whisper, "shouldn't we go back to the canyon first? I mean . . . my things are back there. You wouldn't want me to leave without taking anything with me, would you?"

His brow wrinkled, Forbes's lips twisted while he thought about what she said. He didn't think she'd be convinced so easy. Figured it'd take a while for her to get used to the idea. He frowned. Why the hell was she bein' so nice all of a sudden? Then he remembered. Birdwell. Forbes smirked down at her and shook his head. "Nah. We ain't goin' back to the canyon. Whatever you need, we'll pick up in Mexico."

Disappointment clouded her face and Forbes couldn't resist adding, "Don't you go lookin' for Birdwell to keep you from me. Nor Hogan, neither."

Miranda's eyes flew up to his. "What did you do to them?"

"Nothin'. Yet." He leaned forward, one hand on the pommel of his saddle, the other holding the pistol still aimed toward Shelly. "But I will. I promise ya. You best remember what happened to your pa, girl."

A shaft of satisfaction ripped through him when Miranda's face paled and her jaw dropped.

"What do you mean?"

"I mean"—he grinned—"last time I was here, I went to your pa . . . all proper and everything, and asked for your hand. He told me he'd rather see you dead than hitched to the likes of me." Forbes's grin faded as he remembered the insults Judd Perry had shouted at him. He could still see the shocked, disgusted look on the old outlaw's face at the mere suggestion of a marriage between Miranda and Tom Forbes. The sandy-haired gunman gritted his teeth together so tightly his jaw hurt. He stared at Miranda and added softly, "He didn't give me no choice."

Miranda stared at him, shocked into silence. A torrent of emotion flooded her body, leaving her hands shaking and her knees weak. Rage and pain fought for control of her and finally all she could say was, "*You* killed my father?"

"I *said* he didn't give me no choice!" He glared at the woman he'd desired for so long. Didn't she *understand*? He'd done it for *her*. Miranda's eyes, wide with pain, stared at him accusingly. "Goddammit! I didn't want to kill him! But you and me's got to be together! He wouldn't *listen*!"

She didn't say anything. As he watched her eyes glaze over, a cold resolve settled over Tom Forbes. It didn't matter if she understood or not. He'd waited for her. He'd come back to get her. And by God, he would *have* her!

"You come on over here now. Enough a this jawin'." He waved one arm at her and straightened up in the saddle. "You're gonna have to ride with me. I was meanin' to have you use Farley's horse, but since he run off . . . this'll have to do."

She didn't move.

"Come on now." He cocked his rifle and the ominous sound cut through Miranda's pain-dulled brain.

"Set up here with me." He smiled and patted his thigh encouragingly. "We'll be right cozy here together."

Miranda threw one last glance at Shelly, then walked to his side silently.

Forbes reached down with his left hand, grasped Miranda's forearm, and lifted her up to sit astride in front of him. When she tried to push her hiked-up skirts down over her legs, he stopped her. With one eye on Shelly, Forbes ran his hand over Miranda's leg and allowed himself the surge of pleasure he'd waited for so long. Her skin was so soft. Softer than he'd ever dreamed.

It didn't matter that she cringed at his touch. That would change. With time. She would see that he was right. They belonged together. The day would come when she'd beg him to touch her like this.

His mouth dry, he moved the fingers of his left hand higher and higher up her thigh. She held herself like a statue until he began to smooth his hand over the warm center of her.

Then with more strength than he'd thought she possessed, she pushed his hand away and jammed her elbow into his chest. A rush of air shot from Tom Forbes's body and sudden, fierce anger sparked and grew inside him.

From the corner of his eye he saw Shelly take a step toward him. He halted her with a lift of his rifle. Grabbing Miranda's chin, he forced her head around until she looked up at him, then he lowered his head and ground his mouth against hers. Every twist of her body as she tried to escape only served to inflame the raw desire coursing through him. When he forced her lips apart, she sagged in defeat. Triumphantly he plunged his tongue into her mouth, eager to taste her.

Miranda bit him hard. He yanked back and held one hand to his mouth. When he lowered his fingers again, he saw the slight smear of blood and it was all he could do not to throttle her on the spot.

The glimmer of defiance was back in her eyes. "Don't you touch me, Tom Forbes, or I swear that someday I'll kill you."

He gingerly touched his fingers to his mouth again. Then, before she saw it coming, he slapped her across the face.

Miranda's head snapped to one side and she opened her eyes to look at Shelly through a blur of tears. Forbes's arm snaked around her middle and pulled her tight against him. Then he raised his pistol, pointed it straight up, and fired two quick shots.

With a frightened lunge, the buckboard horses pulled against the rickety brake until it gave way completely. Free of the last thing that held them, the animals raced off down the trail toward the distant town.

Forbes then held the pistol tight against Miranda's throat and motioned to Shelly. "Give me the gun down there."

Quickly the woman moved to obey.

Once he had Buck's pistol safely tucked away, Tom Forbes smiled down at Shelly. "Next time you see ol' Birdwell, you be sure to tell him 'bout me and Miranda gettin' married. You hear?" Then he gave his horse a kick in the ribs and started the big animal out into the desert. Away from town, away from the canyon, away from any chance of rescue.

Shelly stood quietly crying and watched her friend fade into the distance.

"He all right?" Jesse pulled his horse up short beside Shelly and looked down at Buck.

"He passed out a while ago. He's hurt bad, Jesse."

She walked up close to the man and leaned against his saddle.

"I figured somethin'd happened. I passed Buck's horse on the road. By now he's prob'ly at the canyon. Folks'll be comin' along soon." Jesse reached down and absently patted her hand. "Where's Miranda? Where'd Forbes take her?"

She looked up at him, relieved that she didn't have to be the one to tell him. "How'd you know?"

"Don't matter now. Where'd they go?"

Shelly turned and pointed. "There. 'Bout half hour ago, I guess."

"Damn!" He rubbed his jaw angrily and stared off at the open country that had swallowed the woman he loved and the man he hated.

"You go on after her." Shelly pushed away from Jesse's side and smiled grimly up at him. "Don't worry about us. The others'll be along. You go fetch Miranda. They're ridin' double, so you should catch up to 'em mighty quick."

Jesse nodded. He knew she was right. He had to go. He had to leave immediately. The longer he stayed with her, the greater the chance of losing all trace of Miranda and Forbes. But Buck looked like hell and he hated leavin' Shelly alone like that.

"I said don't worry about us."

He glanced over to her and saw her half smile.

"I can see you ain't anxious to leave us here. But we'll be fine. Just leave some water if you can and go get Miranda."

Jesse nodded and lifted the strap of one of a pair of canteens. He held it out to her, and after she took it, he half turned, dug into his saddlebags, and pulled out his extra pistol. He handed it to her butt first, and as she took it he was already turning his horse in the direction Forbes had taken.

He hadn't gone more than a few feet when Shelly's voice stopped him. He turned in the saddle to look at her.

"Jesse, you go careful with Forbes. That man's crazy as a bedbug. Said he killed Judd Perry to get Miranda and that he wasn't about to let you have her."

Jesse nodded, turned back around, and urged his already tired horse to run once more. Deliberately he pushed everything but Miranda out of his mind. Her eyes, her smile, her voice, the soft strength of her in the night when only the two of them existed.

He would get Miranda back. And when he did, he'd never let her out of his sight again.

CHAPTER 20

More horses! Keeping her body in front of the still-unconscious Buck, Shelly spun around, her grasp tight on the borrowed pistol.

Relief rushed through her body so quickly, she thought for a moment she might fall over. Instead she let her arm drop to her side and her fingers uncurl from the walnut pistol butt.

Birdwell raced up to her, his huge horse snorting and shaking its great head. Right behind him came Dave, and she used the last of her strength to walk to meet him. Both men leaped from their moving horses and ran across the few feet of desert sand that separated the two parties.

While Dave folded Shelly in his arms Birdwell dropped to one knee and examined Buck's wound.

"He all right?" Dave asked, his hands moving reassuringly up and down Shelly's back.

"Will be prob'ly. If we get him to a doctor." Birdwell turned his head and looked at Shelly. "Where's Miranda?"

"Gone." Tears coursed down her face as she lifted her head from the comfort of Dave's broad chest. "Tom Forbes took her."

"Goddamned bastard," Birdwell muttered, and pushed himself to his feet. "What about Jesse? He been here?"

She nodded and gulped noisily. "A while back. He left us some water and took out after 'em."

Birdwell grunted and headed for his horse. He didn't make it.

"Hold it, Birdwell." Dave faced the bigger man steadily. With one hand he pushed Shelly away from him. The other hand held a pistol aimed at Birdwell. Legs spread wide apart, his hat down low over his eyes, Dave waited.

"What the hell?" The big man pushed his hair back from his face and glared at Dave. "What's goin' on here?"

"I don't want to shoot you, Birdwell, but you ain't goin' after Jesse and them."

"The hell I ain't." He shoved one foot in his stirrup.

Dave cocked his pistol. The sudden click stopped Birdwell in his tracks.

"You'll have to shoot me to stop me, son."

"Don't you think I won't."

"Dave . . ."

"Stay outta this, Shelly." Dave didn't even glance at her. "I won't kill ya, Birdwell, but I *will* make you some miserable."

"Why? What do you care?" Birdwell jerked his head in Shelly's direction. "If Forbes had *her*, wouldn't you want to go?"

"Hell yes. But if the law told me no, I'd prob'ly listen."

Shelly sucked in her breath.

"The *law*?" Birdwell's eyes narrowed thoughtfully.

Dave nodded abruptly. "Texas Rangers. Me and Buck. We came here lookin' for Tom Forbes. And you nor anybody else is gonna stop me from takin' him back to Texas to hang."

Birdwell's hand tightened on the saddle horn. Slowly, reluctantly he pulled his foot free of the stirrup. "That don't mean spit to me! Law or no, you ain't so good you couldn't stand some help!"

"Didn't say I was." Dave shook his head slowly, his gaze sweeping over his wounded partner momentarily. "You'd only slow me down, though. Between me and Jesse, we can get the bastard before he makes off with Miranda permanent."

"You expect me to just sit and wait while you go after 'em?"

"No." Dave's voice shook with his effort to maintain his patience. "I expect you to go find that damn buckboard, load Buck onto it, and get him to the town doctor. We been ridin' together too long for me to let him die because you're too goddamn stubborn to see the right of things!"

Birdwell glanced behind him at the man lying so still on the ground. He pulled a deep breath into his lungs then blew it out quickly. "Shit." His shoulders slumped, he looked back at Dave. "All right. I won't leave a man to die out here in the desert and I reckon it's your right to go after Forbes."

Dave relaxed a bit but remained ready in case the big man changed his mind.

"But"—Birdwell raised one hand and jabbed his index finger in the air toward Dave—"if harm comes to my girl, Ranger or no Ranger, you got *me* to deal with."

The younger man nodded then turned to face

Shelly. She stepped into the circle of his arms and he held her tightly. In all the years he'd ridden for the Rangers, Dave had never known the fear he'd tasted that morning. Silently he thanked whoever was lookin' out for him in heaven for keeping Shelly safe.

She tilted her head back and pulled his mouth down to hers firmly. Their lips met in a long, frantic kiss and Dave would have liked to stay that way forever, but Shelly finally pulled away. She ran one hand down the length of his jaw and forced a sad smile.

"You go on. Me and Birdwell will see to Buck."

"I know that."

"Go careful, Dave. That Forbes man is out of his head. And I didn't like the look in Jesse's eyes when he took off out of here, either."

Dave nodded and turned for his horse. Once astride the tired animal, he looked down at her and grinned. "Don't you worry. We'll see you in town. *All* of us."

The horse reared up when Dave pulled on the reins, and before she could say a word, man and horse were racing away.

"Ranger, huh?"

She turned and looked at Birdwell.

"Hell, I must be gettin' old." He stared after Dave for a long minute. "Not too many years ago I used to be able to smell the law more'n a mile off." He frowned, disgusted at himself, then climbed aboard his own horse. "I'll be back directly with that wagon, Shelly. You have Buck ready."

Shelly nodded absently, and as Birdwell started off down the trail she crossed her arms over her chest and hugged herself tightly. Miranda. Jesse. Buck. Dave.

So many lives twisting in the hot desert wind.

And everything had happened so quickly. Almost *too* quickly for her to take it all in. A familiar sound reached her then. She shook her head and turned to watch the approaching riders. Somehow she wasn't even surprised to see the Sully boys heading toward her.

They'd been walking for what seemed forever. Carrying double, the horse had tired quickly, and the only way to rest it was for its passengers to walk for a while. Miranda shoved at her hair and tried to take a step farther away from Forbes. He pulled her back close then let his hand drop.

The man didn't seem concerned about anyone following them, but Miranda was sure Jesse and Birdwell would be coming soon. And the longer they walked, the more time it gave her rescuers the chance to catch up.

She risked a glance at Tom Forbes, then quickly looked away again. It was all she could do to walk beside him. She still couldn't believe that he'd killed her father to get to her. And the way he'd said it. As though it was expected. As though killing Judd Perry had meant no more to him than shooting a stock-raiding coyote.

A shudder coursed through her and she clenched her jaws tightly. She couldn't help her father, but if she could only *think,* maybe she could help Birdwell and Jesse. From the corner of her eye Miranda tried to study the surrounding desert. Anxiously she searched for *something* that she could either hide behind or use as a weapon against Forbes. But there was nothing.

She tilted her head back and stared up at the hot, glassy sky. Afternoon already. Thoughts of Buck and Shelly swam before her tired eyes and she prayed that help had reached them in time.

"Want some water?"

She glared up at Forbes and shook her head at the canteen he held in one hand. Even the sound of the warm water sloshing in the container made her thirstier than she'd ever been before, but Miranda wanted *nothing* from the man.

"Well hold up then, 'cause I do." He came to a stop, and when she kept moving, he reached out, grabbed her arm, and swung her around to face him.

Miranda watched him lean his head back and lift the canteen to his lips. She stared absently as droplets of water ran down his chin, along his neck, and disappeared under his shirt collar.

He gulped at the water until Miranda couldn't bear the sight of his greedy lips at the mouth of the container anymore. She looked past him, over his shoulder, and just managed to stifle a gasp.

A dust cloud, about a mile back, heralded the approach of help. Jesse, Birdwell, *someone* was coming. And deep within her, Miranda was somehow *sure* it was Jesse. Deliberately masking any emotion, she turned her gaze back to her captor.

Forbes lowered the canteen, smacked his lips, and wiped his mouth dry on his shirt sleeve. As he replaced the stopper in the flask he said gruffly, "Reckon we can ride again for a while now. Horse is pretty much tuckered, but so'm I."

No. Miranda's heart stopped. They couldn't get back on that horse. She *had* to keep him where he was. She had to buy some time. But already Forbes was reaching for the saddle horn and slipping his booted foot into the stirrup.

Quickly she reached for his arm, and when her fingers curled around his wrist, he froze.

Miranda felt the intensity of his stare and knew that he was just a breath away from madness. The flat, emotionless gray of his eyes seemed to burn through her body, making her want to run screaming into the desert. Instead she forced herself to smile at him. His brow furrowed, and she knew he was confused by her actions. But that was all she needed. To keep him guessing just long enough.

The dust cloud over his shoulder was closer now. Soon he'd be able to hear the pounding of the horse's hooves. Then she would somehow have to prevent him from shooting at her rescuer.

But for now she did the only thing she could think to do. Deliberately she pulled her hand from his arm and reached for the top button of her plain white shirt. As she slipped it free of the tiny buttonhole, she saw Forbes's eyes widen expectantly. Miranda took a deep breath and held it as she slowly opened the next two buttons, giving him a partial view of the valley between her breasts.

"I'm so *hot*," she whispered, fear making her voice sound husky with desire. "I think I'd like some water after all, please."

Forbes's tongue ran across his lips hungrily. He pulled his foot free of the stirrup, lifted the canteen, and handed it to her. When she took it from him, he used the opportunity to run one finger down the vee of exposed flesh on her chest. He didn't seem to notice the shudder that racked her body. His other hand he kept on the saddle horn. Miranda noticed that the rifle scabbard was far too close to his reach and she deliberately took a step back.

He frowned, but when she undid yet another button and then languidly smoothed the palm of her hand over the top of her breasts, he was caught, spellbound, by the motion.

Miranda's straining ears picked up the hollow echo

of the running horse and she only prayed that Forbes was too intent on her to notice. Slowly she pulled the stopper out of the canteen and purposely spilled a small stream of water down the front of her shirt. Wet, the thin, white fabric molded itself to her body and she read the fierce hunger in his cold eyes.

Sudden, overwhelming fear gripped her as she realized what would happen to her now if Jesse failed in his attempt to get her away from this man.

A flash of suspicion shot across the killer's features and Miranda knew that she'd failed. She'd let him glimpse her fear, her revulsion, and now he knew her attempt at seduction for what it was. A desperate ploy.

All at once he spun around. The rider was closer now. The thunderous pounding reached out and wrapped a web of hope around Miranda. She held her breath. He was close enough for her to identify now.

Jesse. Just as she'd known it would be.

Almost before the swell of relief began, she saw Tom Forbes spring into action. He reached across his saddle and pulled the rifle from the scabbard. Instinctively Miranda leaped at him. Her hands closed around the cool metal barrel and she fought the much stronger man for control of the gun.

He shoved at her, screaming, "Let go, damn you! I have to save you! You're mine now! And nobody's gonna take you away! *Nobody!*"

"Jesse!" Miranda's defiant screech cut through the desert silence. She had to let him know that Forbes was aware of him. She had to make him be careful. To watch for his chance.

But she was no match for Forbes's greater strength. In a moment he would wrest the gun from her hands. The best she could hope for was to delay him a bit. Force him to hurry his shot. Make him miss his first attempt. Hopefully Jesse would be able to finish the fight that she had started.

A shot rang out but went wide of the two people struggling in the sand. Miranda knew that Jesse wouldn't risk a direct shot at Forbes as long as she was locked in battle with him. But she couldn't let go yet.

Desperately she clung to the rifle barrel despite Forbes's attempts to shake her off. Her shoulders ached. Her sweaty palms slid over the now warm, slate-gray metal. Every ounce of her strength was concentrated on her hopeless task. But Miranda knew that every second she delayed Forbes gave Jesse that much greater a chance of succeeding.

In one last, mighty effort, Miranda tightened her grip and pulled the rifle toward her, hoping to draw him off balance.

A white-hot pain lanced through her side and she was almost deafened by the accompanying explosion of sound. Her jaw dropped with the shock of the fiery blow. Her turquoise eyes, filled with pain, widened abruptly, and she didn't even have time to scream before they closed again and she slumped to the ground.

Tom Forbes stood over her limp body, his features frozen.

When Jesse drew his lathered horse to a sliding stop, he kept his rifle trained on Forbes's back even as his terrified gaze swept over Miranda. As he watched, motionless, bright red blood poured from her left side, spilling onto her shirt and staining the sand beneath her.

''Miranda . . .''

Forbes turned slowly, his rifle barrel drifting pointedly toward Miranda's head.

"Drop the gun," Jesse ordered, forcing his gaze away from the unconscious woman.

"Nope." Forbes took a step toward his horse, looked past Jesse, and saw yet another dust cloud closing in fast. More of them. And who knew how many?

"I said drop the gun," Jesse commanded, his voice cracking with rage.

"You shoot me, mister, and I swear that with my last breath, I'll finish her off." Forbes looked up at Jesse through slitted eyes. The sun was directly behind the man on horseback, putting Forbes at a disadvantage. All there was to be seen of Jesse Hogan was a wavy dark image against the shimmering desert sun.

He chanced another look at the distance. The rest of 'em were closer now. He had to get out of there fast. "I'm goin' now."

Jesse stared down at the man he'd chased for two long, lonely years. The old killing rage filled him and he wanted nothing more than to pull the trigger and rid the world of Tom Forbes. But could he keep the man from carrying out his pledge? Jesse swallowed painfully and his heart staggered when Miranda moaned softly.

He had no choice. He couldn't take the risk. Memories of Miranda raced through his brain and filled every cold, empty place inside him.

She'd told him once that someday he would have to make a choice. Love or revenge. The day was upon him sooner than either of them would have expected. And when faced with the choice of avenging his past or saving his future, there was really no answer but one.

Miranda. The life she'd shown him. The life they could have together. The love she'd managed to bring to him even when he was too stupid to take it. He chose Miranda. He would always choose Miranda.

"She's prob'ly got a chance if you get her to a doc," Forbes added slyly. "But you best make it quick."

Slowly Jesse nodded. He kept his rifle trained on the other man, ready for the enemy to make the slightest mistake. But Forbes moved carefully. And once astride his horse, the killer spared Miranda's limp form only a passing glance. Then he looked over his shoulder before spurring the animal into a mile-eating gallop.

As soon as Forbes left, Jesse dropped from his horse and ran to Miranda's side. Gently he lifted her from the desert floor and cradled her against his chest with one strong arm. Carefully then he pulled her shirttail free of her skirt and lifted it uneasily to examine her wound.

His breath rushed from him and he almost wept with relief. "Holy God, Miranda," he whispered in her ear. "You liked to scared me out of ten years."

Quickly he reached into his pocket and pulled out a worn, wrinkled red bandanna. Crumpling it in one hand, he held it against her side tightly to stop the bleeding.

Jesse heard Dave's horse approaching only moments later and looked up to see the worried concern in his friend's eyes.

"Jesus!" he cried. "She ain't . . ."

"No." Jesse grinned. For the first time in two years he felt like laughing and dancing and just plain old jumping up and down. "Looks a helluva lot worse than it is. Not much more than a scratch."

"But the bastard tried to kill her?" Dave's fingers tightened around the reins and his horse danced nervously at the smell of fresh blood.

Jesse shook his head. "From what I saw, M'randa was tryin' to pull the gun away from him. Think it was an accident." He looked back down at the woman in his arms. Accident or not, he'd come too close to losing her.

"Which way'd he go?"

Jesse jerked his head in the right direction. "His horse is pretty well shot. Don't think you'll have too much trouble catchin' up to him."

Dave nodded. "You and her be all right?"

"Yeah." Jesse's left hand smoothed down Miranda's shoulder. "Soon's I get the bleedin' stopped, we'll head for town."

Dave nodded. "See you there. Look after Shelly for me."

"Right." As Dave started off Jesse called out, "Watch out for him now. From what I hear, the man's almighty good with that gun!"

Dave raised one hand to acknowledge the warning and then was lost in the rising cloud of dust.

Miranda stirred restlessly.

"Lay still now, M'randa," Jesse whispered, and tightened his hold on the still-bleeding flesh wound.

"Jesse?"

Her eyes opened and he felt himself falling into the glorious turquoise depths. Thank you, God, he cried silently. "It's all right, darlin'," he said softly. "Everything's all right now."

"Forbes?"

"Gone. Dave went after him."

"He shot me. . . ."

"Yeah." He swallowed heavily and fought down the urge to squeeze her. "But you'll be fine."

Tears filled her eyes and her bottom lip quivered.

"He killed my father, Jesse. He killed him so he could have me."

There was nothing he could say. Instead he tightened his hold on her, bent down, and smoothed his lips over hers gently. Jesse knew that he would never be able to touch her enough. In the years to come, he would always remember this day and how close he'd come to losing everything he held dear. And he swore to himself that he would never waste a minute of their time together.

"I knew you'd come, Jesse." She sighed and closed her eyes again. "I knew it."

Jesse smiled and planted a soft kiss on her forehead. "'Course I came, darlin'." He smiled even though she couldn't see it. "We got a weddin' to see to."

A short time later Jesse had Miranda on the saddle before him. Her breath, warm and soft against his neck, and her hand against his chest filled him with a surge of love so overpowering, he trembled slightly at its strength.

She shifted position slightly and he drew her up closer to his heart. He turned his horse around to head for town. He'd feel a lot better once the doctor had looked her over.

The weary animal hadn't taken more than a step or two when a single shot rang out in the distance. Jesse pulled up on the reins and glanced back over his shoulder. Only a minute later two more shots echoed in the stillness.

| EPILOGUE |

One month later . . .

"Still don't see why you had to *shoot* him!" Buck adjusted his sling, then grabbed up a nearby shot glass and tossed its contents down his throat.

"Jesus, Buck!" Dave gripped his mug of beer tightly and scowled at his partner. "How many times do I have to tell you? Forbes drew on me! He didn't give me no choice! I *had* to shoot him."

Buck sniffed, pulled at his too tight string tie, and looked past his friend for the bartender. "You always was too damn fast for your own good!" He lifted his empty glass as a signal for a refill and added, "The boys back home was countin' on a good hangin'. They're gonna be some disappointed."

Dave rolled his eyes, took a long drink of the cold beer, and said shortly, "The cap'n wasn't much upset."

"Hmmph! Capn's all business. He don't care *how* you do it, just so's you do it."

"The wire he sent last week proves that," Dave went on, speaking loud enough to drown Buck and the others out. "Says he's got a job for you to do as soon as you're fit."

Buck frowned. "You still set on quittin', then?"

Shelly walked up and linked her arm through her husband's. Dave looked down at her and grinned before turning back to his old friend. "You bet on it. From here on out, I'm a *rancher*, not a Ranger."

"Dance with me?" Shelly smiled up at Dave and her new husband caught his breath. Only a month of marriage and she was more beautiful than he'd ever seen her. Why, if things kept goin' like they were, he thought, by the time they'd been married twenty years, he wouldn't be able to look at her without shadin' his eyes!

As his arm snaked around her waist and the fingers of his left hand entwined themselves with hers, he told himself he could hardly wait.

They slipped effortlessly into the dance and were quickly enveloped in the moving crowd of people. Buck turned his back and waved the fingers of his good hand for the bartender. Shaking his head, he silently swore, I *told* him womenfolks was trouble!

"Yes, sir, Birdwell," Jim Sully pointed out for the fifth time, "I think goin' back to ranchin' is the right thing to do."

Birdwell nodded, his eyes blank, his head pounding. He'd been listening to Jim for more than an hour now, and if he didn't get away quick . . .

"Did I tell you about the time me and Bill started in a new way of handlin' the roundups back in Montana?" Jim asked as he took another hearty swallow of the saloon's best whiskey.

"Yeah, Jim," Birdwell groaned, "you *told* me."

"I didn't think so."

Jim's face was flushed, his tie crooked, and his words were beginning to slur. But that wouldn't stop him, Birdwell knew.

"It was back in Montana in spring of sixty-six." He paused. "Or was it sixty-seven?"

Birdwell's head dropped to his chest.

Ezra smiled shyly at Miranda. Then the old gambler bowed his head, lifted her hand to his lips, and placed a soft, quick kiss on her fingertips. "You are the prettiest thing I ever saw, M'randa. Even more beautiful than your mother, I think."

Miranda leaned toward him and gave him a hug. "Thank you, Ezra. For everything." She waved her hand down the length of her new, meadow-green gown. "It was so sweet of you to give me this lovely dress to be married in."

The gambler blushed and ran one finger under his collar. Miranda'd never seen Ezra looking more dapper, in his stiff white shirt and spanking-clean black broadcloth suit. With his hair combed and every speck of dust gone from his old bowler hat, she now had a notion of what a handsome rogue he must have been in his younger days.

"Just a small thank-you for the years of family you've given me," he said quietly.

On impulse, Miranda took his hand in hers. "Are you sure you won't come with us to Texas?"

"No." He shook his head, but she could see that he was pleased that she'd asked him again. "No, I'm gonna head down to Tucson, meet up with Pete and the girls."

"But you'll come visit, won't ya, Ezra?" Jesse

stepped up behind his brand-new wife and laid one hand on her shoulder.

"Sure will." He grinned up at the younger man. "You folks expect me next winter, all right?" Then Ezra turned for the bar with a decidedly light step.

"How you doin', Mrs. Hogan?"

"That sounds nice." She smiled and leaned back into her husband's strong arms.

"Yeah, I think so." He watched the dancers in front of him for a long moment before commenting, "Shelly and Dave do pretty good together, don't they?"

"Uh-huh." Miranda turned and looked up at him, smiling. "Of course, like she keeps telling me, she's an old married woman now."

He chuckled softly. "A whole month on us makes her an expert, does it?"

"According to her."

"Well, if we hadn't had to wait for you and Buck to heal up, we could've been married a month by now, too." Jesse curved one arm around behind her, pulling her close to him.

She let her gaze rake over her handsome husband, from his shining new suit to his slicked-down hair. Her heart pounded heavily and she decided that she must be a completely wanton woman. The only thing she wanted to do was leave her own wedding party and hurry Jesse upstairs to the room that awaited them.

"I see what you're thinkin', Miranda," he breathed, and leaned down to kiss her. "And I figure a few more minutes down here, and nobody's gonna notice if we slip out."

His thumb began to move in lazy circles over the small of her back and she locked her knees to keep from falling against him.

And though she'd never thought to be so happy, there was still *one* thing niggling at her brain. It didn't matter that they'd already talked about it. She had to know that he was all right with what had happened in the desert.

Her features clouded over slightly. "Jesse, I know I've already said this, but I'm sorry I kept you from settling things with Forbes on your own."

The smile on his face faded and his green eyes softened as he looked at her. Slowly, deliberately he bent down and kissed her forehead, her eyes, the tip of her nose, and finally her mouth.

His lips moved against hers leisurely, lovingly, and it was a long, full moment before he straightened up again. "M'randa, darlin', Forbes is finished. And"— his hands reached up to cup her face gently—"as far as I go, it was finished when he rode away from you. That was all that mattered to me, M'randa." His eyes roamed over her face and his thumbs traced her cheekbones. "You bein' safe. With me. *Lovin'* me. That's everything."

The proof of his words was etched plainly on his features and she felt as though they had finally put his past behind them.

"But what about you?" he asked then, his fingers lifting her chin slightly. "How do you feel knowin' that Bandit's Canyon don't exist anymore?"

It only hurt for a moment. The brief jab of pain for something that would never be again.

Dave had spent almost a solid week apologizing for burning down the bandit town. But he'd had his orders from the Rangers. He was to see to it that outlaws wouldn't have a place to hole up in anymore. And, Miranda thought, if she were to be completely honest, she would have to agree with the Rangers.

Times *had* changed. The kind of men looking for a hideout now, were not the kind she would have welcomed anyway. Birdwell was right when he'd told her that it was time to let go of the past and move on.

Miranda stared into her husband's eyes, reached up, and smoothed back a wayward lock of his hair. Softly she told him, "I'm all right. Bandit's Canyon is finished, too. But before it died, it gave me my future. You, Jesse."

This time when he bent to claim her lips, Miranda wrapped her arms around his neck and clung to him tightly. She parted his lips with her tongue and felt his gasp of pleasure shoot through her as well.

He was right. Nothing mattered but this. Being together. It *was* everything.

"Here now!" Birdwell stepped up to the entwined couple and deftly separated them. "Save some a that for later, you two!"

A sprinkling of laughter floated up into the air from the smiling people surrounding them.

Birdwell placed his hands on Miranda's shoulders, kissed her forehead loudly, and proclaimed in a booming voice, "Before these here two sneak off, leavin' us to party alone"—a cheer sounded out from the crowd—"we think they ought to dance for us, just once. Make this whole thing kinda official like."

Everyone started clapping and Jesse and Miranda were gently shoved toward the center of the floor. They stood uncertainly for a moment or two, basking in the love and friendship offered them by the waiting people. Then, as the fiddler struck up the soft, sweet strains of "Barbara Allen," Jesse bowed formally to his wife.

"Mrs. Hogan"—he grinned—"would you do me the honor?"

She held the edges of her skirt out and curtsied deeply. Then slipping her hand into his, she whispered, "A pleasure, Mr. Hogan."

Together they glided around the floor with the ease that comes from long practice . . . or love.

FREE

Romance

(a $4.50 value)

Send in the Coupon Below

To get your FREE historical romance and start saving, fill out the coupon below and mail it today. As soon as we receive it we'll send you your FREE Book along with your first month's selections.

Mail To: **True Value Home Subscription Services, Inc. P.O. Box 5235 120 Brighton Road, Clifton, New Jersey 07015-5235**

YES! I want to start previewing the very best historical romances being published today. Send me my FREE book along with the first month's selections. I understand that I may look them over FREE for 10 days. If I'm not absolutely delighted I may return them and owe nothing. Otherwise I will pay the low price of just $4.00 each: a total $16.00 (at *least* an $18.00 value) and save at least $2.00. Then each month I will receive four brand new novels to preview as soon as they are published for the same low price. I can always return a shipment and I may cancel this subscription at any time with no obligation to buy even a single book. In any event the FREE book is mine to keep regardless.

Name _____

Street Address _____ Apt. No. _____

City _____ State _____ Zip Code _____

Telephone _____

Signature _____
(if under 18 parent or guardian must sign)

Terms and prices subject to change. Orders subject
to acceptance by True Value Home Subscription
Services, Inc.

915-3

la teva condició de neobecaria, del
~~departament~~ de que signis tu, la
destinataria de les uniques salutacions
que ens ~~enviguen~~ aquinans amigues
dirigeixen al seu departament

Jo
O
S
E
P

A
I
Me

MUACK!

MUACK!

MUA